I0788582

Not Hear

INSTRUMETAL BOOK 2

by
Elizabeth Borae

Images

Janisphoto - adobe.stock.com "A part of a gold plated flute on a black background. An instrument common in the symphony orchestra"

exty/depositphotos.com "Sickle-cell anemia red blood cells"

AVFC/Depositphotos.com "Flute"

Prikhnenko/Depositphotos.com "Music"

ellander/Depositphotos.com "Music background"

Author's Note

A Brief and Oversimplified Note About Sickle Cell Disease

This story was started several years ago and is set several years before that. It was a struggle to determine how much information to present and how, due in large part to the personal impact of the disease and constantly changing medical science.

In addition to using hydroxyurea, l-glutamine, infusion therapies, and bone marrow transplants, other significant and interesting advancements in sickle cell disease (SCD) have occurred during the interim time. For example substantial progress has been made in gene editing therapies. The body of information about the prevalence of SCD in India has been expanded.

A Story Note

With the exception of the prologue, this is a single POV story told from Anayah's perspective.

Dedication

Steven Chester Jones
1960-1994

Contents

Prologue

Anayah

My phone goes off as I place a clipboard on the counter at the nurse's station.

"Anayah, I wanted to warn you before you saw anything," Mother says. "Seth was in a car accident. He might be there already, and his parents are on their way."

A jolt of fear shoots through me. I spent a large portion of my childhood playing and hanging out with Seth Banik, in part, because our families are very close.

"I'm on it." After ending the call, I direct my attention towards the nurse I'm working with. "Can you access records for floors besides your own?"

"Technically, yes. Is everything okay?"

"I have a friend on his way to the emergency room."

"I need you to escort a family, but while you're doing that, I can ask if they need help in Emergency or possibly ICU. That'll make it easier to get information."

The main hospital at the Benjamin Johnson Medical Center was extremely short-staffed this week, and Human Resources asked me to pinch in here. Usually, I volunteer at the Children's Hospital since I'm sixteen. I don't mind, but their tasks differ from what I normally do. After taking the family to Outpatient Services, my boss tells me to report to Emergency.

I call my father on the way down. "Did you hear?"

"I did," he replies. "I have one more patient, and then I can get down there."

When I enter, a woman at the counter beckons me toward her. "Frequently, in these circumstances, we have an influx of families and teens that need traffic control. If you know them, that would make things easier." She hands me another clipboard. "We need more information like alternate phone numbers for guardians. Two guys were taken to Trauma I; the other two weren't as serious."

"There were four of them?" I ask as I flip through the pages.

Will Cox is in Trauma I. This time I can't stop my heart from galloping.

Seth is there too. "How bad are the guys in Trauma I?"

"I don't know. Here are the EMTs."

"I worked on Will," one replies after we asked. "He was bleeding heavily but responsive when we first came on the scene."

My breath catches. "He's not anymore?"

"He passed out when we moved him to the stretcher," he answers. "Probably the pain got to him. He was coming to when we wheeled him in. His friend was unconscious too the last I saw him. I think his name was Seth, but I didn't work on him."

I clutch the clipboard. Put out that fire of fear that lit me up. Be rational, and do something about the situation.

"I'll be back with the info you need," I tell the nurse.

Will

A doctor is stitching me up when my twin sister, Kyra, bursts through the curtain. Her large dark eyes are red, and I haven't seen her this scared in a long time. She's just over five feet and at the moment looks like a little girl.

I try to smile to reassure her, but it's taking too much effort. "Where's Seth?" I ask instead.

"I don't know. They wouldn't tell us anything for the longest."

I fall back.

"Don't move!" the doctor exclaims. "The glass sliced you up bad."

"I need to know about Seth."

The doctor frowns and yells for someone.

A woman appears a moment later.

"Can we get information on his friend, Seth—"

"Banik," I supply.

"He's one of the four boys in the accident," the doctor explains.

"His parents haven't arrived yet—" she starts.

"I need Will to calm down," the doctor cuts in. "His blood pressure is all over the place, and the sedative isn't helping."

"I'll see what I can do." She leaves the room, and Anayah takes her spot.

Kyra throws her arms around her. "What are you doing here?"

"Volunteering," Anayah replies. "I'm making sure you get escorted safely back to the ICU waiting room or wherever you need to go."

Perfect. Nayah always fixes things. "Do you know about Seth?"

Nayah glances at the doctor, and he nods. "Tell him what you know."

"It's not much," she replies. "Last I heard, he was unconscious, but I'd hoped he'd come out of that by now."

"Can you find out?" I ask.

"You do realize the staff nurse is completely capable of getting that info," my doctor tells me. "Volunteer girl, you can stay back here when you're available. Will's heart rate and blood pressure dropped precipitously when you came in."

She raises an eyebrow. "That's a good thing?"

"Yes. It's been sky-high, and it needs to come down. There are only so many meds I can give."

Nayah and I lock eyes.

"I'll come back," she says.

The curtain moves about twenty minutes later, and Kyra and Anayah appear again along with Anayah's dad, Dr. Kapur.

"Dr. Kapur, I'm surprised to see you in our neck of the woods," my doctor says.

"I know a couple of people in this neck of the woods, so I figured I'd come in for a visit."

My doctor looks toward the monitor. "There it goes. Down… down, down."

I ask about Seth for the hundredth time, and they assure me he's alive but still has ways to go.

"Now, will you let your doctor finish his job in peace?" Dr. Kapur asks. "We need you calmer. You took a hit to the head too."

His phone goes off. "Seth's parents are finally here. I'm going to meet them."

"I'll go with you," Nayah says.

"One of you has her number, right?" my doctor asks Kyra and me. "Because if things get out of whack again, we're calling her."

I try to roll my eyes, but I guess that takes more coordination than I'm capable of.

A few minutes later, Kyra leaves to meet our parents who have just arrived.

"Is she your girlfriend?" my doctor asks.

"Anayah?" I try to scowl, and I'm rewarded with a blast of pain. "No."

Her face pops clear as day into my muddy mind.

Anayah Kapur is hands down gorgeous. Long, thick, dark wavy hair, smooth bronze skin, and green eyes. Her features are so perfect, it's almost unreal, like an anime character. But unlike most good-looking girls our age, she doesn't flaunt it. I suspect she tries to hide it.

I also have the sneaking suspicion she's brilliant, which is why I enjoy sparring with her. We're friends, but I don't think she sees me as the same caliber as everyone else in our circle, and that irks me.

Because I am.

"How long does it take you to stitch me up?" I ask.

"Maybe if you didn't cut every square inch of your body, I'd be done," my doctor retorts. "Did you roll around in the glass?"

"Your bedside manner is atrocious."

"And you love it."

Yeah, I do.

"You don't need to impress me with your vocabulary," the doctor continues. "Don't use your brain too much and let it rest."

"Can I leave when you're done?"

"No, we're keeping you at least overnight. You lost a ton of blood, and this is the first time you've been coherent since you came in. I'm not wild about that knot on your head, even though your initial CT scans were okay."

"I don't feel that awful." Just sorta awful.

"The magic of painkillers. You'll sing a different tune when they wear off."

Anayah

My father and I meet Seth's parents in Emergency.

We hug one another, and Dad leads us to ICU, where
Seth was moved. We enter his room, and I try to control
my reaction, but it's hard to see him lying there.

Seth usually exudes an easy confidence, but he looks incredibly vulnerable. I've never seen him so washed out. His
right arm is in an air cast, and there's a bandage wrapped
around his head.

"Sendakir!" Mrs. Banik rushes to his side and moves
hair off his forehead. She sinks into a chair and grabs his
hand.

Seth mutters something, but it doesn't sound like words.

"He seems to be slowly coming out of it," Dad says. "At
the scene, his only response was to pain — no response to
verbal stimuli."

"In your non-doctor, our friend, Kareem, capacity,
what is your opinion?" Mr. Banik asks.

Dad smiles slightly. "I think he'll be okay. He's in
excellent physical shape overall. It seems he absorbed most
of the impact which rattled his brain a great deal, and it's
taking a while to recover from that."

"There were others in the accident?" Mr. Banik asks.

I leave to finish my shift while Dad gives a synopsis of
their situation. Seth and Will were the most seriously hurt,
the other two guys will be released shortly with more minor
injuries.

Will has been moved to a permanent room, so I clock
out, and head there. Exhaustion is kicking in after the
four-hour adrenaline rush. Mr. Cox plans to stay overnight

with Will, but had left with Mrs. Cox and Kyra for a shower and change of clothes.

Still in medical mode, I scan Will as I sink into a chair in his room, searching for signs of distress. It wasn't too long ago that I would've described him as a tall pole, but he's broader now. Over the last few months, Will's long, gangly limbs have developed a good deal of muscle tone, and his six-foot frame is stretched down the entire length of the bed. His normally eye-catching features are covered by bandages, bruises, and swelling. He has a rich brown skin complexion, and light brown eyes that have a luminescent quality, like they're back-lit.

He fixes those eyes on me. "How's Seth?"

"I know he's your brother from another mother, but you're going to make yourself sick over this."

Will chuckles. "Never say that phrase again. It sounds wrong coming from you."

I scowl at him. "Seth is groggy but talking coherently."

"Good. Progress."

"Have you been able to actually rest much? It's been about five, six hours since you came in."

"I'm tired, but it's a little hard for me to fall asleep." He studies me, concern spreading across his swollen features. "You look exhausted."

I stare at the recliner on the other side his bed. "Don't worry about me. We're the ones who are supposed to keep you calm and happy."

Will chuckles.

So I'm not the greatest person for that task.

"Why don't you switch seats and take a nap?" Will suggests.

"It was a hectic afternoon, and we were really scared." I pause. "I was really scared."

"Please, get the chair, Nayah," he says quietly.

I grab a blanket from the cabinet and pull it over me while sinking into the seat.

This feels amazing. I must be beyond exhausted because these chairs are not that comfortable. "Are you sure you don't need anything else?"

"Nayah, I'm fine."

We're quiet for a moment.

"I'm glad you're okay, Will," I say softly.

He moves a piece of hair from in front of my face. "You're part of the reason why."

An explosion of warmth spreads through my chest as I lightly grab his bandaged hand.

He squeezes mine. "Get some rest."

Still holding on, I drift into sleep.

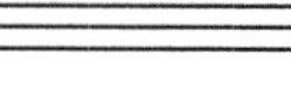

Will

I watch Nayah drift off. That was a powerful wave of emotion. Super strong pull.

I shake my head. Probably the meds. Got my brain and body all messed up. I don't belong to Nayah, and she certainly doesn't belong to me. Anayah belongs to nobody but herself.

But I'm still holding onto her hand and drifting off myself when my doctor comes in.

"I'm leaving. How are you doing?"

"I'm tired and itchy but otherwise okay." I gently lay Nayah's hand next to her, trying not to be obvious about it.

"The first sign of pain, tell the nurses. It'll be intense for the first couple of days, and we need your vitals stable." He gestures toward Nayah. "Speaking of, keep her close."

I scowl at him.

His expression softens to a genuine smile. "Teasing aside, she seems like no ordinary girl, and she stabilizes you. Literally."

That's deep, and I can't make that happen now. I can't even think.

"I've done my good deed for the day. I wish you a speedy recovery, Will."

I thank him, and he leaves.

I glance at Nayah still sleeping soundly.

She is no ordinary girl, which is why I shouldn't start something I can't finish.

1

Perfect Priya

Present

"**A**nayah! Can I come in?" Priya sings outside my bedroom door.

Literally sings.

I stop mid-stride, shutting my eyes. Why is she home so early?

My older sister bursts into the room and rushes me like a linebacker. Her fruity scent surrounds us as she crushes me in a hug. I can't quite pull myself from her grip, but I manage to get a little space between us.

Priya holds me out at arm's length. "My beautiful, brilliant, fearless baby sis making her high school debut! What a way to end the Kapur dynasty. How did it go?"

"It went."

The school lost my schedule, my biology teacher is a long-term sub which ruins my favorite class, the plastic fork broke in my mouth during lunch, and I'm afraid my friends will ditch me in high school. My plan to conquer Southerland High is massively derailed.

She sobers. "Anything you want to talk about? I know a thing or two about navigating the wild waters of high school."

I study her, weighing my response. Priya works at a bank and today's outfit has more polish. Dark blue suit, trendy heels, and her straight, dark hair is arranged in an elegant bun.

Perfect, as always.

Admiration and jealousy war inside me. "No, I'm good."

She flops on my bed and dangles a small brightly colored embroidered bag in front of me. "I bought you a first day of high school gift."

My annoyance subsiding, I pull a jade necklace from the bag and rub the smooth stone. I don't wear much jewelry, but this is beautiful. "Thank you."

"It'll go great with your eyes. I could have done serious damage in high school with your looks." She sighs. "You had one shot to make a fabulous first impression. I should've eyeballed you before you left."

I glance down. Dark jeans, a green sleeveless top, and black ballet flats. "There's nothing wrong with my outfit."

"But it's so conservative. What image are you creating here?"

"I'm a serious school student ready to work."

"But you can be a serious school student with sparkle."

"I need a snack."

Priya plays with my ponytail as we go downstairs. "I wish you'd worn your hair out. It's gorgeous, cascading around your shoulders and flowing down your back. The boys will fall at your feet."

"Then they'll be in my way when I go to class."

Usually, I cut it to my shoulders at the end of each school year. Mother and Priya begged me not to so it'll be longer for her wedding.

My older brother, Balraj, is digging through our refrigerator when we enter the kitchen. He's a junior at a college about an hour's drive from here. We rarely see him during the week, or most weekends, for that matter.

"What are you doing home?" I ask him.

"Nice to see you too. Don't you guys have anything to eat here?"

"Don't you have a meal plan at school?" I retort. "Why are you here?"

"Mom called a family dinner so we can talk about Pri's wedding."

My body tenses.

We always ate as a family when we were little, and it was fun. As we grew older, schedules stopped syncing, and people left for college. Now family dinners occur when we have to discuss something. They feel forced, end oddly, and I don't want to discuss Priya's wedding.

My other brother, Adil, walks into the kitchen. He's a high school senior this year. Adil is slender like my father. Balraj, while not overweight despite all the food he manages to consume, is taller and broad with more musculature. Adil's hair is like Priya's and hangs in his nearly amber-colored eyes. I resist the urge to fix it.

"Did you know about this family dinner?" I ask him instead.

"Yep, Mom told me last week."

"Nobody bothers to tell me anything," I complain. "What if I had things to do?"

"Do you?" Adil asks.

"No." I toss my ponytail. "It's the principle."

Balraj rolls his eyes.

"You've been in a mood all day," Adil remarks. "I'm not used to seeing you so antsy. It makes you shrewish."

I glare at him.

He plays with my ponytail. "Take a breath, Yaya. You'll be fine. Tomorrow will be better."

When I was a baby, Adil called me Yaya because he couldn't say my name right. My family loved it, and the nickname stuck.

I'm still the baby.

"Where's Mom?" Balraj asks. "It's weird to have a family dinner and no food. I thought she'd be home cooking by now."

Priya makes a face. "Are you straight out of the stone age?"

I pull tea out of the fridge and cookies from the cabinet. We spend more time in the kitchen than any room in the house. It's spacious, with barstools at the island and a decent-sized circular table at the windows. Our enclosed porch is towards the back and has large French doors, so it still reads as contiguous space when they're open.

Mother walks into the kitchen carrying several takeout bags. She's a writer and professor at the university teaching creative writing courses. "Excellent. Everyone's here. Who's snack is this?"

"Mine."

"Put it back," she orders me. "We're about to have dinner. Can you four get the rest of the bags?"

We shuffle in a few minutes later laden with packages. How much food did she buy?

"Smells good," Balraj says after kissing her cheek. "We wondered what happened to you. We thought you'd be cooking."

Priya raises an eyebrow. "We?"

"Someone else can cook around here besides me." Mother plunks an entrée on the counter. "I do have a job."

"I don't live here anymore." Balraj digs through a bag.

"If someone had told me we were having a family dinner, I could have prepared something." I tap my nails on the counter.

Mother looks confused. "I'm sure I told you, Anayah."

I shake my head.

"Oh. We're having a family dinner tonight to discuss Priya's wedding."

Priya giggles as I glare at Mother.

"Balraj and Adil set the table," Mother says. "Put the extra leaf in. I got a lot of food, and dinner will take a while."

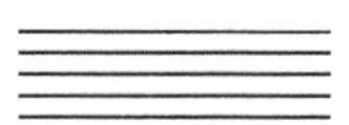

An hour later, I'm ready to poke my eyeballs out.

"The colors and invitations will be…"

Priya's wedding will be elaborate. She's not the last of her friends to get married, but she's been to several other weddings of her peers, and she wants to make sure hers will be memorable.

"We have to get this place for…"

Dinner was finished a while ago, and dessert is gone. I have nothing to distract me anymore.

"The engagement party must be spectacular…"

I make a goofy face at Adil, and he grins.

Then I catch a look from Mother. She is not grinning.

"The band will have to be—"

"Don't you have a fiancée?" I interrupt. "Does he have a say in this, or are you bogarting this wedding?"

"Of course, I'll talk to David about the arrangements. But I need to narrow down the choices and be persuasive about the things I really want."

Mother is excited. Priya's fiancée makes and comes from good money, and he's polite.

Not that we're poor by any means. We've never been in want for anything, and Priya has her own substantial income from a comfortable job as an IT auditor in a major bank.

"What are you bringing to the table in this marriage, Pri?"

"Whatever, Raj. You could only dream of marrying a girl like me."

Perfect Priya.

When we visit my parents' families in India, everyone says Priya is beautiful, like my mother. My features are nearly identical to Mother's, except for our eye color, but no one makes those comparisons about me.

I feel lacking when I'm with Mother and Priya — always trying to keep up. Perfect Priya and her very far from perfect Baby Sister Anayah.

Priya is so polite and personable. Priya dresses so trendy. Priya sings and dances beautifully. Priya is such a talented writer. Priya has a great job and makes so much money she'll be able to care for her parents when they get old.

While I get, Anayah, be nice, don't be rude. Anayah, can't you dress up more, and a little makeup won't kill you. Anayah, your writing is so wooden. Anayah, you have no rhythm; maybe your sister can teach you a few steps.

"Anayah?"

"Yes?" I whip my head around.

"Are you okay?" Dad seems concerned. "You're scowling."

"I'm good."

Mother is giving me another dirty look.

"Would you be my maid of honor, Yaya?"

"Don't you have a best friend to do that?"

"Anayah Kapur!" Mother snaps.

"It's not uncommon, and I can't possibly be the best person."

Priya's already large eyes are humongous. "I'd rather it be you."

It's not like I don't love my sister; I just feel my voice is always drowned out by her. There's a tug in my chest until I look at Mother, whose eyes are shooting daggers at me.

"I'll be your maid of honor," I reply quietly.

"Fabulous! This will be so much fun. We'll make our first shopping trip next week to buy your special outfits."

"Is there anything else to discuss, Priya?" Dad rubs his face.

After Priya declares an end to the torture — I mean meeting, everyone clears the table, and Mother asks me to help her in the kitchen.

"Anayah, you need to be supportive of Priya." Mother shuts the refrigerator after putting the last of the food away. "Be enthusiastic and helpful. Your sister is getting married. It's a very important event."

"Okay." I shove forks in the drawer.

"This is what I mean!" Mother exclaims. "Your response is 'okay'."

"What do you want me to say?"

"Never mind. Just be more… more." She sighs and leaves the kitchen.

I toss the dishrag on the counter and run upstairs to my room, closing the door harder than necessary. After falling on my bed, I stare at the gray walls.

Black, white, and gray colors suit me, and the lack of furniture and knick-knacks keeps me from being distracted. People view me as a goal-driven high achiever. I have to be this way - I'm part of a goal-driven, high-achieving family. Cure disease — Dad did. Win a Pulitzer — Mother's got that. Salutatorian… Homecoming Queen… Cheerleader

Captain… Soccer Captain… Yearbook editor… the list goes on.

Balraj managed a near perfect SAT score and has a 4.0 in business school. Adil is Mr. Popular and in a ton of school organizations. Everyone loves him, me included.

I'm smart, and I've done some things, but that's part of the Kapur way. My family is the one place where I don't want to excel — I just want to belong.

2
Getting in the Trenches

"It's time to get you involved with the kids," announces Katie, the head nurse on my shift. "Come with me."

I click out of the program where I was inputting new inventory numbers and follow her out of the nurse's station. I'm back at the Children's Hospital, and my hours have changed to Wednesdays after school. "Involved in what way?"

We pause to let a kid with an I.V. and his parents pass. After my first month of orientation and training this past spring, I'm usually assigned stocking and working behind the desk. My stint at the main hospital was my first time interacting heavily with visitors and patients.

"We'll ease you in by starting with transporting patients. A bunch of kids have radiology appointments this afternoon, and there aren't enough people to transport them."

We stop at a patient's room, and Katie pokes her head in. "Felicia, can you come out here?"

She appears to be a few years older than me, possibly in college. Katie instructs me to shadow Felicia for a couple of trips before reporting back to the nurse's station for my own transport patients.

As I follow Felicia into the room, a smell of unidentifiable meat greets me, which I find mildly disconcerting. A bunch of helium balloons float a few inches off the ground in the corner, and a teddy bear sits in the chair next to a vase of wilting flowers on the windowsill.

Felicia introduces me to the patient, a girl about my age, and moves the table with a lunch tray away from the bed. "Today, you get a treat because now two people will talk your ear off while traveling to x-ray."

The girl grimaces.

Felicia turns toward me. "Someone will come before you to disconnect the machines. You should only have to push the bed or wheelchair. If you have to move the child's body, hit this button on the bed and someone from the nearest nurse's station will assist you."

The wheels whirl on the linoleum as we push the girl to a set of elevators. The bed isn't heavy but it's unwieldy.

I shadow Felicia for one more patient and then do two of my own. I wouldn't want to do this all the time, but mixed in with the other activities, it makes volunteering more interesting.

A part of me wishes this is the only socialization I'll have to do.

Katie glances at her watch when I return to the nurse's station. "Since you're leaving shortly, I'll give you the lecture and papers I'm obligated to deliver so you can jump in the next time you're here."

We enter a separate section within the station. In this wing, the stations form a large circular core through several floors. Usually, I'm in the outer part, which is open for easy interaction with staff, patients, and visitors. We head to the interior with a few enclosed offices and a meeting room. I haven't been here since orientation and training.

"Needless to say, it's important for families to feel comfortable when they come here," Katie begins after we sit at a table in the meeting room. "Frequently, they don't know what's happening. They're scared and occasionally angry. Because we're talking about children, those emotions run higher."

I'd never thought about that.

"Even when an outline for medical care has been implemented, the process is seldom easy," she continues. "Volunteers can fill an essential function in easing their emotions as we try to carry out the mechanics of their care."

"I'd think performing those tasks and seeing everyone work towards an answer would do that."

"What if there is no solution?"

"There's always a solution. We just have to find it."

"The idealism of youth." Katie chuckles.

I scowl at her. The jadedness of adults. But I like Katie, so I keep my mouth shut.

"You're right, and that's a great attitude, especially if you go into research," she continues. "However, when you're here in the trenches with an individual family, there may be times when you don't have a concrete answer or solution. You'll need to grapple with that reality."

I sit back and bite my lip. "I appreciate your candor."

"I'm not saying it to scare you, though I get the sense you don't scare easily. Volunteers don't need to know much about medicine; they need to connect with people."

"That's not one of my predominant skills," I say wryly.

"You may have a bumpy start, but you'll do fine in the end. I'll give you a booklet and documents to read and sign."

I really like that blue and yellow fish.

The Children's Hospital is new and impressive. There's a primary entrance through the main doors, but I'm on the second floor, where there's an extensive lobby that acts as a waiting area and playroom. The hospital built an enormous aquarium with lots of vibrant colored fish.

A little girl next to me has her nose pressed up to the glass. She's running her finger where her breath fogged up the surface.

That's disgusting.

Then her tongue darts out of her mouth.

Ugh, please don't do it.

"Come over here, honey," a woman calls behind us.

I stare at the tank as the girl runs away, having not good thoughts about my new responsibilities.

Father is running late with his hospital rounds, so he's meeting me in the lobby. He specializes in infectious diseases at the main hospital, which is connected with the medical school and university where he does research.

I'm not one for children, but my father recommended putting in my volunteer application at the Children's Hospital instead of the main medical facility. They have a greater need, and I'd be a better fit because of my age. He also said I'd learn the most here.

Now I get why.

I'm not used to working in an environment without solutions or answers. Having no concrete way of winning makes me uncomfortable. How else can I evaluate how good I am? That mentality makes me hard to take sometimes, which bothers me, but I haven't figured out how to soften the edges without losing ground.

The blue and yellow fish remained in the spot near me, while others like him are on the other side of the tank. Does he have a hard time making friends? I rub my finger on the glass near him.

I have many talents, and comforting people is not one of them. I'm not without heart, but I don't understand the issue half the time. Just solve the problem, and then everyone can avoid all the messy feelings underneath.

I place my forehead on the cool glass and shut my eyes. I'm acting like the little girl. At least my tongue is staying in my mouth.

This new role will spotlight my weaknesses instead of my strengths in the one realm where I thought I had a lock. How does one magically become a people person? It wasn't something I imagined I'd have to develop for volunteering. In hindsight, that wasn't very forward-thinking. I'll have to read the information Katie gave me carefully.

"See you later," I tell the blue and yellow fish while lightly tapping the tank.

A little while later, I look up from my booklet with a start after hearing my name.

Dad gives me a tired smile, but it's still the charmingly crooked one he's known for. He runs a hand through his dark hair, which could use a trim, like Adil's hair. Wrinkled trousers and a lose tie at the neck completes a disheveled look.

Dad tosses me his keys. Since I got my permit a month ago, I drive us home from the hospital all the time.

"Anayah, the light is green."

I press the gas pedal. Volunteering is supposed to set me apart. What if it does the exact opposite? Or sets me apart in a bad way?

"You'll need to be in the other lane because this is a right turn only," Dad says.

I flick my blinker and move laterally.

A horn blares.

I cringe and swerve back into the lane as the driver in the car next to us glares at me through the passenger side window.

"It's usually good to make sure no one is there first," Father says dryly.

I wince. "I'll be more careful."

The highway lights form a monotonous pattern, making it hard to concentrate.

"You're quiet this evening, Anayah, and clearly distracted."

"I have a lot on my mind. Want to go to the science center?"

"Is there a night program this evening?"

I nod. The science museum is where I go when I need space. Clarity. Peace. The planetarium and the butterfly exhibits are my favorite rooms.

"Challenging day on your shift?" Father asks.

"Not yet, but it soon will be."

"Do you need your stars tonight?"

Yes. "No, it's okay. You're tired, and I have homework to do anyway. I asked without thinking."

"I'm sure you'll rally like you always do."

"Yes, Dad."

"That's my girl."

3

In My Way

It's Friday, just after seven in the morning. I'm half awake in my position on the field for early morning band. The director, Ms. Cortez, wants to work out a couple of issues for the halftime performance, and then we need to finish learning the moves for the fourth song of the field show.

I shift my feet to keep the dew from soaking into my sneakers. The sun burned off the fog, so at least it's not dark and dreary — like nobody should march on a field at this hour of the day.

Tara, one of my squad mates, groans as she saunters into her spot in front of me.

I glance at my watch. 7:13. Cutting it close. We're supposed to be on the field and ready to play by 7:15.

"Finally found the field," my squad leader, Samantha, snaps. "I have to tell Mel you're here." She runs out of line as the drum major climbs his ladder.

I sigh.

Band members were placed into groups of four, with a squad leader, who's usually a senior, in charge. As a squad, we learn our marching moves and are tested to ensure we have the music memorized. My friends were placed in groups that are helpful and on the ball.

Mine seems to be the exception. Samantha is a mediocre flute player. Tara is a junior and treats band like it's a social function. I'm not against fun, but I'm here to play music. Good music. There's nothing wrong with Bea, who's a sophomore like me, but I find her company boring. I feel bad about that and try to be nice, but it's hard sometimes.

"To warm up, we'll play our halftime show for Friday." Ms. Cortez stands next to the drum major ladder with her megaphone. "Pay attention to your diagonals in the second piece."

The drum major gives four tweets, and we begin marching as the low brass blows the first notes.

My entire focus is on the music and marching. Play flawlessly, learn the steps, and execute.

An hour and change later, Ms. Cortez calls us to the fifty-yard line. "Good work, but we still need to play catch up. Our first competition is in three weeks, and we have one more song to learn." She grins. "Now for my next announcement: we'll have a special guest with us this spring. V and the Deep Harmonic Overtones have agreed to work with our jazz band and do a joint concert."

A murmur runs through the crowd.

I've heard the name, though I'm not steeped in jazz. I'll have to ask Seth; he might have some of their music. He and Will are talking and gesturing to one another.

The field is on the other side of the building, so it takes time to walk back to the band room. On the way, I fall into step with Seth and Will. A cast is still on Seth's right arm, and Will is also sporting remnants of the accident with bandages on his.

Even though Seth is a close friend of mine, we don't usually run in the same social circles at school. But he seemed to gravitate towards my group of friends during band camp this year, so that may change. Possibly because Will has been spending more time with us too.

"You guys looked excited about the jazz clinic," I comment.

Will gives a whoop. "I don't even know how Ms. Cortez made that happen. She's on fire!"

"Trying out for jazz band this year?" Brooke Campbell asks, popping up on the other side of Will.

"Brooooke!" Will holds his hand up.

I try not to scowl as Brooke slaps it. She does nothing for my disposition.

"I was going to anyway, but now I need to get in," Will answers.

"I went to one of their shows last year in Philly," Brooke says. "They did a free performance on the steps of the museum there. Vivian is usually the vocalist, but she does piano and flute too."

"It would be amazing to work with the trumpet player," says Will. "And if we can actually play with them… unbe-lievable."

"Ms. Cortez has a flute player with the jazz band," Brooke says to me, her eyes lighting up. "I love jazz, espe-cially anything with an Afro-Cuban feel. Do you have an interest?"

I did not peg her for that. "I don't dislike it."

"My dad is a jazz musician," she says. "Maybe when he's home, I'll have more to talk about if I can get into jazz band."

"He's not home much?" Will asks. "Or do you not have a lot to talk about?"

"Both. He travels, and he's not much of a talker. Or someone that pays attention to life. Is your dad a doctor, Anayah?"

Random. "Yes."

"I think I saw him a couple of months ago when I was getting a shot for my trip," Brooke remarks. "There was a picture of the two of you in the waiting room."

I wince. "Yeah, you saw him."

My father is part of a practice though he doesn't spend much time there - only so many hours in a day. Why does he have that photo out? I was doing my first major science experiment, and Dad asked someone to take a picture of us. We were both smiling and hugging each other, so objectively, it's not a terrible photograph. I just don't want all of Southerland to see it. I was thirteen with a retainer and frizzy hair — not exactly a glamor shot.

"He couldn't say enough good stuff about you," Brooke says. "You two must be very close. Following in his footsteps?"

"I guess."

"When do we get to see this picture?" Will asks.

"Not ever."

Ms. Cortez approaches us as we enter the band hallway. "Will, Seth, and Brooke follow me."

The three grow serious as they exchange glances and head down the hall.

I sneak a peek into the band office before someone closes the door on the mini meeting. For such a small room, they crammed a bunch of people in there.

During band camp, Seth, Will, and Brooke emerged as sophomore class band leaders. The sophomores weren't learning the music or steps well enough for this marching band's ambitious program. Seth is sophomore band rep and took charge, and he drafted Will as his right-hand man, like he usually is. Brooke was asked to help in a huge way. She had been drum majorette in ninth grade, and it felt like she stayed in charge right on through to high school.

I was one of the few playing to expectations, but I still didn't come out a leader.

Brooke seems to always get in my way.

I spot Genevieve Larsen's signature long chestnut curls, and make my way to her. Her bright pink t-shirt is hard to miss, though it looks great on her, as does her always meticulously done makeup and hair. Tan complexion, pretty brown eyes, and a small stature complete her photogenic appearance. Next to Seth, Gen has been my good friend longer than anyone else.

The meeting didn't last long because the group is out before the bell rings, and Will catches up with us. The hallway feels close and humid.

"What was the meeting about?" I ask Will, trying to sound casual.

"Ms. Cortez wants to add practices to learn the fifth piece and fine-tune our show for the Florida competition. She asked what days and times would work well."

That's not earth-shattering news, but he's on the inside track. I want to give my opinion. I'm sure I'd have excellent ideas.

We stop short at a people jam in the corridor intersection.

"What was decided?" Gen asks as she waves to another girl across the hall.

"Nothing yet. I pointed out sophomores have a big issue with transportation, but that's not a solution, just something to consider when putting together a plan."

I mull the situation over as I turn sideways to let a kid, who's not paying attention, walk by. "More early mornings?"

"That idea got shot down. There's not enough time before orchestra to make it worthwhile."

"What about Saturdays? Or a second night during the week?"

"Also suggested. We may end up doing that, but we'll have to fight sports events and practices."

We're temporarily parted by a group of giggling girls, a couple of them checking Will out.

"What about making our night practice longer?" I ask him.

"Mentioned too." Will hand clasps a kid at his locker. "We'd still have sports practice to fight."

"At eight o'clock at night?"

"After rehearsal?" Will looks thoughtful. "It's funny nobody mentioned that. I guess everyone figured eight is late enough."

"Lighting could be a problem, but will anyone complain if we stay until nine?" I ask. "We'll be here that late for basketball pep band in the winter."

We stop at the door of their biology room, and Gen waves goodbye to me as she enters the classroom.

"You can mention it to Ms. Cortez at lunch," Will says.

I would love to give a good idea to Ms. Cortez, but it might be weird for me to offer this suggestion when I wasn't at the initial meeting. I don't want to be a busybody.

Will leans against the doorjamb, smirking. I feel he understands my internal battle more than I want him to.

"You can tell her yourself since I wasn't at the meeting." It killed me to say that.

"We'll do it together. I want to make sure credit is given where due." He straightens up so another guy can get through the door. "It's not like you're desperate for attention or anything."

I give him the evil eye. "I'll see you at lunch."

I follow Will into Ms. Cortez's office at the beginning of lunch. Officers and section leaders are in and out of here constantly, but this is the first time I've been inside. A trombone sits under the desk she's eating at, one of three along the walls. A picture of a guy is on top of a MacBook.

Ms. Cortez puts down her sandwich. "What's on your minds?"

"Anayah has a suggestion for our extra practice time issue," Will answers.

She perks up and fixes dark, intelligent eyes towards me. Despite her small size, there's something about her that demands respect. "What is it?"

I'm standing close to Will, so I step forward and explain. "If it's a problem," I conclude, "that should be an incentive to learn the moves faster during regular practice."

Ms. Cortez chuckles. "Not that I don't agree, but we have to accommodate a large variety of temperaments and learning speeds, so I need to be flexible. I'll get opinions from the section leaders and make an announcement tomorrow. Good job."

"Thank you." Hopefully, my help will be sought in other matters now.

"Did that go the way you wanted it to?" Will asks as we leave the office.

"Yes, I'm happy to contribute."

"You don't need brilliant solutions to be a contributing member."

"I know." Many only play their instruments and march, which is fine. "It's just good to be seen."

Will stares at me, which makes me fidget. I focus on Seth hurrying in our direction.

"Where's the fire?" Will asks him.

"Mia is in the hall."

"How many times have I told you to leave her alone?" Will asks.

"Too late," Seth replies. "We got back together this morning."

Will shakes his head. "She just doesn't want to start high school without a man."

"I wasn't too keen on starting one without a girl, so this works."

I make a face. "And you had to pick Mia?"

"What exactly is your problem with her?" Seth asks.

"We've never gotten along." I smirk. "I'm probably not as subservient as she'd like."

"And you wonder why there's an issue."

"She has you on a short leash." I bend over and pat my thighs. "Come here, Seth. Over here, boy."

Will laughs.

Seth narrows his eyes at me as his phone goes off, and then he growls at the screen.

I wave a hand. "Go on, boy."

He points at me. "We're not finished with this."

"The cast takes away from your menacing quality," I say.

Will and Seth both catch a fair amount of female attention, which gets annoying with the fawning girl thing. But Mia Thompson is smart and keeps her cool, so I have some respect for her. It's interesting we butt heads.

The band room door flies open, and Mia steps into the room. "What's taking you so long, Seth?" Her face clouds over. "Anayah," she greets me coolly.

"I see you're collecting your belongings," I reply.

She glares at me for a moment, and then her demeanor changes completely as her attention shifts. "You're a sight for sore eyes, Will."

"How you been, Mia?" he asks.

"Why don't you come with us tonight after the game and find out?"

"Nah, I'm good," Will replies. "Thanks for the invite though."

"Estelle won't be there."

Will's jaw tightens. "I'm good."

She touches Will's arm. "Not all of us think the same way she does."

Will jerks his arm back.

"We should go," Seth says quietly.

"What was that about?" I ask Will after they walk out the door.

"It's in the past. Don't worry about it."

That sounds ominous. Will and Estelle dated for a large part of freshman year, and people identify him as one of the popular kids, like top echelon. He stopped going with his old crowd and exclusively spent time with my friends after he and Estelle broke up. I can appreciate hating to hang out with your ex, but what just transpired makes me think it was more than that.

I walk towards our group eating lunch in the trumpet section.

"What do you think of Gen's interest in Seth?" Will asks.

I stop short. What's with the random questions today? "How do you know about that?"

"We had a chat."

I'm not sure how to answer him without sounding like I'm constructing a thesis. I didn't like the idea when she told us girls. That development would introduce a complication into our comfortable group dynamic that I don't care for, and Seth's dating habits leave a lot to be desired. Break-ups create messes in groups. Will and Estelle are case and point.

"Why are you asking about it?"

"Gen made it sound like you weren't a fan, and now you're not a fan of him with Mia."

"Where are you going with this?"

"I really have to paint a picture for you, don't I?"

"How about asking a straightforward question?"

"Have you ever had a crush? Or is that beneath you?"

I glare at him. "If there were crush-worthy specimens around, I might consider it. Do you think I like Seth?"

He shrugs.

"Ugh."

"He's not bad, and friends fall for each other all the time."

"Not bad is a ringing endorsement."

"No guy around here is good enough for Miss Kapur." Will gives me a wicked grin.

I stomp back to our group. My annoyance is irrational. For the most part, Will is correct — I've never seriously liked anyone, and crushes, one or two.

I appreciate attractive guys. It's not like that's lost on me. But liking someone? To me, that requires more going on, and boys my age tend to be lacking in that department.

I have things to do and goals to accomplish. Ridiculous adolescent romances that won't last are a needless distraction. Why am I deemed abnormal just because I don't want to go out with immature teenage boys?

But the way Will asked about it being beneath me implied things that I'm not happy about. It fed into a painful recognition of my difficulty in drawing people.

My mind flashes back to when we were at the hospital. I had felt super close to him and thought he had too. Apparently, that moment happened because he was on tons of pain medication.

I drop into my seat when we rejoin our lunch group.

"You okay?" Gen asks me.

"Yeah, just Will being Will."

"He always finds a way to wind you up."

"Usually I don't care, but today's comment…"

"Did he say something out of line? That's unlike him."

"No, and I'm sure he didn't mean it to bother me the way it did. It's nothing; forget about it."

I pull out my food but don't have much of an appetite. After taking a couple of bites of my chicken salad, I put the lid back on and stick it back in my bag.

I catch Will's eye.

Something shifts, and his eyes hold me to his — like he's got me locked in a tractor beam. As quickly as it came, it's gone, and I exhale.

What was that?

4

Crisis

"You can be the prince, and I'll be the village girl." It's another Wednesday at the hospital, and today's volunteer session is the first time I'm doing serious patient interaction. I take the prince doll from Emily, a six-year-old with congenital heart disease. The monitor beeps at regular intervals by her bed.

"Save me! Save me!" she cries.

I stare at her.

"Anayah!"

"What?! What am I supposed to do?"

Emily sighs like she's explaining to a three-year-old. "You're supposed to save the girl."

"Why? She doesn't need a prince to save her. This game does nothing to teach female empowerment. How about she comes up with a plan and invites the prince to assist?"

"Work with me, Anayah." Emily stands the prince on the thin, white blanket on her bed. "Should we try this again?"

I have to work hard to keep from sighing. "Yes. I got it."

I'm learning children can destroy your ego. So far, eleven-year-old Jared told me I'm a horrible race car driver and to get someone to teach me his video game. He asked if I drive as slow on the actual road as I do in the game. Eight-year-old Amara said I don't read with all the voices, and that she would show me next week how it's done if she's still here. Now I can't catch on to doll scenario games.

Other than the complete demoralization, it hasn't been as painful as I thought it would be. The kids are appreciative, and it's nice to be appreciated.

I'm walking back to the nurse's station about ten minutes later when I spot Seth sitting in a hallway. His usually calm demeanor looks cracked. The Baniks have been in hospitals far too much this year.

"Hi, Seth. Is it Nina?"

He nods. "Another crisis. My parents are in there with the doctor."

Nina is eleven years old and has sickle cell disease. Crises are very painful and can sometimes result in tissue or organ damage if they're severe or happen frequently. With regular medical care, it's now easier for children to survive into adulthood. This is Nina's second one in a short time, so her overall health is not in a good place.

Our fathers were friends in college, and Seth and his little sister are unofficial family members. As close as my family is to the Baniks, this is the first time I've been on the front lines when Nina has been very ill. I usually visit them after the emergency, when Nina is on the road to recovery.

I swallow as my heart thumps louder. It's like the car accident all over again.

"Did my mom call you?" Seth asks.

Before I can explain, a door opens, and his parents step into the hallway with a doctor. Mr. Banik puts a hand on Seth's shoulder.

"It's so good to see you, Anayah." Mrs. Banik hugs me. "I got off the phone with your mother barely twenty minutes ago."

"I was already here volunteering and ran into Seth on my way back to the nurse's station."

"I don't want to take you away from your duties," Mrs. Banik says.

"Helping visitors feel comfortable is part of them."
Seth chuckles.

Thanks for the vote of confidence, Seth.

"Do you need anything?" I ask Mrs. Banik as she grows teary-eyed.

My eyes get itchy. This is precisely the kind of vulnerability that sharing emotions can bring. I must steel myself.

Seth was right to laugh at me. The physical and concrete — that's what I do best. "I can take you to the visitor's lounge or the cafeteria. Unless you need to stay by the room, and then I can bring food up."

"We better eat," Mr. Banik replies. "It'll be another long night."

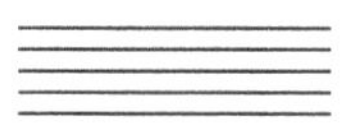

The ride home from the hospital is somber. My father had offered to take Seth with us so the Banik parents could stay in the hospital, and Seth wouldn't be alone. He seems understandably tense and tired.

I pull into our driveway. It's like every light in the house is on. The aromas of curry and naan greet us as we enter.

Mother rushes to Seth and gives him a huge hug. "You're welcome to stay here as long as you need. There's plenty of food in the kitchen. Help yourself."

"Thank you, Mrs. Kapur," he says.

Mother tells me to take him to Balraj's room, and we run into Priya in the hallway.

As Seth explains, Priya stops running the towel over her wet hair. "I'll visit Nina tomorrow after work."

"Thanks, Priya."

"Do you like to dance?" she asks him.

He's quiet for a second. "I don't wile out in my room, but I don't hate it either."

"I'll keep that in mind." Priya continues to her room after they say goodnight, and Seth gives me a questioning look.

I shrug. "It's Priya."

Seth has been here a million times, but given the circumstances, I try to do more to get him settled and comfortable in Balraj's room. To my surprise, he joins me forty-five minutes later in the rec room with food.

I ask Seth what it's like when Nina has a crisis.

He seems surprised by my question. "Sometimes she cries, but other times I think the pain is so intense, it's like tears aren't enough. Her face gets pale or yellowish, and her eyes look sunken. It's awful to watch."

Nina is more mature than most children her age without being a killjoy. She's the right kind of kid for me. The description of her writhing in pain is upsetting, to say the least.

In a blinding flash, I know what I'm doing for my SJRC project. "I'm curing sickle cell."

Seth looks at me like I have two heads. "You say that like you're getting a drink of water."

"Obviously, it's going to take tons of work, but I'm going to do it. We're making Nina better."

Seth gives me a smile.

"And in the process, I'll be inducted into the National Academy of Sciences."

"You couldn't hang on to that moment could you?"

5

Priya's Great Idea

The following Sunday, I'm salivating, thinking about eating last night's leftovers for a late lunch. I need a break from my marathon study session. These AP classes are no joke, and I have to decide how to discuss my goals for SJRC with Dr. Reed.

I stop short after entering the kitchen. Balraj is at the kitchen island.

"You were here two weeks ago, and that better not be the last of the tandoori chicken and aloo chaat you're eating."

"I left the samosas," he replies, giving me a display of half masticated food. "Pri needs to talk to us about her engagement party. Something special she wants to do."

I yank open the fridge, grab the samosas, and pour myself some iced tea.

Am I invisible? I have a life and can't drop everything whenever it suits people. "Once again, nobody tells me anything."

"Would it have mattered?"

I'm fighting the urge to be a jerk back when Priya sails in. "Hello, everyone," she sings. "Where's Adil?"

"Upstairs," answers Balraj. "He'll be down in a minute."

"Adil, we'll be in the tree house!" Priya yells.

"The tree house?" I repeat.

"It's the perfect place to talk about my fabulous idea!" Priya skips out the side door.

Balraj and I exchange looks across the kitchen island.

I grab a fork and shove it into his bowl before he knocks my hand away. "Get out of my food!" he exclaims.

"I don't have time to heat mine," I whine. "You can share. You're not even home most of the time."

We fight over the last few forkfuls of potatoes before heading into the backyard.

Treehouse is a misnomer since most of the old trees were cut down when the development was built twenty-five years ago. My parents sprung for the construction of an elaborate elevated clubhouse with an attached tire swing and two regular swings when we moved here. Mother was always big on us playing outside.

While it was fun when I was younger and you'd think the swings would be more my speed since I was the youngest, the playhouse was more of Priya's and Balraj's thing. The neighborhood kids would come over, and it was popular because the house part created a little distance from the grown-ups without having to deal with some of the hassles of being out in public. By that time, they were teens, and it wasn't like we were all playing together cohesively anymore. I had to work around everyone to get any play time on it and usually entertained myself with the equipment they weren't interested in. I spent a lot of quality time with the pulley — not always exciting.

"Is this thing going to hold us?" Balraj asks.

Priya appears by the ladder, already up in the playhouse. "We used to cram a million kids in here. It can hold the four of us."

We climb up, and I duck my head as I enter. Balraj folds his body into the house after me, grumbling.

Adil crawls in a second later. "This is fun. Brings back memories."

Balraj shoots him a glare. "Let's make this quick."

"I have a super idea for the engagement party." Priya's eyes are dancing, and she looks pleased with herself. "We're going to do a professionally choreographed feature dance."

She flings her arms wide in a flourish and grimaces when one smacks a wall.

"What?" asks Balraj.

I'm with him on this one, for the first time ever.

"A dance," Priya repeats, as she rubs her arm. "And we can get our friends to be background dancers."

"But why?" asks Adil.

"Oh, come on, it'll be fun," Priya coaxes. "The Kapur Kids doing a spectacular dance on a special evening for the last time as unmarried siblings."

"Did we have a first time?" asks Balraj.

"I thought you were throwing like a typical states engagement party?" Adil asks.

"Yeah, dancing and entertainment. Our family isn't the typical states family, and we can introduce some flair. The place has a stage, and since we can't hire a professional group to do a show for us, I thought this would be a good idea."

"Really?" Adil questions.

"One of David's friends, Owen, is a choreographer. As a wedding gift, he's willing to make up a dance routine and teach it to us for a very low price. Think Bollywood."

"There's no way we have the skills to pull that off," Balraj says. "And is Owen really up to creating that level of choreography?"

Her enthusiasm wanes just a bit. "He did a study abroad program in Bangaluru while doing his dance studies. He's not completely clueless."

Balraj gives her a look.

"Are we going to come up with something better ourselves?" Priya challenges.

"Hence the reason for our objections," I point out.

"I think we can do this," Priya says her confidence returning. "It doesn't need to be perfect, it just needs to be us. I promise it'll be fun, and we won't do anything embarrassing."

How can she make a promise like that?

Adil shrugs. "If it means that much to you, Priya, I'm in."

"We need to look good," Balraj says.

"Of course, but you're not outshining the bride-to-be."

"I wouldn't dream of it. But I may need to outshine your fiancée."

Priya rolls her eyes. "Anayah?"

Another occasion where, as the baby, I'll get roped in and dragged along. Boxed in, like this playhouse is doing to us.

Priya pouts. "I need you, baby sis."

I cringe.

"Come on, Yaya." Adil gives me a light punch on the arm.

"I don't like dancing, and I don't want to do it in front of an audience."

"Ladies and gentlemen, we finally found something Anayah is afraid of." Balraj snickers.

"I'm not afraid," I snap. "Fine. I'll do it."

Priya claps her hands. "The Kapur kids are going to be amazing!"

6

A Vague and Lofty Goal

"I want to cure sickle cell," I tell Dr. Reed on Monday when I report to lab. I've been working at a university research lab for a while under Dr. Reed. He has been good friends with my father and family since before I was born.

Dr. Reed's piercing blue-gray eyes tell me he thinks I'm being ridiculous. I receive those looks from him often.

"I'm serious."

"I'm sure you are, Anayah. You seldom aren't." He leans back heavily in his chair. "Curing sickle cell isn't a research investigation. It's a vague and lofty goal, especially for a sophomore in high school. You are still talking about your SJRC project?"

"Of course. What else would I be talking about?"

"I thought you turned into a fifty-five-year-old multi-doctorate scientist on the verge of the Nobel prize."

Dr. Reed and I have always had an interesting relationship. It's like mutual respect combined with mutual annoyance.

It's a big deal that he's my mentor for the competition. Dr. Reed is a big name in genetic research, the field I want to be in one day. His respect is important to me, but at times like this, that's hard to remember.

SJRC is the Sieps Junior Research Competition and is THE showcase for young scientists — a national competition with top-notch level research and prestige.

If you win, you can almost name the school of your choice that has a strong science and technology program. There are also scholarship awards, some for large amounts of money.

While that's important to me, it's not the primary reason I participate in these competitions. I'm good at book and classroom work, exams, papers — you name it, I'll ace it. But to use that book knowledge and apply it to real-life problems; that's where it's at. To start an experiment from nothing, investigate a problem, get results and analyze them to amaze myself and others about the world — I get goosebumps every time I think about it.

Dr. Reed runs a hand through his salt-and-pepper-colored hair. "You need to do background research to understand the disease and what's been done so far. Then you'll have a better idea of where to go."

"I know about sickle cell."

"You need more knowledge than what your biology textbook imparts. Before you design or do any experiments here, I'm assigning a comprehensive research report on sickle cell, complete with footnotes and references."

My jaw drops. "I want to do lab work."

"I want to make sure you know what you're doing," he counters. "The University might not expect much since this is slated as a community outreach project. But if you're working with me, you will do something real."

I hold my chin up and toss my hair. "I wouldn't have it any other way."

"Good. At least we have that understanding. Create a stronger, more focused project. Curing a disease is not an experiment."

He has a point. I get that he's guiding me; I just don't like the direction this guidance is heading, but I'll follow it because I trust it'll lead me to my goal. "Fine."

"Spend the rest of the week in the library. We have a tiny one in this building. Start there before going to the campus one."

BSRI is a research facility that's part of the University Medical Center but also not. Now it's an impressive new and shiny building, large, white, and boxy that probably won't age well. Dr. Reed is a professor at the medical school and heads a research team here.

He stands while gathering papers from his desk. "If you have questions about what you read, besides asking me, you can also talk to Chen, Yessenia, or Jaya."

"Okay."

"You'll thank me later." He walks out of the room.

I make a face at his retreating back and head downstairs to the building's library. I still don't see the need for all this preliminary research, and I'm going to prove it.

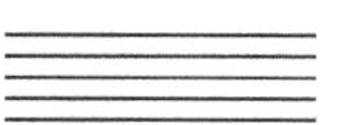

I spend several hours at the library, which was much longer than I had planned. Dr. Reed hadn't assigned a date due but I wanted this finished in a week or less so I could move on, which will be tough. Lab papers, journal articles, and college textbooks are strewn across the table. It's taking forever for me to unwind what they're talking about, and I have pages of questions to ask or research further so I can fill in the gaps.

Begrudgingly, I see Dr. Reed's point.

My knowledge is superficial at best. Red blood cells are misshapen and therefore die rapidly or get caught on one another and destroyed. The disease is carried genetically. I could even do the Punnett square for it.

The actual mechanics of the disease and why it operates the way it does are beyond me, but at least I'm not alone there. I also learned that they can "cure" the disease in a small population through bone marrow transplants. But even if that treatment becomes widespread, and there's no guarantee that it will, that's years away. More research is needed from a treatment and therapy standpoint.

I stare out the window next to me. The sun is setting, and the lights along the walkways throughout the quad are coming on. I didn't realize how late it was.

Father calls to find out where I am and says he'll swing by and get me on his way home from the office. I told him I'd meet him by the lake.

It's a reservoir, but the university landscaped it. The leaves are changing color and planters with giant mums dot the patio. Ducks and geese swim in the lake. It's a short walk from BSRI, and I come here sometimes when I take a break.

I plop down on the bench, setting my heavy bookbag beside me. This is getting super complicated. My heart stutters. I can't fail at this. So much is riding on it.

A figure jogging catches my eye. That isn't unusual on campus, but this figure strikes me as familiar.

"Nayah?" Will calls out. He slows his pace as he reaches the bench.

"What are you doing here?" I ask him.

"Running."

"Obviously. Why are you doing it here?"

"Dad has a meeting. He said I'd probably like jogging on campus, and that I could come with him."

I take in his professional running clothes. "I didn't realize you took running so seriously."

"I do it almost every day but stick with my neighborhood or the park. Or at least I did before the accident. It'll take a while to get back to that level. Is your lab nearby?"

I nod and point to the building through the trees across the green.

He peers at me.

"What?" I ask.

"You seem off."

"That's a crystal clear description."

"Like you got knocked off your high and sturdy pedestal. It's not often you look unsure."

I freeze. Besides the fact that was an unflattering description, it was also eerily accurate. "I'm allowed to not have the answers every once in a while."

"Do you actually believe that?"

First Dr. Reed and now him. I put on armor to operate. Will could poke a lot of holes in it or rip it off if he wanted to.

Whispering in the back of my mind, 'you bit off more than you could chew this time'.

"Seriously, Nayah. Are you okay?" Will sounds worried. "What's wrong?"

I'm going to do this. I'll start by writing the most comprehensive research report Dr. Reed has ever read on sickle cell and show him he doesn't know everything either.

"Everything is great." I shoot up from the bench. "I just hit a little bump. Nothing I can't get over."

Dad shows up, and I ask if he remembers Will.

"Of course. At first, I thought you were a part of the lab team," Dad says to Will. "But, now registering your clothing, that was a silly assumption." He sticks his hand out. "How are you? It appears you're making a full recovery."

Will shakes it. "I'm good, sir."

"Do you need a lift home?"

"No, thank you. My father is here somewhere. Take care of yourself, Nayah." Will jogs off.

"He seemed concerned," Father remarks. "Is everything all right?"

"Would everyone stop asking me that? I'm fine."

"Excuse me for showing concern for my daughter." He smirks. "Will is good-looking."

"I hadn't noticed."

He chuckles. "You did, and that's okay. Let's get dinner. I'm starved."

7

In Charge

My section leader, Mel, runs up to me and drops squad sheets and diagrams into my arms. "Good, you're here."

It's Monday, early morning band, and she seems agitated. Our first competition for the year is Thursday, and we've barely learned the field show in its entirety.

"Samantha is absent," Mel continues. "We're about to have a short squad meeting. It's crunch time for the trip too, and Ms. Cortez told me to grab you to represent your squad. "

Yes! "Sure."

Tara is standing nearby, gossiping with a group of people. She gives me a dirty look when I follow Mel into the band room. If she paid more attention, she'd probably be in here instead of me.

Ms. Cortez is getting the meeting underway as the door bangs shut behind us. "Even with the late practice tomorrow night, we have a lot of woodshedding to do by

Thursday. If you see an area that needs correction, hop on it."

She spends a couple of minutes outlining which sections the band has difficulties with, so we can spotlight those areas with our squads.

"Let's get moving," Ms. Cortez concludes. "We need field time, and unfortunately, it looks like it'll pour any minute. Unlike band camp, I can't keep you in the rain during school."

Metal scrapes against the linoleum as everyone jumps up and heads outside. The wind is getting stronger.

The first two songs are okay because we've performed them during football games and the percussion feature isn't bad either. The jazz piece is a whole different story.

My squad is nowhere in the curve. I've always questioned Samantha's placement of us, but since it didn't look awful, and Ms. Cortez hadn't said anything, I had let it go. But today… how can we be this wrong?

Now I can correct it the way I want. "Tara! You need to take like four steps up, so you're in the curve."

She looks away and stays put.

I set my jaw as Bea and I move. The other squads around us adjust.

This is so much better.

Now, Tara is really out in left field, so she moves up. By that time, we're switching to a new formation, and she's behind.

"Come on, Tara!" I yell.

She glares at me but increases her steps.

Then it starts to rain.

After finishing the piece, Mike blows the halt sequence.

"We'll have to finish indoors," Ms. Cortez says through her megaphone.

Tara stomps towards me. "Don't order me around-"

"Then act like you know what you're doing. Why don't you quit socializing and pay attention?"

Tara leans into me.

"Enough, Tara!" yells another squad leader. "We need to move."

Tara scowls but takes off as Mel comes behind me. "That needed to be said, and Sam isn't always firm enough."

"You're going to be sopping wet." I say to Bea, whose eyes are still huge. "Better get inside,"

I heave a deep breath, trying to calm down.

"You all right?" Mel asks after Bea leaves.

I nod, and we jog towards the building.

"Ms. Cortez seems edgy about this competition," I comment. "I thought she'd be more concerned over the theme park performances and the bowl game parade. Aren't they more important?"

"Depends on what you consider important. They're more high profile, but the field show is kinda the marching band's heart and identity. She wants to make sure it's our best."

"Concert band isn't?"

Mel grins. "I guess it could be. Why be good in only one when you can do both, right Anayah?"

I chuckle.

"Maybe that's something you and your class can do," Mel continues. "I bet you and Brooke are part of the group of people that have a different instrument for concert band than for marching."

I nod. Ms. Cortez encouraged us to get piccolos if we could swing it, and I did. But even before that, the flute I play for concert band is much nicer than the one I had used for marching. I don't want my good flute to get ruined in the weather.

We enter the building and slide into our seats.

Ms. Cortez is clearly not happy to be practicing indoors. She frowns after the band plays the last piece and asks me and five other sophomores to play a portion of the song.

This exercise is like a pop quiz. Ms. Cortez does it more often when she's in a mood, like she is now, but she doesn't usually call on sophomores. It's an excellent opportunity to show what I can do, and my group is good.

Ms. Cortez gives a satisfied nod after we finish and calls another group. We spend the remaining time on the last two pieces.

"We'll have chair auditions for concert band seating in six weeks. That's the third week in October," Ms. Cortez announces as we pack up.

The room grows quiet as she explains the procedure. Chair placement isn't super important during marching band season, but it matters for concert band. Solos and the parts assigned are based on chair, and concert band season is much longer than the marching band one.

"Good job with the solo thing," Brooke says as we leave the band room. "I heard you and Tara had a nice chat."

"She drives me nuts."

"Sounds like she needed to be set straight." Brooke takes off down the hall.

What would it feel like to be friends? Iron sharpening iron. But to get what I want, I need to take Brooke down first.

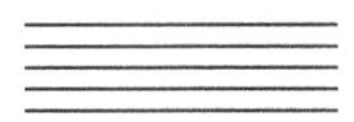

I catch up with Will and Gen. My shoes squeak on the floor, but I barely notice as I try to parse out my next steps for band.

I'm fourth chair for marching band season based on our auditions last spring for the high school. A junior is first chair, and a senior, third. They're decent, but with a little effort, it'll be no problem to beat them.

My real competition is Brooke, who's currently second. We've been battling for flute first chair since sixth grade. Unfortunately, she usually wins. I need a plan for dominating my chair audition.

"Whatcha thinking 'bout, Nayah?" Will asks.

I whip my head towards him. "The chair audition announcement."

"And it makes you mad?"

"No. Determined."

"The battle for flute queen continues." He smirks. "You think you'll actually win this year?"

I stop short.

My bookbag is hit from behind, and someone mutters.

Will turns and faces me, still walking. Still grinning.

"At least I have a shot," I snap.

"Anayah!" Gen exclaims.

Is she serious? He's the one goading me.

Will chuckles. "No, she's right, but I'm going to audition like I have one anyway."

He disappears inside the room.

"Anayah, your mouth is off the charts," Gen says. "He says that stuff just to watch you holler."

"Why doesn't he do that with anyone else?"

"They don't fight him like you do which makes you more..." a sly grin lights her face. "Provocative."

"I'll provoke him all right. I need to push his buttons."

"You do, but you could do it better if you were less defensive. He has a laser focus on you." She winks. "Something to think about."

I'm not the only one he's focusing on. "Are you still interested in Seth?" I ask.

Gen's eyes widen as her face grows pink. "Could you be any louder? Or random?"

"Sorry, it came to mind suddenly."

"Not anymore." As quickly as it came, the color drains from her face. "Do I act like I am?"

"I don't think so."

"If I tell you something, promise not to tell anyone."

"Of course. What's wrong?"

"Nothing is wrong, just complicated." She smiles and flushes. "I like Taylor's older brother, John, and he likes me back."

Taylor Vance is Gen's best friend. Not that Gen isn't a lovely person, inside and out, but from what I've seen of John, he's a high caliber too. Given their difference in grades, I'm surprised Gen was in his ballpark.

"When did this happen?" I ask.

"The weekend before school started."

"So are you two doing anything about it?" This is sorta beginning to sound like fifth grade, and freshman college John definitely is not.

"We're in a holding pattern for now. Taylor has some fears that are real to her and serious, and this makes them more intense. John is stressed and can't do a relationship now. A real one anyway."

And she is? I've never considered myself wise with dating and crushes and such. A lot of it seems nonsensical to me. Way too much emotional randomness and not enough rationale.

But I can comprehend that Gen needs me to keep quiet on a personal and potentially explosive issue. "My lips are sealed."

"Ladies, let's keep it moving." A teacher walks by.

My mind goes back to Gen's earlier comment about Will observing me as I rush to health class. For some reason, that makes me feel weirdly exposed.

And excited.

8

The Competitor

We need to unload the delivery from the band's citrus fruit fundraiser after school today. The upperclassmen made it sound like the greatest thing on earth. I'm skeptical, but it's an important band morale function, and I want to help.

Kyra and Taylor are on the sidewalk with me. I don't know what kind of fruit truck I expected, but an eighteen-wheeler was not it.

Will rushes out the cafeteria doors. "Let's dive in."

We join the seniors at the truck, who've started taking boxes inside. A couple of the guys seem especially happy to see Taylor. She has long blonde hair, blue eyes, and a nice height. I've known her nearly as long as Gen, but not as well. Like Mia, Taylor has a cool reserve to her, but I find Taylor much nicer and more fun. She has the popular thing going for her, like Will and Seth, but Taylor has been more of a floater, instead of becoming part of a clique. This year, my friends seem to be gradually forming a close group.

I grab a box and almost fall over.

We shuffle back into the building and add them to a small pile in the cafeteria. By the time we get back out, a small human conveyor line had formed from inside the truck to the building.

Taylor and I squeeze in next to Will and Seth inside the truck.

Boxes are cleared systematically from the front of the truck, and we're working our way back. The line stretches, and instead of passing the boxes, we're tossing them to each other, with lots of yelling and hooting.

Kyra joins a new line forming on the opposite side of the truck. We haven't been talking a ton because the work is hard, but our line is at a brief standstill while they untie something. The citrus scent fills the truck.

"Are you doing SJRC this year, Kyra?" I ask. "I noticed they have a programming category."

"I'm not sure yet." She grabs a box and hands it to a senior next to her. "I have a lot going on with drumline. Will is entering."

My eyebrows shoot up as I take some rope from him. "You're entering The Sieps Science competition?"

"You make it sound like it's impossible."

I toss the rope off the truck. Will is smart, so it's not impossible; he's just not serious. I never imagined him entering.

Our line gets going, and Seth passes a box to Taylor. "What made you decide to enter?" he asks Will.

"My dad is making me. Kyra did it the last two years, and now he thinks it's the greatest thing ever — that I should go into the sciences."

"I didn't know you hated it so much." Kyra passes a box. "I can't stand how you ace those classes without lifting a finger."

"I don't hate science. I just don't want to spend all my free time on it. I got things."

Will's cavalier attitude and disdain towards science grate on my nerves. SJRC is my competition, and he's acting like it doesn't matter. "Yeah, those video games are so important."

"I also play this thing called the trumpet and run. Some of us like to be outdoors." Will tosses a box at me.

I stumble as I catch it. "I like the outdoors, but choose to interact with it on a cerebral level."

"So you're the only one who's smart around here?" He tosses another box at me, hard.

"No, and could you work on your aim? Kyra is a coding genius. Matt's graphic novels are amazing. Xiang is a brainiac despite acting flighty sometimes." I hand the box off. "Gen is a brilliant dancer, and Taylor, an exceptional cellist."

"And I'm something that doesn't belong?"

"You don't apply yourself."

"I'm in half your classes. How do I not apply myself?"

"You fool around."

"That doesn't mean I don't work." Will chucks another box at me and it sends me hurtling to the side of the truck.

"Knock it off!"

His jaw ticks. "Sorry."

This argument has a sharpness that's not usually there. Will tends to let things slide off his back, and I haven't said anything untrue.

An hour later, we're about two-thirds through the truck, and everyone looks tired. My thighs are killing me; tossing those boxes requires a ton of squatting. Joe suggests a fifteen minute break before wrapping things up.

Taylor, Kyra, and I compare our arms as we get out of the truck. Their arms are pinkish and rubbed raw. Mine have angry red welts from the box corners hitting my skin and purple bruises from harder tosses.

I growl. "I'm going to get Will when we're done."

We're grabbing water from the vending machine when the guys join us.

"What projects are you two working on?" Kyra asks.

"I'm curing sickle cell." I take a swig of water.

Will laughs hard. "Who cures a disease for a high school science project? What are you trying to prove, Nayah?"

I will die before telling him my actual reasons for trying to win SJRC. Yes, I want to win, but really, I need my family to start treating me with respect and not like the baby. He would roll hearing that.

His laughter dies. "Nayah?"

I bend over and stretch. "I'm not trying to prove anything." I straighten up. "I'm trying to help Nina."

Will's eyes soften a touch.

That pleases me, which then annoys me. I toss my ponytail. "What is your project about if mine is so ridiculous?"

"Music."

"That's not a category."

"Biochemistry is. I believe music's effect on cortisol and other antibodies would qualify as scientific research, wouldn't you, Anayah?"

My jaw drops.

Will crosses his arms. "Unless you plan on doing high level genetic editing and manipulation to cure sickle cell, which I doubt you have the expertise to perform, you may also end up in the biochemistry category. Last I heard, pain management is hot right now, and would be considered an acceptable downgrade from curing the disease on the DNA level." Will flips on the tractor beam. "Do I sound serious enough for you yet, Miss Kapur?"

I work hard ignoring several other unwelcome physical sensations. Pain management isn't the only thing hot right now. "How do you know about sickle cell?"

"Our uncle has it," Kyra answers.

"I'm also capable of reading," Will says with an edge.

I recall the numerous journal articles and studies I read. He read that material? Maybe he skimmed other general articles.

Joe walks past us. "Let's finish this."

We follow him back to the truck and climb in.

"How did you become interested in music therapy, Will?" asks Taylor.

"Camp. One of the kids there was on the autistic spectrum, and his family uses music to help him. We went to a center on a field trip, and they let me play my trumpet for them. The specialist was specific, but it's mind-blowing to help like that." He's holding a box. "Come on, Nayah. You're holding up the line."

I scowl, but move more quickly. "Do you even care about the competition?"

"Yeah. This project is interesting, and it might do something real." Will tosses me a box and grins. "And I always play to win. It's time someone taught you a lesson."

His smile disappears and the tractor beam is back.

I squirm, holding the box. Why is this happening again?

He looks away, releasing me, and I exhale, handing the box to Kyra. I have an uneasy feeling the lesson I'm about to learn will be one of the hardest I've ever had.

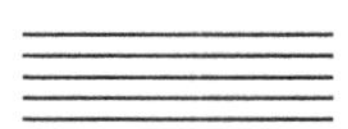

"Did you review my report, Dr. Reed?" I'm standing in the doorway of his office the next afternoon.

"Yes. Why don't you come in and shut the door?" He waves to a chair. "Have a seat."

I make myself comfortable while Dr. Reed pulls my report up on his laptop.

"This was good. You had information I wasn't familiar with."

Of course. "Thank you."

"Did you see why I had you write the report?"

"I did."

"So are you going to cure sickle cell?"

I make a face. "My pronouncement was late and over-simplified. However, many things are still unknown and need study."

"True. If you really want to do this, you need to narrow your focus. What made you interested in sickle cell in the first place?"

I tell him about Nina and Seth. "I suppose you could say I want to end her pain. Eliminating sickle cell would be the ultimate solution."

"Yes, but not a practical one, for you, in the immediate future. Other things can be explored."

"Such as?"

"Did you come across articles regarding pain management with sickle cell?"

Will can not be so dead right on this. If my research project follows his prediction — I will never live that down.

Even in his absence, I can feel his taunt. His promise.

It's bringing the same unwanted sensations I experienced before. This just adds credence that I'm weird because this situation should not act as a source of attraction.

Pull it together. "Yes, I saw articles on that topic."

There's a moment of silence, and then Dr. Reed's phone makes a wind chime sound.

"What did you think of them?" he asks.

"The articles? They were very interesting."

"Anayah, you can't possibly be so obtuse right now."

I exhale. "You're suggesting narrowing my focus to researching the reduction or elimination of the pain involved with the crises?"

"It's a good direction. It's still a very lofty goal, but there's a slight possibility you can reach it, on what will most likely be a lower level."

I can barely understand his statement. "That's a lot of qualifiers."

Dr. Reed shrugs. "I'm trying to be honest and realistic."

"But there are drugs that reduce the pain already." Last ditch effort to steer him away from this topic.

"There are only one or two FDA approved drugs that address the pain associated particularly with crises. That's an embarrassingly small number given the extraordinary level of pain this disease produces. Research has been done on other possibilities, and I want you to explore those."

I groan. "Don't tell me you're assigning another paper?"

"I am, but include outlines for a specific research investigation and experiment. The readings you do for your paper should give you ideas."

At least we're finally talking about actual lab work.

"Please keep in mind you're only a high school student, and your submission needs to be to SJRC by the middle of December. You cannot outline an experiment that will take three years and hundreds of subjects."

"I realize that."

"I'd prefer if your experiment didn't use any human or animal subjects. Those require so much paperwork."

"Okay."

"Keep it simple — low cost, community outreach project. I don't need the new director breathing down my back while he tries to prove himself."

“I got it. Can I go?”

Dr. Reed directs his attention towards his laptop. “Yes, you can leave.”

9

Let's Dance

Priya promised a dinner meeting about the engagement party dance at any place we named the first Saturday of October. Balraj being Balraj, named an expensive Indian restaurant about an hour away from here.

I'm looking forward to dinner, even if it means enduring more wedding talk. To my surprise, we stop by the Baniks on our way, and I make room for Seth in the backseat. Priya is buttering him up good if she's asking him to be part of the dance. This is much better than being squashed in a tree house.

The host greets us at the restaurant. "As requested, your table is not as close to the other guests."

He takes us to a table with a pleasant view of the gardens in the back and a little privacy.

"This is perfect," Priya says.

We sit down, and my eyes widen as I scan the prices on the menu. Priya agreed to this, so I suppose she knows what she's doing.

She claps her hands. "This is nice."

"Priya, this is really nice," Adil says. "Are you sure about this? I didn't realize what kind of restaurant Balraj had picked."

"Pri is fine," Balraj declares. "I bet she's been here before, and they even gave her a good table."

"I knew what I was in for and happy to do it. Order what you like." Priya shakes a finger at Balraj. "Within reason. No expensive bottles of wine, mister."

"But I can order a glass?"

"One glass and I'll order it. I'll get one myself."

The server comes and takes our drink orders.

"Were you able to ask Gen if she could be in the dance, Anayah?" asks Priya.

"She wants to do it, but her ballet schedule is intense since she began a professional program this year. Theoretically, it should work, but she needs time to breathe."

"I'll count that as a go, and my three friends said they would. I have one last person to ask." Priya fixes Seth with a sweet smile. "Would you be a part of the dance for the engagement party?"

"Are you that desperate?" he asks.

"I want my family with me, and you're part of the family." She gives him a big hug.

"Laying it on a little thick?" Seth jokes. "I'll do it, but I might not be able to get to every practice."

"We'll give you private lessons when you can't make it."

"I'm not sure how good I'll be."

"You'll be fine," Priya assures him. "Owen said to get enthusiastic people with a little rhythm."

"I'm not exactly enthusiastic."

"You'll be interested enough with Anayah and Gen involved."

Seth gives her side-eye.

"Everything is set." Priya squeals. "I'm so excited!"

"How's the other wedding stuff going?" Seth asks Priya. "Are we going to eat as good as we are tonight?"

"Sure, everything is going great!" Priya says, too brightly.

He raises an eyebrow.

"Honestly, it's stressful," Priya concedes, coming down several notches. "It's fun planning some parts, but everything is expensive, and everyone has their own ideas about how the wedding should be done. This dance is one of the few things I can control and enjoy. But I'm sure you didn't want to hear all of that."

I'm shocked she's so undone about wedding planning.

Priya's phone goes off, and she groans. "The only time he calls is when there's a problem. I'm sorry, I have to take this… Hi Alan, what's up?… No! The report stays as it is. Alan, can you give me a minute? I'm doing a family dinner." She looks at us. "I'll be right back."

After she walks away, Seth says, "I'm glad I don't work under her."

"I'm sure they deserved whatever they got," I say.

The server appears with our food, and we're diving in when Priya returns.

"They can't do anything over there…" she grumbles. "How is it?"

We respond with grunts, our mouths full.

Priya takes a few bites and then pulls her tablet out. "I have pics of the outfits I'd like us to wear."

She's slick. Wait until our bellies are full of good food and then ask about the important stuff.

She passes the tablet over to the boys. "That's what I picked for the guys."

"Yeah, they're fine," Balraj says.

Adil and Seth nod. That was easier than I thought it would be. They must have been nice.

Priya swipes a few screens and then hands the tablet to me. "And this is what I want us to wear. I'll wear the one in pink, and you'll be stunning in the green one."

"I don't like it."

"Shocker," Balraj says.

Even Adil lets out a snicker as a couple turns and gives us an odd look. Probably wondering who let the children into the nice restaurant.

"Anayah, they're typical lehenga cholis, and gorgeous," Priya says. "You'll have all the guys in the audience drooling."

"Exactly what I don't want," I say. "I'm surprised you'd want guys drooling over your younger sister at your engagement party."

"I might call you baby sis, but the guys are definitely looking at you." She glances at Seth.

He shrugs. "Guilty."

My jaw drops. "You have a girlfriend."

"I look, but you're not the love of my life. I can assure you Mia looks. She's probably planning her next boyfriend as we speak."

"You two are messed up." This is what I mean by ridiculous teenage romances that don't last. This nonsense Seth has going on with Mia barely qualifies as romance.

"Anyway," Priya butts in. "At least this is in a controlled environment and will be to my benefit."

These people cannot be my family and longest friend. "You are unbelievable."

"I was afraid that would be your reaction, so here's plan B." She swipes a few screens and hands me the tablet.

"That's better, but it has so much stuff on it."

"It's an engagement party," Priya says. "Bright colors. Happy day."

I point to another outfit on the page. "How about that one?"

"This is something the aunties would wear."

"Then I'll look like a very young auntie."

"Fine. But since you're getting the boring one, I'm buying the first one."

"Suit yourself. You should eat. Your food will get cold."

The boys are shaking their heads like I'm being ridiculous.

Priya may have bowed to what I wanted, but the win is bittersweet.

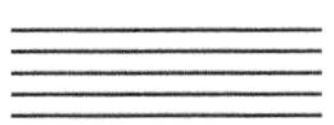

Today is the first dance rehearsal. Priya scheduled them for Sundays from three to five.

Owen's place is an old mansion that his family converted into apartments. He kept a large section for his living quarters and dance studio.

We enter the main dance room, which might have been a large ballroom or dining room, and Seth is already there. We talk about band for a bit before growing quiet. I'm mentally preparing myself for the agony that is about to commence.

Gen breezes in. "I'm so excited! I get to learn another dance form. This year is like international year with Ms. Cortez's salsa lessons and now this."

I shake my head, smiling. As much as I don't want to be here, Gen's enthusiasm for all things dance is impossible to rain on.

An hour later, Owen has tested my patience. He's having Gen, Priya, and me do harder dance moves, and I have the steepest learning curve.

I exhale in frustration.

"You're doing fine, baby sis. Together, we will stun the crowds." Priya does a hip shake.

We'll stun them all right.

After another hour, towards the end of class, Owen takes me to the side. "Anayah, I want you to watch Priya and Gen. Can you two take it from the top?"

I watch. "I don't get it. I did the same thing."

"Technically yes," Owen replies. "But it looks like you're trying too hard."

"I don't dance, and this is difficult."

"Anayah, try to relax," Gen suggests. "The moves go with the music. Your body should want to do what you're asking, if you let it."

I take Gen's advice and try to relax.

"That's better, but it's still stoic." Owen scratches his chin. "Can you channel emotion into your dancing?"

I narrow my eyes. "What emotion would you have me channel?"

"What are you feeling?"

"Rage."

"Okay." Owen looks a little scared.

Priya chuckles. "She's not going to stomp you to pieces, Owen."

"Let's see what rage does," says Gen. "Listen to the music and dance."

I close my eyes to concentrate.

"Rage works for you," Gen exclaims when the music stops. "Very intense."

"Definitely a different interpretation." Owen claps his hands. "But it'll work."

Priya gives me a thumbs up.

I surprise myself and smile back.

10

In Spades

One week later, I'm back in Dr. Reed's office.

"Your best bets are proposals two and three," says Dr. Reed. "Number one is much too broad, and I don't like number four."

"Don't like?"

"If I'm helping you with this, I want to be interested in what you're doing. Pick a proposal."

"Pick a proposal now?"

"Are you turning into a parrot? Yes, now. Time's a wasting. I don't have all day."

This choice could be a determining factor in whether I win, or make the process easier or harder. And Dr. Reed is forcing me to rush it?

"You're not choosing a marriage mate."

"I know. This is far more important."

Dr. Reed chuckles. "A part of me wonders if you believe that."

"Depends on if you're speaking in relative or absolute terms and time frame. Obviously, I don't feel that—"

“Anayah!”

“I choose proposal three.”

“Good. Talk to Yessenia about how you’re going to get blood samples.”

“You don’t have some?”

Dr. Reed gives me a withering look. “No, we don’t have blood samples lying around the lab, and you’ll need specific types of samples. Hammer that out with Yessenia.”

“Okay.”

“Chen can give you a crash course in the chemistry you’ll need to complete this experiment.”

“Got it.”

“Those two items are due by the end of next week along with a written report on your progress. Two pages should suffice.”

“Why do you want a progress report? You’ll be here.”

“Not all the time, and it’s best you learn this principle - document everything, especially here.” He smiles. “I’m excited by your experiment.

I’m surprised. Dr. Reed doesn’t smile often.

“Hop to it. I need to make some phone calls, and then maybe I can get into my lab and do some real work like you.”

I can finally start my experiment.

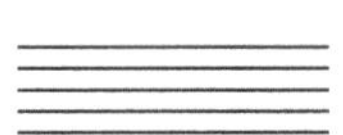

Our family brought dinner over to the Baniks on Saturday. After we ate, the parents threw us out of the house, so we’re kicking a soccer ball around the backyard. There’s not much sun today, and it’s brisk.

Nina is still weak and watches us from a bench on the patio. Priya is being a good sport hanging out with us outside. With engaged status, she could stay with the adults indoors.

"Your sister seems stronger." Priya's flat flies off as she kicks the ball towards Seth. "Is she back at school?"

Seth 'dribbles' the ball and then kicks it towards Adil. "No. She's not strong enough for that. She can't even do a full at-home program right now. It's taking longer than usual to get back to her normal, and this will probably be a bad year for her."

I didn't realize she was still so sick. I chase after the ball Adil had just kicked to me and send it to Balraj. He launches it into the practice net.

"How do you guys manage that with work and school?" Priya kicks at a leaf pile.

"We've changed our schedules, so someone is around most of the day."

"That must be exhausting." Adil grabs the ball from the net. "We could pitch in and sit with her from time to time to give you guys a break."

Priya seems game, but Balraj is frowning, and I have an awful feeling my face looks more like his than Priya's or Adil's.

"Anything to help would be appreciated. I know everyone's time is limited," Seth says. "Do you volunteer every Wednesday at the hospital, Anayah?"

"Yep. It's good for college applications." I kick the ball.

Seth gives me an odd look. "You don't care about the people at all? It's a children's hospital."

"Sure, I'm not a complete ogre. But that's not what motivates me to go. The primary reason I volunteer is to help get me into a good school."

That sounds cold and another excellent reason people don't draw close to me, but I'm not lying about my true motivations either.

"I'm not judging; it just doesn't sound like you," Seth remarks. "What about helping Nina?"

"That's completely different," I reply. "Of course, I care about Nina. If it makes you feel better, I had a hard time coming up with a research investigation until you told me how bad things get for her."

"There may be hope for you yet," Seth says.

Priya rolls her eyes. "Yaya is fine. I don't know why she said all that crazy. We know she cares about people."

I stare at her, touched. "Thank you, Priya. That's kind of you to say."

She shrugs. "It's true. And Seth, we'll definitely pitch in and help you out. You look exhausted."

He does have serious bags under his eyes. I should have noticed that before.

"I stay up late with Nina while my parents get work done," Seth explains. "Depending on what my parents have to do, I go to school late or leave early. The district issued me a special pass for it because of the circumstances, but it's not great for my grades."

Should I cut down on volunteering at the hospital and help Nina-sit? I'm supporting strangers more than a family I love.

"Coach has been hassling you too." Adil kicks the ball to Seth. Besides varsity soccer, Adil plays for the same soccer club that Seth does.

"He was understanding at first." Seth knees the ball. "But missing practices is showing in my performance." He does a neat sidekick and sends the ball towards me.

"And I'm sure you're worried about Nina," Priya says softly.

"I am." He crosses his arms. "Two so close together… It's not good."

We're quiet for a minute.

Priya claps her hands. "We're here to cheer you guys up, not make you sad. Why don't we do a little soccer game?"

I pull my hair back into a ponytail. What would help the Baniks? Searching for a way to ease the pain? Will my contributions in that area be helpful? Am I really going to unearth anything to help Nina?

"Yo, Anayah, heads up."

I step back in time to receive the ball properly and kick it to Seth. I wish my focus had been more on what my project might actually accomplish instead of SJRC.

"Anayah, what's with you?"

I turn in time to see the ball whizzing by me. I chase after it and kick it to Seth again.

Not that Nina wasn't a factor. She was a big one and still is, but not the driving motivation. My win was and still is.

"Seth," Nina calls out.

Seth jogs towards her. "What's up?"

"I'm going inside."

"Are you feeling okay?"

"Yeah, I'm just a little cold."

"Are you in pain?" Seth asks.

"I'm fine."

"Nina."

"Dad will make me lay down if I complain, and I don't want to miss stuff."

"We're not doing anything."

"It's more than what I'll be doing in my room, by myself."

"How intense is it?" Seth asks. "I can give you aspirin if it's mild, but Mom or Dad will have to give you the stronger stuff if it's bad."

"Aspirin should be good."

"Why don't we all go inside?" I suggest.

"Will just sent a text," Seth tells me as we head in. "He and his family are on their way over with dessert."

My heart does a body slam. "I didn't know they were coming."

"I guess our moms bonded when we were in the car accident, so mine invited the Coxes over."

I pull my hair out of my ponytail and shake it out. "Will cheers you up better than us."

"You guys are fine, and you and Will together are always ridic. The night is about to get real fun."

I'm sure he's right.

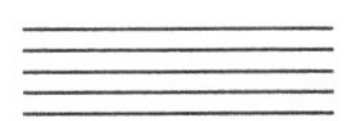

"What's your actual experiment?" Kyra shuffles cards for Spades next to me at the card table in the rec room. She's got her long thin black braids piled in a bun and a UConn women's basketball t-shirt on.

I sneak a glance at Will sitting across the table from me in an olive green hoodie. He's grinning slowly.

I put my hand in front of my mouth and rattle off the project title.

Kyra deals. "What? I can barely hear you."

"Yeah, Nayah, what was that?" Will cups his ear.

I repeat it, staring at the ceiling.

He laughs and slaps the table. "What did I tell you? Pain management." Will sorts through his cards. "What's your bid, Nayah? What can you do?"

"Would you give me a second? Kyra just finished dealing." I study my cards. "How's your experiment?"

"Fine," Will replies.

Kyra takes a bite of cake. "Don't rag on Anayah for her experiment and then be cryptic about yours."

"I'll have a banging project," he says.

I snort. "Banging?"

"Yes, Anayah, in my sentence, it's used as a colloquial for superb, fantastic, beyond expectations-"

"I know what banging means." I move a couple of cards around in my hand. "I'm questioning whether it's the correct word to use in connection with your experiment. Especially since you speak of it in the future tense." I look at my hand again. "I can definitely do two. Maybe three. And if things go well, possibly five."

"Could you narrow that down to one number?"

"What can you do?"

Will holds up four fingers.

"Then we can bid six," I reply.

"Put us down for seven," Will says to Seth.

"Will!"

Seth writes down our bid, chuckling.

Will glances at me. "We'll be fine."

I glare at him.

Kyra and Seth decide to go easy for the first round and bid five.

Will's attitude towards SJRC continues to irritate me. Like he can waltz in and produce high-level, scholarly work with no real effort and seriousness. That burns me up, and some of that attitude stems from his overconfidence. Which also burns me up.

"Did you even start your experiment?" I ask Will as I toss in my card.

"Yeah. I have a mentor-"

"Who?"

"Mr. Titus."

Kyra and Seth take the book.

Seth throws in a card.

I snort. "Your SJRC mentor is the new drama teacher?"

Kyra and Seth take another book.

Kyra lays down her card.

Will scowls. "What's your problem with him?"

"Are you sure he's up to the task?" I don't bother hiding my disgust.

"He actually has a degree in music therapy."

"How did he end up here then?"

"Is it your business? Why are you acting like such a snot?"

"Maybe because you're such a jerk," I snap.

"Both of you, stop acting like you're five." Kyra picks up their third book and lays down a card.

"Are you paying attention to the game?" I throw down my card.

"I am," he retorts. "But I need you to be."

"You only have a mentor so far?"

"No. I'm having difficulties finding the right materials, but I'll be fine." Will slaps down his card.

We finally take a book.

Will throws in a card.

"I might believe that when you actually have an experiment."

"You will not be disappointed," Will says. "You'll be mad at me for a completely different reason, since you're so desperate to win."

"I'm not desperate." I slam down my card. "A desire for excellence is not the same as desperation."

Will takes the book and lays down another card. "I agree, but that's not you right now. How did you feel when your mentor said to do a different project?"

"He didn't." I toss my hair. "He merely guided me so I would have a different outlook."

Will rolls his eyes.

Even Kyra giggles.

I throw my card in.

"Nayah!" Will throws his hands in the air. "What are you doing? You cut me."

Whoops. "Sorry." I grab the book and lay down another card. "Was that part of your four?"

"No talking across the table." Seth smirks and then takes the book after everyone goes.

"We only need one more book," Kyra sings.

Seth throws down a card.

Will lays his hand facedown on the table. "We got this."

I toss in my card.

"I still maintain you're desperately trying to prove your dominance." Will throws in a great card. "Why?"

We take the book.

He throws down another.

"I have a reputation to maintain."

After Seth throws in his, I take the book and throw in another card.

Kyra exhales.

"She's probably mad Priya is getting more attention than her with the wedding," Seth says.

I give him a light kick under the table, and he flicks one of my books over the edge.

Will tosses in a card and takes the book. He throws down another card.

I hold back a fist pump. We're going to get our bid.

Kyra tosses her card in. "You're letting their drama distract you, Seth."

Will looks at me, the corners of his mouth turning up a little. "Is what he said true?"

I'll be cold and dead in my grave before I admit anything to Will. No fear. I slam down my card. No weakness. Besides, it's far more complicated than that. "You guys don't get me at all."

"Relax, Kyra." Seth throws in his card. "We can still get our bid."

Will grabs the book and then holds up his last card. "Can you?"

He puts the card in.

"Really?" Seth takes his turn.

Will's smile widens as he leans back in his chair. "Show them what you got, Nayah."

I grin back, and our eyes lock for a fraction of a second, ratcheting my heart rate up. I slap my card down and do a dance in my seat.

"Seth!" Kyra throws her card in the pile. "I told you."

Will gathers the cards. "That is how we play the game."

"How did you two do that?" Seth exclaims. "You were arguing the whole time."

"I'm in Nayah's head."

"No, you're not."

He flips on the tractor beam. "Yeah, I am."

"Turn it off," I growl.

"Turn what off?" Kyra asks.

"He knows."

"Why is it so effective, Nayah? Or are you gonna dodge that question too?"

"Why do you keep using it?" I shoot back. "Answer that question first."

"Like I said, always entertaining," Seth says.

11

The Maze

The next Saturday, I'm standing in the middle of a dank, musty cornfield in the dark. I had bent down to tie my shoelaces, and everyone was gone when I stood back up.

I listen to the wind blow the dried out leaves on the cornstalks. Never realized how dense corn grows in a field. There's not much in the way of lighting, and the cloudy sky hides the moon, giving everything an inky blackness.

Why do I let Gen talk me into these things?

I call out as I walk to see where everyone is. It's the middle of a corn maze, so I'm on a path, but I'm not sure how to get out of here.

The path Ts. Which way did they turn? You'd think you'd be able to hear seven teenagers. I turn right.

"RAH!"

I scream.

Seth doubles over in laughter in front of me.

Gen runs around the corner with Will right behind her.

"You guys okay?" she asks.

"Fine." I stalk past her, turning the corner.

"You aren't actually mad at me, are you?" Seth asks as he catches up to me.

"No." I cross my arms.

He throws an arm around my shoulders and drags me towards him in a sloppy hug. "You're cider is on me when we get out of here."

I can't help but laugh. He's so ridiculous sometimes. "Okay Seth, you're forgiven."

"Gen, are we supposed to look for clues?" Taylor asks from Will's other side.

"Yeah, Matt and Xiang got it handled."

They're a little further ahead, poring over a paper. "We're good," Matt yells back. "We only have two more clues, and then we should be out of here."

Most of us have lived in Southerland all of our lives, but Li Xiang and Matt Bellinger are newer, moving in the last three and four years. Matt lives next door to Gen, and Xiang moved four houses down from Taylor.

I like Xiang, but I know her the least of the girls in our group. She bounces from ideas and activities at a moment's notice, but focuses enough to be near the top of our class.

Whereas Xiang is all over the place, Matt is almost the opposite. Serious, levelheaded, and structured, I'm surprised he and Xiang get along so well. I suppose they balance each other out. In some ways, they're much alike — Xiang is sunshine, and Matt is one of the nicest guys I know.

He doesn't believe it, but he's decent looking — dark brown curls and intense dark blue eyes framed by black-framed glasses. Xiang is pretty too and just cut her long hair into an angled chin length bob which makes her look older.

"What time does this place close?" Taylor tightens her scarf. "I don't want to be trapped in here."

Gen sneezes. "They keep track of the groups that come in and out, so that doesn't happen."

"Besides, we can protect you." Will flexes a muscle.

Gen and Taylor giggle.

Can I lose any more brain cells? I sidestep a dirt rut in the path.

"Was that a mega slide I saw when we came in?" Xiang turns and walks backwards.

"Yeah, it's a huge chute, and they give you sacks to slide down." Gen sniffles again.

Xiang gives a whoop. "Can't wait to try it out."

We're definitely five years old again.

Seth nudges my shoulder. "You can't tell me you aren't a teeny bit curious about sliding down a giant adult-sized slide."

"Nope. I'm surprised you could come tonight and without Mia."

"Mia wanted to go to a party."

"And you being the dutiful boyfriend didn't go with her?"

"This was more fun; she'll survive one party without me. My parents are both home tonight, so they told me to go. That it might be one of my few opportunities for a while." Seth's mouth forms a thin line. "I'll probably have to quit the soccer team."

"Wait, seriously?" Will is on my other side. "Even with us pitching in?"

Seth nods. "They don't even like the time I spend with band. I don't wanna talk about it."

He joins Xiang, Matt, and Kyra.

"Way to bring down the party, Nayah."

"I didn't know that was coming. I was just making conversation."

"You might wanna work on that."

"I'm sorry I'm not as gifted at meaningless banter as you, Will."

"I'm available for lessons anytime. For you, I'll give a special discount due to the severity of your case."

I give him side-eye. "I'll pass."

Taylor giggles from his other side. "I'll take you up on those lessons."

I slow my step, so I'm walking with Gen. "Taylor, cannot be serious."

Gen shrugs. "She could do way worse. Will is smart and nice, and looking very good lately."

I sigh. "When did life get so complicated?"

Gen rubs her pink nose. "What do you mean?"

"All this pairing. You and John—"

Gen narrows her eyes at me.

"And you can't tell me something isn't going on with Matt and Xiang."

"What about you?" Gen asks.

"What about me?"

"Any boy make your heart thump louder?"

Taylor drops back. "What are we talking about so secretly? Are you eyeing one of the boys, Anayah?"

"I was getting the dirt on that," Gen replies.

"I thought you were," I say to Taylor.

"Seriously? Who?"

"The giggle with the lesson?" I ask.

Taylor waved a hand. "He's gorgeous, so yeah."

What sense does that make?

Gen nudges me. "There has got to be at least one boy."

"Why does there have to be anyone?"

Taylor whips out some lip balm. "Your standards are high, but come on…"

"No boys until I get my postdoc. I have things to do."

Taylor snorts as Gen looks like she's rolling that around in her mind. "Okay."

"I liked it better when we were all just friends, hanging out and playing," I say. "It was simpler."

"We're out!" Xiang jumps up and down. "We beat the maze!"

That is cool.

"Time for the slide!" she exclaims.

I grimace.

Twenty minutes later and one slide trip down, I'm huddled next to Matt at a nearby picnic table, checking out pictures on his phone. Will sits on the other side of him as we're laughing at a funny shot he got of Seth and Will.

"I don't post much, but that one has to go up." Matt swipes to a great picture of Gen and me.

"Posting that one?" Will asks.

I've never seen that expression on him before.

"I wasn't planning on it. Why?"

Will looks away and shrugs. "Just curious."

"Can you send me a copy?" I have a nice collection of pictures on my computer.

"Sure." Matt taps his phone.

"Me too," Will says.

I raise my eyebrows at Will trying to ignore the odd sinking sensation in my stomach. "You want a picture of Gen?"

Will's face goes blank. "Why is it weird that I want a picture and not Matt?"

"Matt is always doing this. I've never seen you take a picture." I pause. "Is that why you asked if Gen was still interested in Seth back in September?"

"Gen was interested in Seth?" Matt asks.

Will and I gawk at him.

"How did you not know that?" Will asks.

Matt shrugs. "She never said anything. It's not like it was obvious."

Will laughs hard.

"Oh, come on, Will," I say. "It wasn't that obvious. I had to be told."

"Well, you're you," Will says.

I glare at him. "It wasn't obvious to Xiang and Kyra either."

"Everyone knew?" Matt asks.

"Don't feel bad. Gen had to tell us girls. Will probably figured it out because he was staring at her all the time."

Will scowls. "Whatever. It doesn't matter anyway. Nothing is happening, and I'm not trying to make anything happen."

"How long have you liked her?" Matt asks.

"I don't like her."

I snort. "Okay, how long have you not liked her?"

Matt snickers.

"Keep it up, Nayah. At least I'm confident enough to admit it when it does happen."

"I have nothing to admit. Why do I keep having this conversation with people?"

"Because you make it overly obvious that you don't care, which usually means somewhere deep inside, you do."

I growl. "What do you care?"

"That's a valid question. I thought you liked Gen?" Matt asks Will.

"I don't like her."

"Anyway, it seems you care about Anayah's interest more than the average person would, especially given whatever it is you have on Gen."

Will stares at Matt. "Who's side are you on?"

Matt shrugs. "Just making an observation."

I smirk at Will. "Are you secretly in love with me, and made this crush on Gen overly obvious, so you don't have to admit what you feel deep down inside?"

Matt lets out a peal of laughter.

"I didn't make anything obvious," Will says. "You don't fool me, Nayah. And you can't hide from me either."

We engage in a glare lockdown. Then he clicks on the tractor beam.

The corners of Will's mouth turn up. As suddenly as it went on, it shuts off. Will looks straight ahead, chuckling.

Matt glances between us. "The next time you two do that, could you warn me because that was incredibly awkward, and I don't want to get incinerated."

I huff and jump up. "I'm finding the others."

As I walk away, I catch Matt asking, "Why are you messing with her like that?"

I slow my gait.

There's silence for a moment.

"I can't help myself," Will replies.

It feels like something is forcing me to look behind, and I obey.

Will's tractor beam is back, even from this distance.

My foot catches on something, and I pitch forward.

"Anayah, are you okay?" Kyra walks toward me.

"Yeah, let's try that slide again."

Anything is better than this crazy head space I'm in.

12

The Traitor

Priya's car is in the driveway when Adil and I get home from school the following Thursday. Priya is usually not home until after five.

Mother is talking rapidly on the phone at the kitchen island when we walk into the house, and she quickly gets off. "I have very important news to tell you."

My heart stops as Adil and I exchange glances.

"Is Dad okay?" he asks.

Mother looks confused. "Your father is fine. The engagement is broken, and there will be no wedding."

That was absolutely unexpected, at least to me.

"What happened?" asks Adil.

"Priya just said the wedding was off and ran upstairs to her room. That was three hours ago. She hasn't come out, and she won't let me in. Anayah, you need to find out what's going on. I want to know what's happening."

Adil gives Mother a strange expression. "And I'm sure Priya could use comfort and support, especially from her sister."

"Yes, of course," says Mother. "That too."

As annoyed by this wedding as I am, I'm not calloused to the fact that a broken engagement must be gut-wrenching. But I am the worst person for this task.

I knock on Priya's door.

After asking who it is, the lock pops and the door opens. Priya's hair looks like she walked through an electric field, her eyes are red, and makeup is smeared on her face.

This is not her.

Priya locks the door behind me, shuffles back to her bed, and climbs in, throwing her turquoise comforter over her head.

Usually, her room is bright because of the windows, and she always has her curtains open. But everything is shut tight and dark except two tiny strips of light on the sides of her curtains.

How do I speak to a comforter?

I study the room, stalling. Priya has a dusty rose and turquoise theme going. There's so much stuff and color. Attractive colors, just not for me.

I take a deep breath. "Mother told me about the engagement."

Priya remains silent.

"I'm sorry."

Not a word from the comforter. Is she still alive under there? What am I supposed to say? "Do you want me to get you something? Tea? Juice? Water?"

Priya's head emerges. "Tea would be nice."

"I'll be back."

Being proactive is good. At least I don't have to talk right this minute.

Adil and Mother are still in the kitchen.

"What did she say?" asks Mother.

"She wants tea."

"That's it?"

"Neither one of us is real talkative right now."

Mother sighs and goes back to the papers she's reading.

Adil gives me a thumbs-up.

About ten minutes later, I return with two cups of hot tea and shortbread cookies. I don't know about Priya, but I didn't have a snack, and I'm hungry.

Priya emerges from the comforter.

I sit on the edge of the bed, hand her a cup and offer cookies, which she takes.

We sip and nibble for a bit.

"David broke off the engagement." She sounds loud in the heavy silence.

"Why?"

"He said our families don't mesh, which meant we probably won't mesh in the long run."

"He's blaming things on us?" Of all the weak-minded excuses — this is his relationship.

"Not exactly. We're both stressed out."

"You're better off without him. He doesn't know how good he's got it."

A ghost of a smile appears.

"He did you a favor," I continue, on fire now. "He's spineless and doesn't deserve you. What if you found out after you got married that he's a weak, irresponsible, un-grateful-" I catch the expression on Priya's face. "I'll stop if you want me to, but I'd like to go on. This is a great SAT exercise if I increase the difficulty."

Priya smiles wider but then the sadness immediately returns. "But if I deserve better, why is my heart breaking?"

She starts sobbing.

Oh no. Feelings, crying, and she's using clichés. I wave my hands around. "Tell it to stop."

"What?" That slowed the tears, but she looks confused.

"Tell it to stop," I repeat. "I'll do it." And before I process the absurdity, I bend over and put my hands on my hips. "Heart, stop breaking, because I'll kick you into cardiac arrest, and then the only thing that'll save you is a defibrillator." I shake my head. "The traitor."

Priya stares at me. Then she laughs, hysterically.

She's scaring me.

"I guess I should go downstairs and tell Mom," Priya says with a sigh.

"She is dying to know what happened, but only if you're ready to share. Mother can sit a bit."

Priya smirks. "Let's wait together a little longer, shall we?"

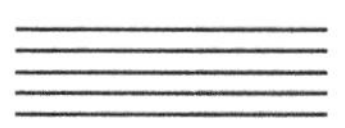

Despite the grilling Mother gave her during dinner, Priya seemed to hold her own. Until she gave me a look that said she wanted to die again, so I inserted myself into the conversation, and she escaped.

"Anayah, you could have helped her more," Mother says. "Your sister is worn out."

"It's not my fault they broke up."

"Of course not, but if you could have calmed Priya down, she might have been more equipped to save things."

The best action is silence because what I really want to do may get me grounded for a month.

"Priya has a lot to worry about," Mother goes on. "Demanding job, a relationship. The younger sister should help the older."

In two seconds, I will blow my top, grounding or not. "I'm going upstairs."

"No concern at all. Fine, go upstairs."

I slam the door to my room and sit at my desk to work. I have tests in every class before vacation, and I plan on being in the lab more this week to run my experiment.

But my concentration is blown.

Is my purpose on the planet to ensure Priya's existence is wonderful?

I feel the shadow, dark and heavy.

13

The Chair

"I have the chair placements," Ms. Cortez announces the next day. "We'll start with the flutes and work our way back. First flutes - first chair, Brooke. Second chair, Anayah…"

I had a near perfect audition. How did she beat that? What did she play? I shuffle down two seats.

"Another year we're stand partners, and we're first," Brooke says. "How cool is that?"

I give her a tight smile back.

"Trumpets. First trumpets- First chair, Joe. Second chair, Ron. Third chair, Seth…"

There's a low murmur in the room.

I'm so preoccupied with my thoughts that I almost missed that. The trumpets have a lot of talented players. Seth must have had a great audition to get third chair.

"Second trumpets- First chair, Will…"

My eyes bug out of their sockets as I watch him move.

Joe, Ron, and Seth turn and congratulate a beaming Will.

He seems to have caught Ms. Cortez's attention. Will has no problem getting noticed, but he rarely clowns around in band, so Ms. Cortez must see something else in him. What does he have that I don't?

I exhale. Plenty. Will infuses people with energy and can get them to accomplish almost anything. He could convince a mouse it was a horse and leap a fence, and it would probably find a way to succeed.

"Will's cute, huh?"

That breaks me from my Will reverie, and I turn to face Brooke, who's grinning at me.

I shrug. "He's all right."

Will is much more than that, but I'm not going to gossip about boys with Brooke. I barely do it with my close friends.

Brooke giggles. "Or was it Seth you were staring at and giving longing sighs for?"

"I wasn't staring at anyone."

"Right."

It's going to be a very long year.

Thirty minutes later, Ms. Cortez ends practice early to share additional information. "For some sections, the chair auditions will determine who the section leader will be next year."

That means there's a good chance Brooke will be a section leader next year as a junior. I'm pretty sure that's unusual.

Brooke as section leader. Again. Brooke's shadow is the next largest I've always lived under.

Always Brooke. Never me. I'm always second best.

"Chair challenges," Ms. Cortez continues.

Someone claps and yells from the audience.

"Chair challenges are the only way to get to a higher seat. Essentially it's a re-audition for the chair," Ms. Cortez explains.

I perk up. We didn't have this in junior high.

"Rules. You can only challenge the person next to you. No jumping six chairs at a time."

"Aw," someone yells from the audience.

"Please inform the person you're challenging before telling me."

"Awkward time," someone else yells.

"Yeah, not fun. We'll set a date for the challenge. Best audition gets the chair."

"YEAAAAAHHHH!!"

Ms. Cortez laughs. "Would you guys let me get through this? Only one challenge for the same person every three months. So if you challenge now and fail, you can't do it again until February. Questions?"

Nobody says anything, but my mind is racing.

I can challenge Brooke for her seat.

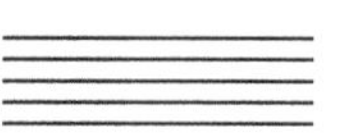

"So Brooke continues her reign as flute queen?" Will teases me as we leave the arts wing for second period.

I literally growl.

"Seriously?" Gen gapes at me like I morphed into something. "You're second chair as a sophomore. That's phenomenal."

"It really is, Nayah," Will says. "You and Brooke must have killed it in auditions."

"You did well too, Will," I say, a smidge chastened. Objectively, I should be thrilled, and instead, I'm being completely into me. "And you, Gen."

"I'm mediocre, but at least I'm not any lower than I was before." Gen's face contorts. "What died out here?"

I drag my brain from thoughts of chair challenges and take a whiff. "Someone probably blew something up in the chem classrooms again. Unless another biology class is dissecting something that's actually dead."

"Speaking of labs, did you get to yours yesterday?" Gen asks.

"No, I didn't get a chance. Priya told us David called off the wedding."

Gen's eyes get wide. "Poor Priya."

"She say why?" Will asks.

"He blamed it on us."

"Did you guys argue with them a lot?" Gen asks. "Or maybe the parents were pushy?"

"David's parents and my mother were giving lots of opinions. But the rest of us? We were taking orders all the time."

Will grins.

"Shut it, Will."

Will's grin grows wider. "I said nothing."

"I know what you're thinking."

"I guess parents can make things rough." Gen plays with her hair. "Don't people complain about their in-laws?"

"Then fix it." I snap. "All this whining. He promised to marry her, and then he broke that promise. He should have worked harder."

"I'm not taking sides with David." Gen touches my arm. "I'm team Priya all the way."

I guess for the moment, I am too, despite her shadow.

Gen scoots into the classroom, but it seems like Will is studying me.

"What?" I ask him.

"How hard do you think a guy should work for a girl?"

"That's a weird question."

"You must have some ideas to say it."

"The excuse sounded weak, and it came suddenly. It'd be different if their goals were different or personalities didn't mesh, but parents? I feel like you could work that one out."

"Maybe he got afraid."

"I get that, but it's unfair to raise her hopes by asking her to marry and then bring them crashing down."

"That's true if he wasn't serious to begin with. But what if Priya asked for something he couldn't or really didn't want to do?"

"Like what?"

Will shrugs. "I don't know; it's a hypothetical. But it does happen."

"I don't do well without data, Will."

The bell rings.

"You made me late!" I exclaim.

He snickers. "I didn't tie you to the door."

I make a face at him and then rush down the hall. Was Will hypothesizing or speaking from experience?

14

Missing

Istorm into Dr. Reed's office. "Where's my anti-in-flammatory drug?"

"I don't know what you're talking about." Dr. Reed doesn't even look up from a paper he's reading.

"My anti-inflammatory compound for my experiment. I put it in the cabinet in the lab. It's half gone."

"'I don't know' was your cue to talk to the others about it. I don't have time to help you search."

I scowl and turn to leave.

"Shut the door on your way out."

He's infuriating sometimes.

I came to lab today, singing. I never sing, but there I was amusing myself with a happy little tune because today is experiment day. My singing turned to growling when I searched the cabinet for my anti-inflammatory.

I run into Jaya in the hallway.

"Jaya, have you seen—"

"No time. Gotta go." She didn't even stop.

I stare at her as she continues around the corner out of sight.

I get being in a rush, but seriously? I set my jaw and enter the lab. Yessenia is pouring something into a flask so I wait for her to finish.

"Do you need something?" she asks absently.

"My anti-inflammatory is half gone."

"And what do you want me to do about it?"

What's with the rudeness today? "Can you help me find it?"

"Like it's a dog, and it's lost? If it's gone, then it's gone. Talk to Chen."

I glare at her but she's so preoccupied it has no effect. I bang out of the lab.

I find Chen in the office next to the lab, jabbing at some key on the computer like it's not obeying him.

"Chen, where's my anti-inflammatory compound?"

"What?" he looks at me, half dazed.

"My compound. The one you helped me order a few weeks ago. It's half gone. I don't have enough for my experiment."

Chen snaps his fingers. "That was yours. I forgot you'd ordered it."

"What did you do with it?"

"I didn't do anything with it. One of the chem fellowship students had an awful headache—"

"He took my stuff?" I exclaim. "What is wrong with you people? You guys ingest anything that's around here?"

Chen shrugs. "He's a chemist. He probably knows more about what should go in pain relievers than the companies themselves."

I pace the room.

Chen pokes the key again.

"Would you stop jabbing that key?" I exclaim. "Obviously, whatever you're trying to do isn't happening!"

"He said it was good with whatever he mixed it with. Felt great afterward."

"It was in a locked cabinet. How did he get in there?"

"A quarter of the people in this building have a key to that cabinet. We all keep supplies in there."

"I don't have enough to run my experiment."

"We can order more. Relax."

"I have to submit by the middle of December. I can't wait another several weeks for it to come in. The guy couldn't buy aspirin?" I storm out of the room with my coat without bothering to clean up.

Nobody is taking this seriously. Me seriously. It's like being at home, and I never thought that possible. Baby of the family. Baby of the lab group. No respect anywhere.

My eyes get itchy, and I give them a swipe. What is wrong with me? Of course, you're the baby. And babies cry.

Dr. Reed's office door opens just as I'm passing it.

"Anayah?" he asks. "Where are you going?"

"Home." I keep walking.

"I thought you were running your experiment today?"

I stop and turn, glaring at him. "Impossible when the principal component is gone."

"I told you to talk to the others about it-"

"I did. They're no help. It's gone. I can't do my work. I'm going home."

Dr. Reed rubs his temples and mutters something about children.

I flush and ball my hands into fists. "Yes, Dr. Reed. I'm a sixteen-year-old baby, and now I'm going home to cry about it."

"Anayah, please come back so we can-"

I round the corner of the hall and keep walking. I have no idea what my next step is, but I need to get out of here.

On Thursday, Dr. Reed's lab team and I gather in the lab.

Today I came much calmer and clear-headed than Tuesday and apologized to Dr. Reed. I was childish and unprofessional, and need to leave my mommy issues at home. He waved it off and said we all botched this one.

"I contacted the company," Chen says. "It'll take three weeks to get another batch here."

"That won't work." Dr. Reed runs a hand through his hair. "Anayah is on a tight time frame, and we can't waste three weeks waiting for what we need. Is there a location that we can physically pick it up at?"

"Yes, but it's three hours away." Chen drums his fingers on the metal counter.

Dr. Reed presses his lips into a thin line. "Anayah, can you drive there to get it?"

I stop spinning on the lab stool. "I only have my permit. Plus, will they hand over a drug compound to me? I'm a minor."

That baby feeling is coming back, needy and dependent.

"Chen, contact that company," Dr. Reed says. "Find out what needs to happen to pick up the anti-inflammatory."

"Okay."

"Now," Dr. Reed snaps.

Chen gets out his phone and leaves the room.

Jaya had mentioned Dr. Reed chewed them all out for not being more helpful. I almost feel bad for them. Dr. Reed discusses some issue Yessenia is having with her housing.

"I ordered the drug," Chen says after he returns. "They said they couldn't give it to anyone under eighteen, but as long as the person has the pickup ticket, they could give it to them."

"I have half a mind to make you take her," Dr. Reed says to him.

"This is not all my fault," Chen complains. "I can't go. I have papers and exams."

Dr. Reed exhales. "Yessenia or Jaya?"

"My car's broke," Yessenia replies and then intently studies her fingernails.

"I might be coming down with something." Jaya gives a half-hearted cough.

Yeah, I didn't think that was happening.

"You guys are so pathetic, it's almost comical," Dr. Reed says.

"It's six hours roundtrip just driving," Yessenia says. "This is not a small errand. You should make the chem guy pay for expedited shipping or something."

I perk up. "I like that idea."

"He can also throw in lunch for the lab group to pay for our pain and suffering," Jaya says.

Chen laughs. "Poor Jaya — this has been so hard on you. How about telling your boyfriend to wait ten minutes?"

"You were going out?" I exclaim. "I thought you were rushing to class."

Jaya snorts. "I would have stayed and helped if that were true. All in favor of making Chen ask his friend to pay for shipping and lunch?"

Jaya, Yessenia, and I raise our hands.

"All in favor of letting Dr. Reed take back control of his lab group?" he asks dryly.

"All you, Dr. Reed," Yessenia says.

"I will strongly suggest to Chen's friend—"

"Why is he suddenly my friend?" Chen interrupts.

"Is he not?" Dr. Reed asks.

"Depends on your definition of friend."

"You and Anayah have been spending too much time together," Dr. Reed says.

"I'd like to think of him more as an agreeable acquaintance."

Dr. Reed rolls his eyes. "I'll strongly suggest to Chen's agreeable acquaintance that he assist with this situation. If that's unsuccessful, Anayah, your dad said he'd take you as a last resort."

I'm surprised. "How's he going to do that? He has patients."

"He said he could clear a day that was lighter. Now I trust this is the only time this year I'll have to deal with nonsense of this sort?"

We all nod.

"Good, because I have to deal with enough of it from other sources who are far less entertaining than the four of you."

"Glad we're good for something," Yessenia says.

"Time to get to work," Dr. Reed says.

I hop off the stool, for the first time feeling like a full-fledged member of the team.

15

Mani-Pedi

“Are you sure it's off?”

Priya sighs. “Yes, Mom. It's over.”

I cringe. That sounds so sad.

Football season is finished, and my research project has come to a standstill, so I find myself home on a Friday night, organizing photos on my tablet at the kitchen island.

Suddenly single Priya apparently does not want to hang out with her friends, so she's sitting next to me, eating a pint of ice cream. She's worked late almost every night this week and goes straight to her room when she comes home. Tonight is the first time she's broken that pattern.

“I bet you two will make up tomorrow, and things will be fine.” Mother gives me a significant look, tapping her fingernails on the island.

What does she expect me to do about anything?

“I'm sure Anayah believes you'll work things out,” Mother continues.

I stare at her.

“Anayah?”

I put my tablet down. "How about we not talk about David for a night? How about we not talk about any boys for a night?"

Priya's face lights up. "Come on, Yaya, let's go somewhere where there'll be no boys."

"Priya, that's not what I meant. I was just trying to-"

"It's a fabulous idea. I have to figure out what we can do that you're old enough for." Priya drags me upstairs to her room with the pint in her other hand. She locks the door and then flops on her bed. "Mom is tiring sometimes."

She shoves a spoonful of ice cream in her mouth. "My fault for not moving out when my loans were paid off," she says with a mouthful of ice cream. "But then I was with David and figured-" She sets the pint on her night table. "Well, that's that. No use crying over spilled milk. We could go apartment hunting this week. Want to move in with me?"

"You're on the weirdest rebound."

"There's no way Mom and Dad would allow you to be in my care for a long period anyway." Priya jumps up and throws open her closet door. "Tonight we can stay in and watch a movie, and tomorrow do a shopping spree. I have to return these wedding outfits. Sunday will be a spa day, and we should get our nails done one day this week. And-"

I close my eyes. "Priya, don't you have other people you'd rather do this stuff with? Friends that make you feel better when you're going through things?"

Priya gives a short laugh. "Your friends do that. Mine don't always work like that. I'd give it a 50/50 chance; you're like ninety-six percent."

The commentary on her friends is sad, and ninety-six percent? How arbitrary is that number?

Priya rattles off two movie titles that I can be happy with. "I'll make us popcorn."

Priya made good to schedule all the activities she had mentioned. If it had to happen, this was a good week for it. Chen's 'agreeable acquaintance' actually felt bad when he heard he had derailed my experiment, so he offered to take me to the facility to pick up the new batch on Friday. Chen suddenly decided that maybe a day off from classwork would be a good idea, and came with us. Jaya and Yesenia still didn't want to come, but to my surprise and delight, they ordered me a new lab coat with my name embroidered on it, and a cool pair of goggles.

Starting next Tuesday, anytime I'm not at the hospital volunteering, I'll be in the lab.

So it's Monday evening mani-pedi.

"This is great," Priya says.

I make a face.

"What's wrong?" she asks. "That color is perfect for you."

"While I appreciate the foot massage part of the pedicure, I absolutely despise having paint on my nails."

I get a look from the nail technician.

Priya chuckles. "Why?"

"It's unnecessary, and when it starts to chip and peel, it looks unkempt and disorderly." I scowl at my toes.

"You don't have to discard your femininity to be treated fairly."

"What are you talking about?" I exclaim. "I only want to be neat, and you start in on the psycho-babble."

"No matter how hard you try, you can't hide your natural beauty."

I glare at her.

"You're not getting any sympathy from me. And the way you dress—"

"I pay attention to my appearance, so people take me seriously, but I prefer to keep my wardrobe nondescript. There's nothing wrong with that."

"Okay, I'll leave you alone." Priya smiles. "I'm glad we got to do this. We never hang out anymore. When you were four, I used to braid your hair in two fat pigtails before bed every night."

"I remember that." That was back when I loved having a big sister.

Priya closes her eyes. "I was so happy when Mom told us we would have a little sister. Someone I could dress up with and share secrets with. You were so pretty, like a little doll, and smart as a whip."

This is news to me. "I thought you and Balraj were more pals."

"I had fun hanging with Raj. He was always looking for a good time and usually found it. But you seem like you're on a clock. Relax and smell the roses from time to time."

"I smell roses. I do stuff."

"But it's good you know your mind, and won't just roll over. Like Adil will sometimes."

What is with her tonight? Is she going to bash everyone in the family? "Adil does not roll over, and he's very kind."

"Adil is sweet. Too sweet for me sometimes, but you adore him."

"Adore is a little strong."

"I'm a little jealous of him because of that. I annoy you sometimes, don't I?"

It feels mean to admit that out loud.

"I'm hard to take, as David will readily tell anyone." She swallows. "I was going through my own teen drama and trying to be popular, so I didn't notice at first that you weren't coming to me as much and snapping at me more.

But when I did finally notice, it sort of hurt. I don't know what I did wrong."

I fidget in my chair. Priya has always been Mother's favorite. The day I told Mother about being one of the few third graders chosen for orchestra was the same day Priya's story was selected for a national anthology. I got forgotten. It sounds like a small thing, but I was crushed, and my heart still squeezes when I remember it. That episode started my discontent within my family in earnest. I had already been unhappy about moving out of the neighborhood where my friends lived, and switching elementary schools.

"You had grown closer to Adil, and I was off to school." Priya exhales. "It's at times like this I wish I'd done something about it. I missed a lot."

A part of me kinda wishes she had. I miss the way we were too.

16

Intentions

Seth has soccer practice today, and I told him I'd relieve Will for Nina-sitting so he could take Kyra to work at the library. Mother drops me at the Baniks at five.

"Nina is upstairs," Will says after I step into the house. "We were gaming until she got tired, so I suggested she take a nap."

"How is she?" I have to remind myself that babysitting is necessary because she's sick.

"She's doing." Will looks unusually serious as we head up the stairs. "Nina puts on a good front, but it's wearing on her."

"She'll be okay." I pat Will's back.

He stops in the upstairs hall. "I keep telling myself that. It's hard to watch, but then, I guess you see it all the time at the hospital."

I nod. "The kids are amazing. It's like they can face their illnesses like grown-ups but still be kids. I don't know how they do it."

"They got people like you to help them."

That was incredibly kind, but a stab of guilt goes through me. He says that like my sole motivation is to help them when that's not true.

I turn abruptly and enter Nina's room.

She's in bed, and she sits up quickly as she says an excited hello to me. "Can we play a game?"

"I gotta take my sister to work." Will smirks at me. "And then I have an experiment to work on."

I cross my arms. Just that quickly, we go from solidarity to competitors. Oddly, I can't decide which I like more.

"On what?" Nina asks.

"A way to help people feel better through music."

"That sounds cool. Could it help me?"

Will's eyes soften as he ruffles her hair. "I hope so."

"I want to help you with your project." Nina gives him a sweet grin.

"You can help me make the graphs."

"No, I want to do something real."

"Something real?" Will questions.

Stick it to him, Nina. I take a seat in the chair next to her bed.

"Don't you need like test subjects?" asks Nina.

"We designed a project without human subjects, so we're good there. I was studying the chemistry."

"How's that going?" I ask sweetly.

"Get off my back, Nayah."

"She might have a point, Will."

I love Nina. I give Will a broad smile.

He scowls at me and then turns to Nina. "Nayah is only trying to get under my skin."

"But if you're studying how music helps people feel better, shouldn't you test it on people?"

"Yeah, and that would be a great experiment. But sometimes we start with the chemically human body stuff and then try the results out on people."

Nina does not look convinced.

"Brilliant explanation, Will."

"At least she knows what I'm talking about. It's called communication, Nayah."

"Do you two like each other or something?" Nina asks.

Where did that question come from?

"I can't speak for Nayah."

"But he can speak for himself. He's afraid to admit he loves me."

Will gives me an odd look.

"Anyway, I can be a part, right, Will?" Nina pleads.

"An experiment with people is complicated," Will replies. "And especially with kids. And you're Seth's sister, and I'd have to get tons of forms signed and…"

Nina's face falls as he rattles off a list of issues. "I just want all of this," she gestures towards herself, "to mean something."

Will closes his eyes. It's like Nina shot him. "I'll work something out, Nina."

Her face lights up, and she almost falls out of bed, trying to hug him. "You're the best! You won't regret it."

Will is a better person than I, because I wouldn't jeopardize my project and chances of winning to please this little girl.

Another stab of guilt goes through me. That seems unbalanced.

"Why don't you get some sleep, Nina?" Will suggests. "Anayah will be here until Seth gets back."

"I'll be downstairs if you need me, Nina." There's a monitor set up in her room if something goes awry while she's sleeping.

"Stop smiling," Will says as we go downstairs.

"Your project just got a hundred times harder."

"My project will be a hundred times better."

"Only if you can incorporate the right changes in time."

"You doubt me?"

"Y-"

I stop my descent down the stairs as Will turns.

We're competing for the same prize, and I was about to engage in some serious gloating, but to tear him down? I don't usually do that, and I've done it to him lately. Is he that big of a threat to me?

I start walking again. "You're in this debacle because you couldn't say no to a ten-year-old."

"Debacle? I only see shining opportunity. You decided to cure sickle cell because of that same ten-year-old. I came up with the easier project."

"One day, it'll happen."

"Just not this science fair?"

"Shut up. You doubt me?"

"No."

He said that with no hesitation and crosses his arms like he's challenging me.

That unexpected, breathtaking confidence boost scrambles my brain, so I inexplicably go on the defensive. "Don't you have to get home? Remember that lesson you were going to teach me?"

"I haven't forgotten, Nayah."

I squirm. "You think I need to be dethroned?"

"That's not what I was going after."

I put my hands on my hips. "Then what?"

"And take all the fun and mystery out of it?" He ruffles my hair like he had with Nina — without the affection.

I smack his hand away. "I bet you don't have any lesson to teach me. You said that to irk me."

"I'm glad it's working." He puts on his bookbag. "Call if you need anything."

"Not likely."

"I meant with Nina. I'm not a miracle worker."

I hurl a pillow at him as he walks out the door laughing.

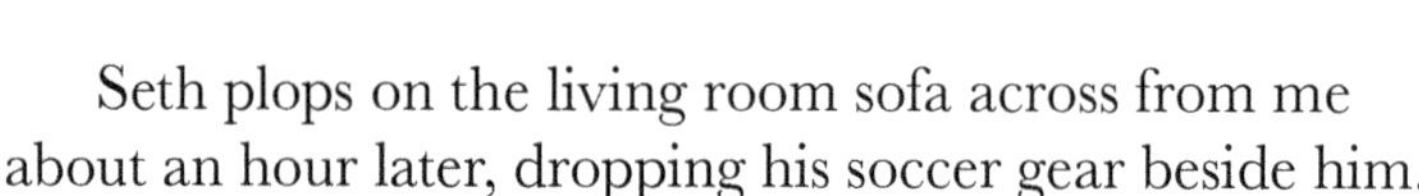

Seth plops on the living room sofa across from me about an hour later, dropping his soccer gear beside him. "How's Nina?"

I shut my bio book and throw it on top of the mound of stuff spread across the couch. I wasn't getting much work done. Will completely unnerved me, which was probably his ridiculous intention. This isn't a sports competition where you can intimidate your opponent and make them choke.

My unfinished homework mocks me.

"Are you okay?" Seth asks.

"Yeah." I wrinkle my nose. "You smell like stinky boy."

"Because I am one. I hope I can shower quick before my parents come home. Nina?"

"Nina went to sleep after Will left."

"Will wore her out?"

"They played video games, and Nina convinced him to change his entire SJRC project so she could participate as a human subject."

"I keep telling her to give Will a break. He loves Nina to pieces, and she knows it. She plays him better than he does his trumpet."

"You're kidding?"

"Nope. You two get into it sometimes, but I thought you knew he had a few good qualities."

"I do, and he seems to understand me on an annoyingly accurate level."

"Yeah, better than me."

I don't believe that but won't argue the point. "I thought his camp counselor thing was just a job but he's actually really good with children."

"It's a job he really likes. Does that change your view of him? Some girls get all gooey when they find out a guy likes kids."

"You know Nina is one of the few kids I can be around for any time."

"And yet you volunteer at a children's hospital."

"My father's recommendation. He said I'd learn a lot there, and he wasn't wrong."

"Hello!" Mrs. Banik calls out.

Panic crosses Seth's face. "In here."

Mrs. Banik walks into the living room and stops short. "You're a nice surprise, Anayah."

That comment is a surprise. I've been a little sparse this year, but I used to hang out with Seth after school regularly. "I'm visiting Nina."

"That's very kind of you. I'm sure she was thrilled."

"She was for the short time she was awake."

Mrs. Banik pauses. "And you two have been chatting while she's napping?"

"Yes," Seth answers slowly.

"I bet you're getting a lot of attention from the boys at school, Anayah."

"No, not much."

Seth snorts. "You attract plenty of attention. They're just afraid to do anything about it and get shut down brutally."

I toss my hair. "Makes my life less complicated. A bunch of Neanderthals anyway."

Seth rolls his eyes. "They aren't all like that."

"We'll need to review house rules when your father gets home," Mrs. Banik says to Seth. "Who can be over here and when. And where in the house."

Seth groans. "Mom, it's not like-"

"It's okay, Seth; we'll talk later."

I smirk. "Seth has some problems with gentlemanly behavior, as I'm sure Mia could attest to."

"Who's Mia?" Mrs. Banik asks.

Seth shifts in his seat. "A girl I used to date."

"Used to?" I ask. "When did that end? Not that I'm surprised."

"A couple of days ago."

"Why didn't we meet her?" his mom asks.

Seth scowls at me.

"Don't look at me," I retort. "I don't know why you didn't bring her home to meet the family."

"So Anayah, I take it this Mia wasn't the nicest of girls?" Mrs. Banik asks.

I shrug. "To be fair, she's all right, but I've never gotten along with her."

"Well, that wouldn't have worked anyway then," Mrs. Banik says.

"Since when does Anayah get voting rights on my girl-friends?" Seth exclaims.

The unflappable Seth getting exercised. I'm sure I'm wearing the smuggest look.

"Anayah would choose very well for you. Shall we have her arrange a meet-up?" Mrs. Banik gives him a sly smile as she waves and heads towards the stairs. "I'm changing my clothes."

Seth exhales after his mom disappears. "Beyond awkward. She was so distracted over that she didn't even notice my soccer stuff."

"She didn't know you were at practice?"

"There's knowing, and there's knowing. I think my parents believe I miss more practice than I do."

"I have homework to finish, so I'll get going." I pause. "Are you actually upset over Mia?"

"Getting dumped is never a fun experience, especially when the same person does it to you twice."

I wince. "Then I'm sorry, Seth. I should have been more sensitive."

He shrugs. "It's fine. I didn't expect you to be."

I snatch my backpack to hide how much that comment really hurts.

"Anayah, I didn't mean it like that."

"It's fine. You're right. I'm saving any guy who might genuinely like me grief by pushing him away."

"That's not true. You'd be great for—"

I was out the door before he finished. I'll walk home. Twenty minutes should be long enough to walk off my irrational frustrated energy.

17

The Challenge

This is a big week with the rival game coming up in a few days and the school activities connected to it. It's surreal — Huskie spirit week is a big deal here. There's blue and silver everywhere, and it's only Monday.

"Brooke, can I talk to you?" I ask when band practice is finished.

"Sure, what's up?"

I hesitate for a moment. Brooke and I have had an unspoken rivalry of sorts, but for all intents and purposes, it's outwardly friendly. What I'm about to say may change that. "I'm challenging you for your seat."

Brooke's face goes blank. "I guess you gotta do what you gotta do. When were you planning on telling Ms. Cortez?"

"Now."

"I'll go with you to set the date." She shuts her flute case and grabs her bookbag.

Ms. Cortez was talking to Joe and Will and asks us what we need.

"I want to challenge Brooke for her chair," I answer.

Ms. Cortez raises an eyebrow and looks toward Brooke, who shrugs.

Joe gives a low whistle. "Once we whipped the sophomores into shape, they became bloodthirsty beasts."

"Nah, Nayah's always been like that," Will says. "Straight up, rip your heart out."

"Boys, that's enough," Ms. Cortez says. "Wait outside, and we'll finish our discussion there."

They leave the room.

"I didn't realize your issue was of a sensitive nature or I would have done that at the outset," Ms. Cortez says. "Anayah, would this have anything to do with the announcement that the first chair would likely be section leader next year?"

I meet her gaze. "Maybe."

She laughs. "Fair enough." Ms. Cortez consults her calendar. "Part of the reason I asked was because we're headed into a busy period, and I'd rather do this after the break so we can focus on the upcoming performances."

"January will be a better month for me too," I reply

"That's fine," Brooke says.

"Good. So we'll table this and revisit the chair challenge in January to set a date."

I follow Brooke out of the office, marveling at how well she's taking this. Brooke has the confidence that comes with being at the top and not feeling threatened.

That annoys me further. She doesn't even see me as a threat.

I walk into the band room after school for jazz band auditions. It's a long shot, but I'm trying anyway.

I hear Brooke's voice in the hall and shift my attention toward the back of the room to see who's here, so I can avoid her.

Seth.

He did jazz band in junior high, but…

I walk over to him. "I'm surprised you're auditioning."

He throws a cleaning cloth into his case. "So will my parents."

"Didn't you quit soccer so you could stay home more? Are you going to have time for everything?"

"I don't know, Anayah."

"Have you told them that it's too much for you?"

"Dad doesn't think I do much to help."

"You're with Nina all the time."

Seth shrugs. "So I babysit. A lot. Big deal."

"It is when she's sick like that. Keep asking us for help babysitting, especially if you're doing jazz band. We'll help you."

18

Eureka!

Today is all about my curiosity. Solving problems from the ground up and analyzing results.

This is the fourth time I'm running the experiment. I did two trials yesterday, and today is the real deal, exactly three weeks after the mishap with the components.

It's quieter than usual because break is this week. Dr. Reed has been at a conference for the last five days but plans to be in this evening after his plane lands. It's a good thing he doesn't have a wife and kids; they'd never see him.

Chen walks in. "How's it going?"

"Smoothly, as expected."

"You should know by now that research and experiments seldom go smoothly and rarely as expected."

"Since my drama happened before the experiment began, maybe it's taking pity on me."

After telling him to have a good break and he leaves, another number on the printout draws my eye. It's not directly related to my experiment, so I paid little attention to it before, but it's not what I would expect.

The number on a previous printout is similar. My breath catches with the weird sensation that my world will never be the same.

As I bang my pen on the metal counter, my brain is like a pinball machine with tiny balls of thought hitting ideas and passing conclusions in such rapid succession they can barely be grasped.

Two hours later, it's night, and I rub my face with my hands while sitting in the library.

I want my Daddy.

I want my Mommy.

I may even want Priya.

That's a milestone, but Priya is great for building confidence.

Am I out of my league this time?

Shove down the emotions and move forward. What do I need?

Answers to my ten million questions. A plan. A redesign.

A new experiment to test a different hypothesis. I think I stumbled on not only a way to dial down the pain but simultaneously increase the blood count.

I pull out my notebook and start scribbling.

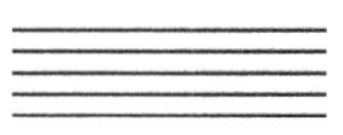

"You're still here, Anayah?" Dr. Reed stands next to me in the lab. It's almost 8:30.

I hand him the printouts. "Take a look at these, please."

He studies the sheets and then presses his lip into a thin line. "How did you get these results?"

"When the anti-inflammatory went missing, I tweaked the experiment in case we couldn't get the second order in time. I added a chemical compound to the anti-inflammatory hoping it might fill the gap. Even though we got the new batch, for fun, I ran both versions anyway."

Dr. Reed smiles faintly. "For fun?"

I shrug.

"It appears your boost did much more than that," Dr. Reed says. "What made you choose it?"

"I ran with a few things Chen showed me. He's a good chemistry teacher."

"That's why he's in my lab. It also looks like you were chasing the proverbial golden ball through the door that study opened a year ago," Dr. Reed commented. "The one you included in one of your reports."

He sits on a stool, studying the sheets. "We need to design a separate-"

I hand him my notebook.

"We have work to do," Dr. Reed says after scanning my brief experiment outline.

His phone goes off. "Yeah, Kareem. She's here with me." He nods. "I'll tell her." He taps his screen. "How about answering your phone every once in a while."

I check it and grimace. Dad had tried to contact me many times.

"You would do this just before break," Dr. Reed says. "We need the team here. You understand what this may mean?"

"I do." And I'm thrilled he's taking this and me seriously.

"Can you come in tomorrow?"

I shake my head. "Parade and bonfire for the big game is tomorrow night."

"You cannot be serious?"

"It's for a grade in marching band. I need to be there." Not to mention the whole band solidarity thing, but that's paling in significance to this.

"What about during the day?" Dr. Reed asks. "I can't imagine you'll be doing much in school tomorrow."

Pep rally. I have no problems missing it, and Ms. Cortez would swallow that absence easier.

"I can guarantee you whatever you'll do here will be far more educational," Dr. Reed continues.

"That I can sell my parents on, especially if you say something."

"Done. Be here at 8 AM sharp. I'll contact the rest of the lab. Let's get cracking."

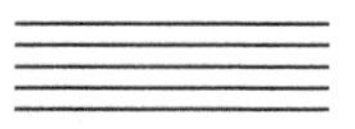

The next day, I'm waiting by the lake for Adil to pick me up. Today was the best lab day. I'm a real Kapur, on the brink of something amazing.

It's still too early to declare everything good. We have tons more experiments to run, reports to write, and research to do. And of course, there's no sure way of knowing until it's actually tested on humans. Even if the science technically works, it may not perform as expected in real life.

But this is enough for the lab to produce a paper, and I'll get named on it. Like high up, which is great for a sixteen-year-old. I have material for a slam dunk of an SJRC project.

I pull out my phone to ask my friends when we can get together so I can tell them the news. I had just hit send when I see Will running on the path and call out to him.

He jogs over. "Hey, what happened to you today?"

132

"I was at the lab. Dr. Reed called the whole team in to help work on the results of my project."

Will actually stops moving for a moment. "Is that normal?"

"No. Usually, everyone works on their own stuff. I might have actually found another way to reduce the pain." I smirk. "And you doubted me."

"That's funny, because I recall explicitly stating that you could."

"After some major teasing. Anyway, this proves I'm a figure to reckon with. A person deserving respect."

He's quiet for a moment. "You didn't think you deserved respect before?"

That sounds terrible when he puts it like that. "Of course I did."

"You sound weirdly unsure of that."

"I'm not, but I need to make everyone else understand."

"Everyone else, who? You don't need to convince us, and I'm pretty sure your family thinks you're great."

I snort, though everyone was appropriately excited. Dad was practically giddy, and Mother gave me a big hug and congratulated me.

Will walks around the bench. "Don't get me wrong, Nayah. What you did was incredible." He gives me a mega-watt smile. "Congratulations."

I try to hold it together as my body turns into a gooey lump of girl.

"But it doesn't change how I fundamentally think of you."

"As a clueless, stuck-up person?"

Will gives me a strange look.

"What?" I challenge. "Am I wrong?"

"I'm trying to decide if you're being argumentative or being you."

"I'm always me. Argumentative or not."

Will laughs and then grows serious as he laps the bench again. "Don't pin everything on this, Nayah. Someone can come and take it away."

"Still trying to snatch my prize so you can teach me a lesson?"

"This wasn't the lesson I'd imagined. I'm on your side. It's the big, bad world you need to worry about."

His earnestness has me flustered, like he wants to bolster me in the big, bad world.

So, I do what I usually do when in that state. "Why do you keep circling the bench?" I exclaim glaring at him. "It's weird."

"I ran a few miles, and I shouldn't stop dead to sit or stand. But I should find my dad. He's probably done with his meeting."

"Will?" another voice calls.

We turn.

Like Will, Mr. Cox has a fluid confidence, but he's rather serious while Will generally is not. They have the same eyes, but Will takes more after his mom than dad. Mr. Cox is an inch or two shorter, with a much broader and muscular frame. Darker complexion, closer to Kyra's color. For a dad, he's quite handsome. Father and son both arrest attention in very different ways.

"I thought you were running?" Mr. Cox asks Will.

"I am. Was."

His dad raises an eyebrow.

"Anayah just finished a lab session," Will explains sounding mildly exasperated. "We haven't been here the whole time.

Mr. Cox says hello to me. "Didn't you do SJRC with Kyra last year?" he asks.

I guess Will wasn't kidding when he said his dad was into this. "I did. We went to Nationals together."

"I remember that. Are you doing it again this year?"

"Yes. I've done the competition every year since sixth grade. This year, I'm doing my research at BSRI under Dr. Reed."

"A young lady with ambition. I like that." He claps Will on the back. "You could learn a thing or two from her."

Will glares at me.

A slow grin spreads across my face.

"What is your research about, Anayah?" his father asks.

Wow, he's really interested. "I'm exploring ways to reduce the pain involved in a sickle cell crisis."

His father's face softens. "I'm glad to hear that."

I suddenly remember Will's uncle has it. I wonder if that's his mom's brother or his dad's. Usually, I think of Nina when I do my research, but it impacts Will's family too.

"She might have found something important, Dad." Will beams at me again.

I can't go to goo in front of his father. I clutch the bench.

"Very impressive." Mr. Cox gives Will a sidelong glance. "I'm surprised you hang out with this one, Anayah."

Will shakes his head. "Dad!"

"I'm never bored when Will is around," I remark.

His dad chuckles. "That I can believe. Anayah, it's been a pleasure talking to you. Visit us anytime. I'd love to hear how your research is progressing."

He sticks his hand out, and I shake it as Will's eyes widen.

I'm sure I'll be there — I do hang out with Kyra. But a personal invitation from his father seems significant, and judging from Will's response, that conclusion is well founded. "Thank you. I will."

"See ya, Nayah." Will flashes me one of his light-bulb smiles.

I let the gooey giddiness overtake me this time. "Bye, Will."

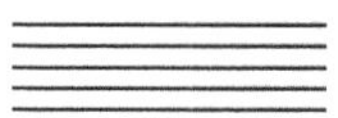

I scoffed at what Will had said on Wednesday. But after the whirlwind of the parade and game, I'm giving it thought as I try to write my SJRC report on Friday.

As he said, my find has caught people's attention, and those close to me are proud. But how they treat me hasn't changed. Mother still lectures me. Priya is still trying to dress me. Balraj continues to treat me with his usual disdain. Father is beaming at me, but then he did that before too. My friends still act like my friends. Good thing too, because I couldn't handle them changing on me.

The difference seems to be in my own mind.

I'm not sure how I feel about that. I try to shrug it off and get back to my report. Get my win, and then I can move on with the real, big-time research at the lab. It's ironic how quickly SJRC has been pushed to a secondary position when it was so important to me a couple of months ago.

I tell people I deserve respect all the time. Of course, I know I'm worthy.

Hypothesis: I don't pin it all on my accomplishments.

Experiment: Strip my accomplishments away and observe what remains.

The silence in my brain is deafening.

Results: Nothing

Conclusion: I am nothing without my accomplishments.

I slam my hands on my desk. No. I refuse to believe that. There must be a fundamental flaw in my reasoning.

There are lots of things about me I don't get — and don't like.

I swallow. Focus on the graphs on the screen. Numbers. Those are safe and make sense.

There's nothing wrong with being a winner.

That's who I am.

Will's warning flashes through my mind. I growl. Get out of my head.

No one will take this from me.

19
Project Submissions

I walk into Dr. Reed's office Monday. SJRC submissions are due this week. My project is a thing of beauty if I say so myself. Seventeen pages complete with an abstract and references, tables, and pictures. Round one of the competition is the paper. From those selections, they whittle the field down by half for round two oral presentations on the regional level.

"This is good, Anayah," Dr. Reed says as he reviews my materials. "And I don't say that to everyone."

He hardly ever says it, and I've gotten that compliment twice already during this experiment.

"Your results are beyond the scope of a high school science project," Dr. Reed continues. "People outside of SJRC will ask about your work, and the University won't like being caught unawares." He smirks. "This year has been especially exciting with the new dean of sciences and department head, along with BSRI's new director. We'll have to take additional and more structured reporting procedures."

"Is that a problem?" There's a hidden significance to this conversation that I'm missing — like the big, bad world is about to encroach on our happy little lab.

Dr. Reed steeples his fingers. "Not necessarily, but it could complicate things. A high school student has never spearheaded our doctorate and commercial research, and I'm in the dark under this new regime."

I rise after he signs a few more forms. "You spend a lot of time in your office. I thought you were in your lab more often."

"Welcome to being on the top," he replies wryly. "You may spend more time dealing with nonsense than the stuff that matters."

I raise an eyebrow.

"There are days when I wish I were in your shoes, when the research was the most important thing, and I could concentrate on it. Get your prize, Anayah. You'll definitely be in the running for one."

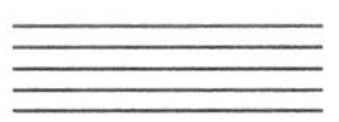

I tried to keep an ear out for how Will's project was coming along. He's been unusually quiet about it, and I don't want to seem like I'm desperately seeking information.

I corner him after band. "Did you submit yet?"

"I'm doing it during bio today. Wanna see it?"

"Absolutely." This is better than I'd hoped.

He fishes out a dark brown leather folder from his bag and hands it to me.

"This is a nice portfolio," I comment.

"It's an important project. I'd like to hear your thoughts."

That was a serious response. I get to reading as Gen and Will chat about the upcoming band trip while we make our way down the hall.

Will was not kidding. This research is excellent and the paper, fascinating. I turn the pages faster and faster. His approach was different, and he presented his findings in clean and academic language without sounding pretentious. It reads and sounds like Will, but yet not Will, or at least not the Will I'm used to.

I barely notice when we reach their classroom.

"You're going to be late again." Gen sounds like she's trying not to laugh.

"I don't care," I say.

Gen scoots through the door as the bell rings.

"Nayah, I have to get in. It's good?"

I snatch my eyes from the paper and meet Will's questioning gaze. "It's fantastic."

"Good. That means a lot coming from you."

My heart thuds. "Thanks."

"You should get going." That tractor beam is back. "You're already late."

"Will, talk to your girlfriend later," his teacher booms.

Will rolls his eyes, releasing me from his beam.

I exhale and rush away.

I mumble some excuse to my teacher and don't hear a word of class.

Will executed a dead serious experiment.

I underestimated him. I knew he was smart, but this is — I'm embarrassed to admit I thought we weren't on the same academic footing.

If he didn't act so goofy all the time, I wouldn't have done that. Why is he hiding this? He's teeming with intelligence and ability and wasting it. No wonder his father is on his back all the time.

Will is a serious contender for my prize.

Having him as a worthy competitor will make SJRC this year more fun. I'll thrive on it. This is better than gloating, and if things go right, I could still do that too.

A pair of backlit brown eyes flash through my mind. My stomach drops, and my face heats.

No.

I slam my health book shut more forcefully than necessary.

There will be none of that.

It's only a science project.

20

Winter Concert

It's the night of the winter concert, the first Thursday of December. Usually, we're in coats this time of year, but it's warm, and I can get away with a heavy jacket.

I love concerts. All of our hard work comes to fruition, and we can show off. I have a solo tonight so I wanted to look nice but still be comfortable. I chose a black calf-length dress with a little flair and black flats. My hair is up in a simple bun. No makeup or jewelry except a watch. I'm tingly with anticipation and arrive at the high school early.

Not many kids are here and they're mostly seniors. Kyra is helping with the percussion setup, and Will is warming up on his trumpet.

I take a seat by him. "Congratulations on making jazz band."

"Thanks. Seth and I are gonna have a blast."

Will keeps surprising me lately. First, his chair placement, then his project, and he also made jazz band.

To get in as a sophomore means he must have made serious advancements.

He's dressing differently too. Even for concerts, he used to look more casual than everyone else. But tonight, his dark brown vest and pants are classy, and the Burgundy tie and white shirt, which he rolled up to the elbows, look sharp. He could be plunked into a 1950s jazz band at a ritzy club.

"So you do know how to dress?" I ask.

"I can make it happen when I want to." He gives me a cocky grin. "You like my threads?"

I cross my arms. "It's better than your usual train wreck."

His grin grows into a mega-watt smile. "That's a definite yes. You always get extra mean when you're trying to cover-up."

"As opposed to my standard mean?"

His chuckle dies as he seems to contemplate me more seriously. "Why do you dress in a way that downplays your looks?"

I almost slide off my chair. Where did that question come from? "What of it if I do? Not that I'm admitting to anything."

"What happened to always being you? It's one of your best qualities."

My body floods with warmth. Really? "I am being me."

"I bet you would dress differently if you dressed for you without reference to anyone else."

"I don't dress to impress anyone."

"Including yourself. Because you're afraid that impression is all people will take away from you."

My breath catches. Man, he's good. Two can play this game. Engage. "At least I don't leave the impression of being a goofball when I can do much more."

Will stills.

"What are you afraid of? That you may actually blow the competition away with your intelligence?"

"I don't hide my intelligence."

"Don't insult mine by denying it. I bet you let very few people see what you're fully capable of."

He glares at me. "Am I suddenly worth bothering with because you decided I'm super intelligent?"

I jerk back. "I've never felt that way, Will. I thought we were friends."

"We are, but that doesn't mean you see me like our other friends, and that gets old."

Lesson learned.

I'm clamoring for people to respect me, and one of my closest friends feels I don't respect him. And he may not be as far from the truth as I'd like. "I'm so sorry, Will. Please believe me, that I never, ever felt you weren't worth my time—"

"It's fine, Anayah. I just don't like being discounted by you."

We're not fine. He didn't call me Nayah. I swallow, the stab getting deeper. "I don't discount you. I just admire different things."

Will raises an eyebrow. "Like what?"

I shrug, my face growing warm. "I've always been jealous of how easily people gravitate towards you."

"That's not a big deal."

"It's huge." He has no idea how much I would kill for that ability. "And Matt would back me up on that."

Will's backlit eyes dig into mine.

It's hard, but I let him do it. I rarely let people see past the armor.

"You're not as bad as you think," he says gently.

I snort and look away, because suddenly, my nose feels like it's filled with cloth. "Are you kidding me? I like emanate the human version of bug repellent."

I try to laugh, but to my horror, it comes out like a weird half sob.

"Come here, Nayah." He throws an arm around my shoulders and hugs me.

At least he's back to calling me Nayah.

"You're good. Anyone worth your time sees you. Hears you. And you can tell everyone else to get lost."

We sit in silence for a moment, my head still resting on his shoulder.

"I'll make a deal with you," I say. "When you blister people with your intelligence, I'll blister them with my beauty."

"That day may come sooner than you think." Will flashes me a mega-watt smile as he drops his arm. "I have a competition to win. You'll need your whole beauty arsenal for SJRC. Not that you need much."

I try to ignore how hot my face is getting. Again.

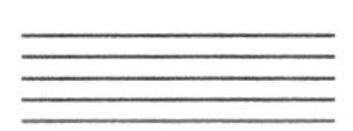

Brooke has the flute players come into a practice room one by one for tuning. I enter the tiny space and shut the door.

The room descends into a heavy silence. Watching so much activity in the hall through the windows and not hearing any of it is weird.

Brooke beat me out for jazz band. Only three flutes auditioned, and we were close together in score. Ms. Cortez chose the third chair senior who auditioned, and then made an unusual decision to have a second flute player and selected Brooke.

Brooke dressed carefully tonight. Her light brown hair is blown out straight, and she has more eyeshadow on than usual, making her brown eyes seem larger and rounder. A sleeveless electric blue dress sets off her look nicely.

She instructs me to play B flat and then C and declares me good.

"Don't you have a tuner?" I ask.

"Ms. Cortez didn't have enough and asked if I could do it by ear."

That's not going well. I'm definitely sharp. "Brooke, I think-"

"Do you have to argue about everything?"

I wasn't even annoyed with Brooke, but if she wants to make everyone sharp, be my guest.

I enter another practice room.

Tune myself.

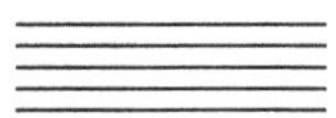

Ms. Cortez furrows her brow as the band plays scales and then asks the flutes to play a B flat.

"Did you tune everyone?" she asks Brooke.

"Yes."

"Flutes sound sharp."

Brooke flushes as Ms. Cortez asks to hear me play. "That's correct."

"I adjusted myself."

Brooke gives me the dirtiest look. "Are you trying to show me up? You couldn't say something?"

"You cut me off," I snap.

"Girls, we don't have time for this," Ms. Cortez says. "Anayah, tune the second flutes in the band office, and I'll do the rest of the first flutes. Everyone else, get on stage."

I glare at Brooke as I walk into the office. You want me to make you look bad? That's all the challenge I need. Give me an inch, and I'll take a very public mile.

My solo is with Brooke and an oboe player at the beginning of the last piece. It's a relatively large solo for concert band.

I glance at the darkened audience and try not to fidget too much. The stage lights are hot, and Brooke seems tense. For the first time, she probably minds being my stand partner as much as I dislike being hers.

Ms. Cortez nods at the oboe player, who begins the solo.

And one…

He's playing in the wrong key, but it actually doesn't sound bad.

Four…

However, it will if Brooke and I play the piece as written. He'll correct himself.

Eight…

Or not.

How can he not figure this out? Is he that nervous?

Twelve…

I lift my flute. One of the three of us will sound wrong. It won't be me, and I'm still ticked at Brooke.

Sixteen…

I begin my solo by matching the oboe's key.

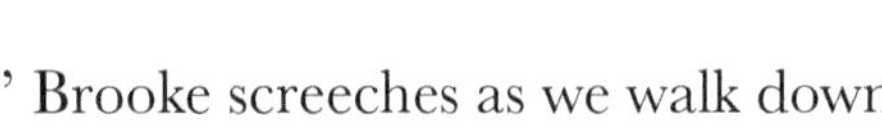

"What was that?" Brooke screeches as we walk down the band hallway after the concert.

I give Brooke a level look. "What was what?"

A few kids glance at us as they enter the band room.

She jabs a finger in my face. "You played something completely different and made me sound awful."

"She played to match the oboe," Ms. Cortez says behind us. "He was in the wrong key."

Brooke and I whirl around as a jolt of fear shoots through my body. "Are you angry with me?"

"On the contrary. That was quite impressive. Someone was going to sound wrong." Ms. Cortez gives Brooke a sympathetic look. "It's a shame it was you since it wasn't your fault. The person you should yell at is the oboe player."

Ms. Cortez continues toward the band room doors.

"My father finally comes to a concert, and this happens." Brooke growls. "You want first chair so bad? Game on. And it'll take more than just playing a few notes on key."

She turns on her heel and stalks off.

I grin. Finally, Brooke sees me as a threat. Someone to reckon with.

21

The Whirlwind

Balraj is sitting at the kitchen table chewing on something when I come down for dinner Saturday evening. "Did you drop out of school? Why are you here?"

"Maybe I'm anxious to see my family."

Adil snorts. He's doing homework on the other side of the table.

"Pri said I'll want to be home tonight," Balraj explains.

While we're eating dinner, Priya walks into the kitchen from the side door, beaming.

"Good, you're all here." She motions with her hand towards the door.

David walks in, and Priya grabs his arm. "We're back together! The wedding is on!"

Mother squeals as she runs and hugs Priya and David.

The rest of us stare at them.

As far as I'm concerned, David did not hold on to Priya as he should have.

"Priya, you never fail to deliver," Balraj says.

I stifle a disgusted sigh. I suppose Balraj is unconcerned. As long as he's amused and entertained, he's good.

"David, we need to talk," Dad announces. "Would you follow me into my office?"

As Mom quiets down, David goes pale, and even Priya looks surprised.

Adil and I exchange glances.

Dad doesn't intercede like this often, and his office is serious. I only got talked to twice in there. One was for sending snotty messages from Priya's phone to a boy she liked when she was in high school. Said boy was the reason she wouldn't take me skating earlier that day and teased me in front of her friends.

The other occasion was when all four of us got in trouble for playing dodgeball in the house and breaking Mother's favorite vase. She was away; Dad was at work; Priya was in charge. Rainy day during summer vacation. There was something about all of us getting into heaps of trouble together that was great.

At least Dad will say something. When he does step in, it's the final word.

Dad and David leave, and Mother excuses herself to call Seth's mom.

"Have a seat, Priya." Adil pulls out a chair and pats it. "Are you sure about this?"

She plops down with that nauseating, dreamy expression in her eyes. "Yes, I love him."

"That's beside the point." I'm stopping this girl from selling herself short.

As Balraj laughs, Priya gives me one of those 'little Yaya doesn't understand' looks.

"People love all kinds of people they have no business being in love with." I hope my green eyes are laser beams burning a message into her brain. "Will David treat you like you're valuable? Is he going to be there for you?"

150

"Baby sis brings up some valid points," Adil says.

"She does, but David approached me."

"Groveling?" I cross my arms.

"He said it was wrong of him to give up on us because of our families," Priya explains. "That he did made him question what kind of guy he was."

I'm not convinced or happy, but I have to begrudgingly admit he at least said the right things.

"That was the only reason he ended your engagement?" Adil asked. "You don't have to share if you don't want. I'm just curious."

"That was the blow-up that ended things." She pauses. "But the real issue was having kids."

She never mentioned that before. I have a quick flashback to my weird conversation with Will in the hallway. "Were you for or against?"

"I'd like kids because I like our large family, but it was never a deal breaker," Priya replies. "David wasn't exactly planning for children, but if it happened, he wouldn't be upset."

"What's the problem?" Balraj asked. "It seemed like you guys could work with that."

"Exactly. But our parents…"

"I could see why that would be a pain," says Adil. "But there's a good chance our parents will get grandchildren out of someone."

"I know. But Mom was pressuring me, and David is the only child, and his parents wanted me to convince him. It was turning into a nightmare."

I understand better why there were challenges, but to just up and leave? I'm still not a fan.

"He said if I gave him another chance, he would never leave me again, no matter what happens. I told him I'd be more considerate of his feelings on things. That's the short story. We spent hours talking and sorting things out."

We're quiet for a moment.

"I won't sentence him yet," I say. "Hopefully, Dad is in there raking him over the coals."

"Balraj?" Priya asks.

"Whatever makes you happy."

"I love you all!" Priya exclaims. "I knew I could count on you!"

I feel like face planting.

We're still sitting at the kitchen table finishing our meal when Dad and David come out. Mother never reappeared.

Priya jumps up and grabs David. "We have to visit David's parents. Tell Mom I said goodbye."

And then they're off.

The kitchen is strangely still.

Dad sits in her seat at the table. He removes his glasses, rubs his eyes, and reaches for food.

I'm dying of curiosity. "What did you and David talk about?"

"We have an understanding." Dad shakes his head. "I should have said something sooner, but Priya is a whirlwind. I could have protected her better."

"She's a grown woman, Dad," I say.

"We protect our own, no matter what age. And Anayah, don't bring any young man in here that doesn't believe you're the sun, the moon, and the stars, you understand?"

Balraj snorts.

Dad gives him a piercing look.

"You don't have to worry about a thing," I reply. "That's so long off."

"You say that now… I wish I could have kept you all at the age of five." An expression crosses his face that I can't quite decipher. "No one will hurt mera bachchi."

I wince — my baby girl.

He shakes a piece of naan at Balraj and Adil. "And don't get me started on how you two should treat young women. Do we need a review? Balraj?"

"What?!"

Dad glares at him.

Balraj goes back to his plate.

Dad sighs. "I'll be in my office."

The sun, the moon, and the stars. Only Dad would think of me like that.

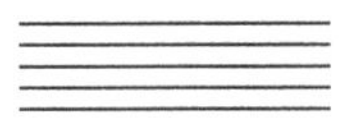

Balraj is in our fridge when Adil and I walk in from school on Friday. "How come you guys never have any food in here?"

"How about going to the store with all that free time since you're on break? Why don't you go out with your friends for dinner?"

"I would, but Mom called a family dinner to discuss Priya's wedding arrangements."

I glance at Adil.

He shrugs.

"You have got to be kidding me?" I exclaim. "How come no one ever tells me about these things?"

Balraj smirks.

Mother walks into the kitchen carrying several takeout bags.

Two hours later, we are yet once again gathered around the kitchen table for another family wedding meeting. Dinner has been eaten. At least there's still dessert.

"David and I made things simpler," Priya announces.

I hope she starts with her explanation.

"The ceremony and the reception will be at a different venue, but it's closer and cheaper. We're cutting the invite list down by at least half-"

Mother gasps. "Half? We had to cut people we shouldn't have before."

Priya narrows her eyes. "We're cutting the list down."

Mother crosses her arms but says nothing further.

"We're keeping the large engagement party, but that'll be the only thing we'll throw before the wedding."

"This sounds fine," Dad says.

"Don't forget the dance is back on!" Priya throws her hands in the air.

I groan. I forgot about that.

"Owen said we can have our old slot back."

I am literally banging my head on the table.

Mother glares at me while Adil and Balraj are smothering laughs. Priya is so preoccupied with her wedding binder, I don't think she noticed.

"Anayah, come with me to the porch area," Mother says. "I left dessert out there."

She shuts the door after we step out there. "What is your problem?"

"Nothing. I just don't want to do that dance."

"Of course, you don't. Anything pretty and nice and fun you never want to do."

My jaw drops. "That is categorically untrue, Mother."

"How many times do I have to tell you to be enthusiastic and helpful? Your sister needs you. Carry the cake in. I'll grab the other things." Mother opens the porch door, grabbing the plastic utensils and napkins.

I snatch the cake.

Nothing is going to change, is it?

22

A Universal Argument

After six buses, thirty-six hours, and seeing sides of people I never thought I'd see, everyone is happy to be in Orlando for our band trip. Breakfast was at 8 AM this morning with a nine o'clock departure for the field show competition, which is part of the bowl game activities. The day is pleasantly warm and sunny. The field show competition is at a local high school stadium. There's a fair amount of confusion as we disembark from the buses and get our instruments from the instrument truck. We're led to a section of field that's a holding ground for our band.

After a while, the director asks Brooke and me to follow her, and we join Seth and Will.

"I need the four of you to get the band warmed up. I'm taking a large chunk of kids, mostly upperclassmen, to run through some things on the field for the general field setup. We're the second band performing, but we're by far the largest group here, so they want to make sure everything is set up properly. We'll join you when we're done."

Ms. Cortez takes off. I'm glad to be someone in charge, but this is a major assignment off the cuff.

"Suggestions on what we should work on?" asks Seth.

I rattle off a few things we could practice. Seth asks Brooke if she'd conduct after he and Will gather the band to explain what's happening.

I turn to Brooke, who has her arms crossed, after Will and Seth take off. Since the concert, Brooke and I have said little to one another. I try to focus on the goal at large. We're here to perform well as a band. It's not all about me.

It was painful, but we decided what measures to run through in each piece. I step to the side to let Brooke handle it from there.

Even though our performance was in the morning, the actual awards presentation wasn't scheduled until four in the afternoon. We had the option to wait on the air-conditioned buses after lunch, but most of us were interested in watching the other bands perform.

There are a large variety of bands here. Some are more jazz-like, others drum and bugle corp style. As Ms. Cortez said, ours was by far the largest and sounded the most like a full-fledged band with all the instrumental sections. However, because of our size, we couldn't produce the fluid formations that some of the other groups could do. I was curious how that would play out in the final standings.

Our band is used to winning or at least being near the top, so we were disappointed not to rank in the top three, especially since we won several specialty awards. The band was in a solemn mood when we exited the stands.

"You performed well," Ms. Cortez says before we got back on the buses. "Which is evident by the specialty awards. Our percussion section is outstanding."

The band cheers.

"Hats off to the band front and our ladies who walked away with a best auxiliary award," she continues. "Great job. You had stiff competition out there."

We clapped for the twirlers.

"Joe, you can work an audience. It was an excellent performance, as always, and you certainly deserve that award."

Joe raises his trumpet as his section gives him high fives and slaps on the back, and the band cheers for him.

After the band quiets down, she continues with a more sober expression. "This was an excellent experience for you. It's good to compete with a wider variety of musical groups and watch their performances. We can learn from this. I look forward to hearing the judges' comments, and we'll listen to them together to find out what we can improve. Great job everyone; you should be proud of yourselves. Let's get back on the buses so we can clean up and eat!"

We give a hearty cheer to that plan.

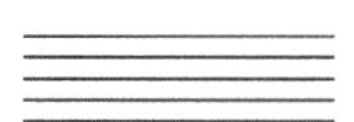

Today all instrumental groups do their assigned park performances. Orchestra performed at another park this morning and has just returned. Our performance isn't until late in the evening.

We're heading to an inventions building and ride when Will drops back and walks alongside me like he wants to talk.

My heart does that body slam it seems to do way too often around him.

"Joe's been asking about you and Brooke," Will says quietly once there's some distance between us and the others.

"Been asking what?"

"Asking, like he's interested."

My stomach plummets. To hide my disappointment, I glare at him. "I'm not getting involved with that nonsense."

"I told him that but figured you should know."

"Thank you." I break eye contact, faking an interest towards the bright flowers in the beds beside us. "I'm surprised he noticed a couple of sophomores."

"Most guys don't care about that"

"They care about looks, I'm sure."

Will shrugs. "Won't lie; good looks will catch anyone's attention. Depends on the guy, if that's all he's after."

"What kind of guy are you?"

"I thought you knew me better than that."

What kind of friend am I? First, I don't think he's smart enough, and now I act like he's some shallow jerk. "I do." I grimace. "I really needed that lesson."

Will chuckles as he opens the door for us. "Be nice to Joe."

What? I stop short. Such an abrupt change of subject. "Am I ever mean to him?"

Will gently presses my arm to urge me forward through the second set of doors. "Never, but in your determination to focus, you're sometimes less than sympathetic."

True, but that truth hurts.

Will winces. "That came out bad. I know you care, but I know you, and other people might not get that, so—"

"It's fine. You know how much of a people person I am." I glance around. We had lost our friends.

"Relating to folk when we don't get their situation is tough." Will points and I follow him to the left. "It's just that you go after everything hard, and it's not like you pretend, so yeah, everyone knows when you're having diffi-culty relating."

That was such a bizarre explanation, I explode into laughter, which draws looks from a few people nearby. Most people would write me off as a jerk and go on about their business, but Will hasn't.

"Anyway, he's a nice guy and my friend, so try to be tactful or something," Will finishes like he's at a loss.

"You're right; I should work on that."

I don't have time for this stuff, especially if it's not for Will.

I shake my head. No. I don't have time for this stuff. Period.

Focus on my work.

And the music.

Time flies by fast and we're getting ready for the parade. It sounds weird, but I concentrate so hard on marching and music, it's hard to be aware of the parade itself. I grab fleeting impressions during the few moments we're not playing as we march the straightway.

This was one of those experiences that's so new and quick that it's hard to grasp. But I force myself to take more notice of what's around me. As we march, the people along the paths cheer.

People save and work hard to come here. It's a once-in-a-lifetime experience for some.

And we're a part of that experience.

Unfortunately, I couldn't hold onto those good feelings as I tried to go to sleep that night. I kept tossing and turning re-running my conversation with Will. It was like he was trying for me for Joe instead of for himself.

Which shouldn't upset me because I don't want any guy trying for me.

Except apparently Will.

Focus on the music.

The following morning my sheets look like I was fighting someone.

Thankfully, we didn't have to leave for the Citrus Bowl parade until 11 am. Besides getting practically no sleep last night, the other late nights and early mornings are wearing on me. We barely made it to breakfast on time, and we were in good company.

The festive atmosphere at the parade site is cool, and everyone is excited. There are floats all over the place and as a college bowl game, many of the spectators aren't much older than us.

Our drum major calls for us to fall in.

Like the park parade, this one is over much too soon, though it's longer. We spent so much time preparing and fund-raising. There's so much anticipation, and then these performances are over in the blink of an eye.

I gaze around the staging area, soaking it all in and anchoring it in my mind before we hop back on the bus.

As I take my seat I reflect on Mel's words earlier in the year, and I think I have a better idea of what she meant. This was great, but it's only a part of what we do and can do as a band. Another way to play music together.

Music first.

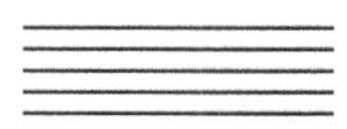

We're leaving, but it feels like our trip is far from over. We're at the studio park for the day, and the bus trip is like a mini trip in itself.

We aren't having much success with these rides though. This is the third line we've been in because the rides for two other attractions got shut down.

"You think we'll always be together like this?" Taylor asks suddenly.

"No," I reply.

Gen gapes at me.

I shrug. "We'll go off to college or work. Possibly move, get married, and have kids. We won't be like this forever."

"I meant close like this, good friends," Taylor clarifies.

"Probably not," I reply.

Will laughs.

"Why are you so negative?" Gen asks, exasperated. "We can stay close if we work on it."

"Why do you believe it's unlikely?" Xiang asks me.

"I don't mean to be negative, and I agree with Gen. If we work at it, we can, and I will. But people grow up and change."

Taylor bites her lip.

Gen gives her an anxious look. "We'll work hard not to leave each other. You have nothing to worry about."

"Priya and Balraj didn't stay in touch with most of their high school friends," I remark.

Gen narrows her eyes. "Anayah."

"Were they close?" Matt asks.

Balraj has many friends, but I wouldn't say he's close to them. Based on Priya's previous comments, I guess she's not as tight with hers as I am with mine.

"No, I guess not," I reply.

Will seems to be assessing me. Again.

I meet his gaze head-on. "What do you think?"

"Everything you said was sound."

"That doesn't sound like you agree with it."

"That wasn't your question."

"Are you planning on drifting off?"

"No, but I'm surprised you're-" he stops short.

"Planning on sticking around?" I cross my arms. "I love my friends."

"You're also into science."

"I can love them both."

"What if you have to choose between the two? What if your career demands all of you?"

"Do you think I'd love my work more than my family and friends?"

He's quiet for a moment. "I don't know. The Anayah I know, my Nayah wouldn't, but as you just said, people change."

I gape at him, not sure how to respond to that. How can a single sentence be the best thing I've ever heard and simultaneously hurt so much? "You should know I'd never change like that." I snap.

"Why would I?" he retorts. "How about acting like you need people every once in a while?"

"You want me to hang all over you like those girls in school do?"

"Girls don't hang on me. Are you gonna let yourself fall for some high school guy? I can hear your brain-"

"You hear nothing. I'd fall for any guy worth my time."

"You're either desperately proving yourself to people or haughtily insisting you're better. Which is it?"

"I won't act needy to boost your ego."

"Stop trying to make this about me, Anayah. It's not inflating someone's ego to tell people you appreciate them."

"Stop pretending it isn't about you. Clearly, my behavior has offended you, or we wouldn't be having this discussion. You want me to stand here and tell you I need you? How large is your head?"

"You don't get it. This is why people don't want to be around you."

I snatch a sharp breath.

Will cringes. "I'm sorry, I didn't mean-"

I hold my hand up, surprised at the lump in my throat and the tightness in my chest. This is what happens when there's no music to focus on.

"You two are arguing like you're having a private conversation in a living room," Matt says quietly.

My friends are gaping at us.

"Sorry. Nayah-"
"Forget about it."

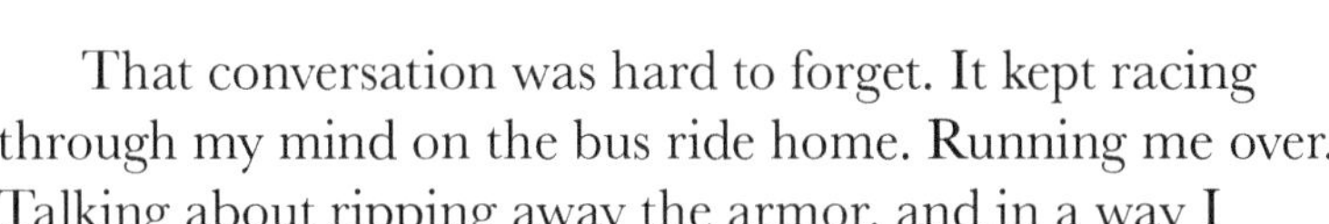

That conversation was hard to forget. It kept racing through my mind on the bus ride home. Running me over. Talking about ripping away the armor, and in a way I never saw coming.

Maybe I don't appreciate people as well as I should. Will may have a tiny point there. It's just that people are so… people.

But don't I tell my friends I appreciate them?

I guess not enough, according to Will, and it's not like they leaped to my defense.

"Penny for your thoughts?" Kyra asks.

"I appreciate you. I really do."

"I know. Don't worry about Will. Your shot about not hanging over him like other girls was a direct hit. I love it when you take him down a notch."

I play with my hands. "You think he wants me to hang over him?"

"I do, and I'm glad you're not letting him win, or at least you're making him wait and work for it."

Kyra makes it sound like I have iron-clad control over this situation, and it does appear to be turning into one.

A restless excitement engulfs me.

I'm being irrational, which is why I hate this stuff. But it would be nice to have a guy like Will like me.

I take a deep breath. Remember the plan. No boys. No drama. No misleading, foolish emotions.

"He's right though," I say. "I'm not always appreciative, and I don't want to be that way with my friends. I don't know what I'd do without you all."

"Then it's good you don't have to worry about that."

Admitting that need didn't make me feel weak or vulnerable, and Kyra's assurance gave me more power.

Will was right. Again. It's scary he can do this. He is inside my head.

How did that happen? That's worse than him taking my armor.

"Speaking of-" Kyra says.

Will asks Kyra if she'd switch seats with him for a bit.

"Is it okay?" Kyra asks me.

I sigh. "Yeah, it's fine."

Will sits down. "Nayah, I'm-"

"I don't want to talk about it. I told you to forget about it."

We sit in silence for a minute.

I whirl on him. "I didn't swear you to secrecy, but you took what I told you in confidence and threw it in my face."

"I shouldn't have. I don't know what's wrong with me."

"It hurt." I can't believe I admitted that to him.

"I'm so sorry, Nayah. The last thing I'd want to do is hurt you."

It feels like that night with him at the hospital, but I don't understand why. "I need my friends, and I don't say it. I view it as a weakness, and that's wrong. I'm glad everyone puts up with me."

"We don't put up with you. Why don't you see yourself the way we do?"

Another deafening silence as I look out the window.

23
A Diplomatic Answer

I've always kept myself well occupied, but I'm in a constant state of motion now. With the tighter wedding schedule, my free time is taken up with Priya. We've had more lab meetings to determine how to proceed and duplicate the experiment. Volunteering at the hospital is busier, and I'm more in tune with the patients.

Dad is next to me at the kitchen table reading his tablet as I do my homework, and Mother is fixing herself lunch.

"I was able to book the same place for the engagement party." Priya sits at the table. "But it's soon, January 14th."

Mother puts a bowl down. "That's next week."

Priya nods. "Next Saturday."

Mother exhales.

"My science presentation is that day." I received notice that I'm in regionals.

My parents exchange looks.

"I can't get any other date," Priya says. "I had to beg for that one."

"What time do you actually present?" Dad asks me.

"I don't know. We have to be there by eleven."

"My guess is you won't be able to stay for the other presenters or the awards ceremony. You can join us at the party after your presentation. There'll still be plenty of time to celebrate as a family."

I glance at my sister. I don't think either of us is satisfied with this solution.

"You two should be happy," Mother says. "Priya gets her engagement party where she wants it, and Anayah gets to present her science project."

She's right; I shouldn't feel cheated. The fact my parents are letting me come to the engagement party late is an acknowledgment of how important this competition is. Under any other circumstance, it would have been a closed discussion.

"Anayah, can you get one of your friends to take you?" Mother asks. "We'll be busy here."

Yeah, too busy with Priya to bother with me. "I can drive myself if I use one of the cars."

"We may need the extra vehicles," Mother replies. "We'll have to run errands in the morning."

"We won't need that many cars, Neeti. Anayah, you can take one." Dad goes back to reading his tablet.

"Thank you." I walk out of the kitchen.

Somehow I feel Priya won again.

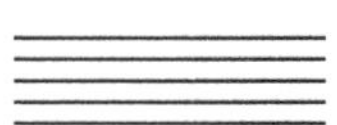

The next day I'm at the lab still fuming over yesterday's conversation about my use of the car for regionals. Rationally, it's not a big deal, but the way Mother seemed to act like I'm in the way really bugs me.

Running me over like Will's comments had.

166

Only Will and I worked things out. I don't think a similar conversation with Mother would end the same way. She'd probably just tell me how ridiculous I am and to be better.

Those ruminations make it difficult for the lab to be my happy place. I absently say goodbye to Dr. Reed as I pass his office.

"Before you go, Anayah, I need to talk to you about the future of your lab work."

Dr. Reed gestures towards the chair, and I sit down.

"The department rolled out a preliminary agenda, of sorts," he continues. "After you present your findings, the University wants further research done."

"Of course, I plan on continuing this project for the next two years' competitions."

"It's more complicated than that. The department is planning a full-scale research investigation with the entire lab team involved."

"That's fine. This is much larger than SJRC."

"They plan on providing funding and want us to submit papers and research for journals like JAMA."
Dr. Reed steeples his fingers, tapping his pointer fingers together.

Funding and JAMA? That's a huge deal. Suddenly, I realize what Dr. Reed is trying to express without saying it. "Are they taking my project away from me?"

Dr. Reed purses his lips. "The diplomatic answer is of course not."

I arch an eyebrow, attempting to appear poised, but a shot of fear lit my body. How can I be a real scientist if people take my work away?

"I'll fight to make sure this remains your project," Dr. Reed says. "But I'm in an awkward position mentoring a high school minor doing nearly doctorate level research at a university lab. The University is starting to make their presence felt."

I feel lost, and that's not something I'm used to.

"I'll find out what needs to be done to make you an official lab team member. That might afford you some protection. Since you're not a student here, we may have to make you an employee of the university, which will be interesting since you're only sixteen. We'd have to track your hours."

"I'd like that, just tell me what would be expected. I'm grateful for all your help, but I don't like sitting around while you do things for me."

"Let me do some prep work before you charge in. You'll have your chance if I don't miss my guess. In the meantime, there's plenty for you to do to advance your cause. Your biggest lack right now is your knowledge and experience. You can't do much about experience in the short term, but you can increase your knowledge. If I were you, I would get my hands on everything possible to understand the world in which your research lives."

Immerse myself. "You gave me a head start on that already. You said I'd thank you later. Thank you."

Dr. Reed gives me a small smile.

There's another area in which I'm woefully ignorant. "Is there a way I can get a copy of that agenda? Or the University's budgets, goals, and plans?"

"That's a very broad request, but I can try to get materials along those lines. To play the game, you need to know the players, right?"

I nod.

He plays with a pen. "Earlier I said the University is asserting themselves. In many cases, there are one or two people or a small group that are actually the ones doing the talking."

I mull that over. "Who is it in this case?"

"I don't know. Like I said, we're in the midst of a regime change, and people are jockeying for position."

I exhale. Nothing is concrete.

"Meanwhile, we'll continue like nobody has said anything," Dr. Reed concludes.

It sounds like these people will take this and not think twice. Like they personally slapped me across the cheek.

Engage.

Is it never ending? I won't be able to gain everyone's respect, no matter how hard I try, and I can't keep winning things for their approval and admiration.

What does that make me?

Silence has never been so loud.

24

Anayah Hits a Wall

"Anayah!" Mother yells in the hallway Saturday.

I force open an eyelid. Six in the morning.

Mother cannot be serious. It's an engagement party. It's not even the wedding day.

"Anayah!" She swings my bedroom door open. "You must help."

I wince and roll out of my bed. Walk bleary-eyed to the bathroom.

Fifteen minutes later, knocking on the bathroom door. "Stop wasting time!"

Ten minutes later, pounding on my bedroom door. "You need to go to the store."

I throw the door open.

Adil stands in the hall. "Why is she pounding on stuff and yelling for you?"

I growl. "I don't know, but I'm tired of it already."

Mother is pulling pots out as I enter the kitchen. "There is a list of things on the counter that I need you to pick up from the store. No dawdling today."

I grit my teeth as I pick up the list and walk out the door.

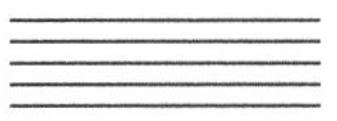

Mother flies into the enclosed porch as I finish my cereal. "How can you eat?"

"It's an engagement party, not a funeral."

"Don't be smart. I need you to go to the dry cleaners. The ticket and money are on the counter."

"I have to get ready soon. I need to change, pack, and go over my presentation one more time."

"You practiced enough last night. Go to the dry cleaners, and stop being so selfish." She marches out of the kitchen.

I throw my dishes into the sink, pick up the ticket and the money, and bang out the door. It feels like my chest is in a vise, being slowly squeezed to death.

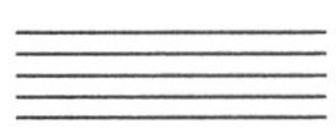

"Anayah!"

I shut my eyes. The vise got tighter.

"What is it, Priya?" I walk into her room.

"Can you run to the party store for me?" She hands me money. "David remembered something we should have, and neither of us has time."

"I don't have much either."

"This won't take long, and it's the least you can do for us today since you're coming late because of your little science thingy."

My mouth falls open.

She gives the money a sharp shake and holds it in my face.

The least I can do? Little science thingy? I snatch the cash from her and stalk out of the room.

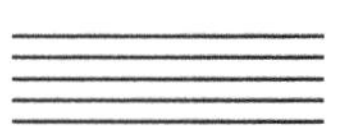

I walk through the front door and lean against it. Weirdly, the house is quiet. I tiptoe upstairs and wordlessly give Priya her stuff before storming out of her room to mine. I walk around a pile of books and papers and fall onto my bed.

I need to get ready. Take a few minutes to calm down. Relax. Slow my breathing. Steady my heart.

"Anayah!"

I close my eyes.

I hear Mother enter my room.

"Where are the cardamoms?" she asks. "They're not in the bags."

"I didn't get any from the store."

"Why not?" Mother puts her hands on her hips.

"It wasn't on the list."

Mother closes her eyes and rubs her forehead. "I can't make besan laddu without it. Anayah, you'll have to go back and get it."

"I don't have time!"

"Why are you being so difficult today?"

"I'm not. I've done everything you've asked me."

"But with a rotten attitude."

My heart stops. It goes from overdrive to nothing.

"We could have not allowed you to do the presentation at all. There are other years," Mother continues. "Go to the store." She stomps out of my room.

I'm never enough.

I scream and punch my wall.

Yelping, I bend over and massage my hand.

Punching walls really hurts.

I find an ice pack and ace bandage in the bathroom. Wrap my hand and take ibuprofen. The pain is so intense it drives me to find my parents, in the kitchen, and I ask Dad to look at my hand.

He shoots Mother a look. "I told you something was wrong." He examines my hand. "What happened? It's swollen."

"Long story."

"We should have this checked out at the hospital." Dad grabs his phone as he stands.

"I'll go to a doctor if it gets worse, but I'm sure an ice pack is all I need."

"I told you it was nothing, Kareem." Mother shoves tablecloths into a huge bag.

Dad frowns. "All right, I'll trust your judgment."

Mother tries to balance the overstuffed bag on a chair. "I guess you're not going to the store then."

Dad and I look at her.

She sighs. "Adil!"

"I need to finish getting ready," I say.

"Anayah, come right over after you're done presenting," Mother calls after me.

I don't respond. Forget Priya. Forget the engagement party. I'm staying for the competition. She can feel what it's like to come in second place for once.

25

A Place

It's hard to drive Adil's car with my hand hurting so much, but I'm glad the regional competition is held at our high school. I don't have to worry about navigating the venue and can concentrate on my presentation.

I register at the tables in the front lobby and get my room assignment and entrants' packet. We're in groups of six to ten presenters per classroom, organized by project type. I recognize only one name on the list of presenters for my room, and he slides into the seat next to me.

As we wait, I scan the project titles that will be presented in my room. I'm the fourth presenter.

"Anayah Kapur," says one of the judges.

I stand and smooth my plain black suit with matching black heels — professional, low-key. I wanted to put my hair in a bun, but that wasn't happening with my hand situation. All I could manage was a ponytail, and it was work making that neat. No makeup or jewelry.

For some absurd reason, my mind flashes back to the conversation Will and I had at the Winter Concert about how I dress. I try not to scowl. He's not even here, and he's in my head. So what if my outfit is plain? It's about my project, not me. I'll sacrifice dressing the way I want to get the respect I need to win.

I begin my presentation, very comfortable with my research, forgetting I'm at SJRC. I'm talking about the science and loving every minute.

The judges seem impressed. They ask challenging follow-up questions, but I think they're satisfied with my responses.

I return to my seat after they're finished. Another student has left already, so it wouldn't look strange if I did.

I massage my hand.

Selfish. Ungrateful. Rotten attitude. Your little science thingy. Guess you're not going to the store.

I sit back and listen to the other contestants' presentations.

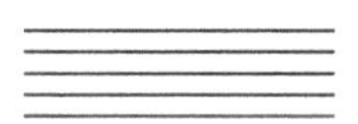

I'm about to go back inside the high school when Matt calls asking if I'm okay.

"Yes, of course."

"Where are you? Adil and I have been searching for you."

"Why? I'm at the school."

"We thought you were done hours ago. Why didn't you answer your phone?"

I check. Sure enough, I had missed numerous calls and messages from friends and family.

"I put it on silent for the presentations. I took a nap, and I'm about to go for the awards presentation."

"You have got to be kidding me." There's a pause. "Hold on a second."

"Is everything okay?" Adil asks me

"I'm fine; everything is fine," I reply, exasperated.
"Why aren't you at the engagement party?"

"We would be if we weren't out here looking for you," he answers with an edge. "Where are you? We're coming to get you."

"I'm at the high school. I have a car. You don't need to get me."

"We're coming anyway."

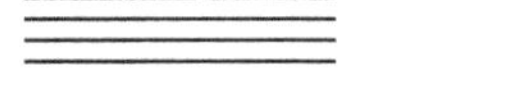

I enter the auditorium with the other presenters.

Most participants will be given either a first or second award. The top twenty-five projects get ranked and go to states. The top five projects receive prizes and scholarships, and the top two an automatic bye to the national competition.

Before they begin, Will sits next to me. "What are you doing here, Nayah?"

I take in his outfit — a crisp white dress shirt, black dress pants, and a sharp tie.

Will is a ridiculously handsome guy.

What is my problem? Pull it together. "I'm about to beat you."

"Aren't you supposed to be at the engagement party? I felt bad for missing it. "

"After all that grief you gave me when I handed you the invitation?"

"That was having a little fun at your expense. But seriously, you shouldn't be here."

"I'm exactly where I should be. My time."

Will stares at me for a moment, and I don't have the strength to hold his gaze.

176

"Please don't do this, Nayah."

"I need this. I win and get things done. That's who I am. "

"No, Nayah. This right now, is not you. It's like you're searching for a place and fighting to be heard. You have it. We hear you."

How many times can this boy rip off my armor? He said that with such force, like he can make me believe it because he said so. I take a deep breath, close to losing it and not understanding why.

They announce the general awards, and we'll get those certificates afterward. Just before they proceed to the top twenty-five standings, there's a slight commotion at the end of our row. Matt and Adil make their way down and sit on my other side.

"What are you doing?" Adil whispers sharply.

"Waiting for the awards ceremony to continue."

"Priya is beside herself."

"Because her dance is ruined?"

"No," he snaps. "She's scared something happened to you. What is wrong with you?"

Adil is rarely angry with me. Ordinarily, that would give me pause.

"We can talk about this later," I tell him. "They're about to announce the top winners."

Adil turns a different color as Matt's arm shoots out like he needs to restrain him.

As they get closer and closer to number one, my excitement mounts. I'm sure I'll place, but Will hasn't been called either, and I'm sure he'll place too. He's sprawled calmly in his chair, chin resting in hand.

"Fifth place is awarded to…"

I squirm. Neither of us has been called yet. I glance at Will again.

He raises an eyebrow at me.

I turn away, flustered. What is with me today?

"Third place…"

It's neither Will nor me. My foot bounces up and down. There's no way Will can beat me, is there?

"This year's runner-up is Will Cox."

I breathe a sigh of relief as Will disentangles himself from the seat and heads to the stage.

That was way too close.

Will shakes hands with the presenters and gives them a broad smile as he accepts his award. It's like his confidence and intelligence are spilling around him.

My cheeks are warm, and my nerves are off the chart. What is going on with me?

"First place goes to Anayah Kapur. Congratulations."

I join Will and the third-place winner on stage, all smiles as I accept the ribbon and certificate. This isn't the euphoria I was anticipating. The discovery in the lab made me far more excited.

I stare at the audience as they clap and have a sudden urge to laugh hysterically. I feel like I'm eating a pie I stole.

Maybe nationals will bring the high I'm expecting.

The judges conclude the awards presentation, and we're dismissed.

It's 5:45, and the engagement party should be in full swing.

I find Adil and Matt in the lobby. "I did it!"

Matt's face is blank. "Good."

"Congratulations," Adil says. "Let's go."

"Why aren't you happier?"

"If you had delivered this news after coming to the party like you were supposed to, I would be. But instead, everyone is upset because you're not where you should be. So no, I'm not happy, Anayah."

I cross my arms. "I thought, at least, you'd be in my corner, Adil."

He looks disgusted as he slams open the exit doors.

I won, so why do I have this deep need to be comforted? Like everything is wrong?

I feel someone close behind me and turn.

Will rests his hand on the small of my back. "Let's go," he says gently.

I fight an insane urge to get that solace from him.

Adil is hurrying down the sidewalk. "I'm not covering for you."

"I don't expect you to," I reply. "I have every intention of telling the truth, and I already told you I have a car here. I can drive myself."

"Leave the car," Adil commanded. "We'll get it in the morning. I'm not letting you out of my sight."

I frown. "Why does everyone think I'm not capable of doing anything?"

"No one thinks that, Anayah. You're capable of doing anything you set your mind to. But I don't trust you, so you need to get in the car and keep your mouth shut."

I feel like I've been slapped. I slide into the car.

Will is in the back seat with me. I guess Adil offered him a ride to the party. I sneak a peek at him. He gives me a sad half-smile.

I flush and look out my window.

Nobody says a word the whole way to the engagement party.

26

Copernicus

We enter the banquet hall, and Gen rushes over.

"Where have you been?" She gives me a huge hug. "Was there an accident? Are you okay?"

It's dawning on me how bad this is going to be. A realization that's coming far too late. I'm glad Will is standing behind me, like a strong post. "I'm fine."

"I thought you were coming right after your presentation."

"I was, but I didn't."

The briefest of frowns flits across her face. "You should find your family. They're pretty upset, and Matt didn't go into detail."

"My parents will probably want me to apologize to Priya for ruining her dance."

"Our dance, Anayah," Gen reminds me with a raised eyebrow. "We all worked hard to pull it off. And it went okay, just not as spectacular as it could have been since we had to do some last-minute shuffling." She pauses. "Did you do this on purpose?"

"Yes."

Her jaw drops. "Why? What is wrong with you?"

Everything. "Nothing. I got my award. Priya got her party, and my absence didn't stop anything."

"How could you-"

"I earned this," I snap and feel a hand on my back. I try to rein myself in.

"When the real Anayah comes back, we'll talk." Gen turns on her heel and stalks off into the banquet room.

Mother rushes over, and Will's presence diminishes behind me.

No, come back.

"We were worried." Mother hugs me. "Afraid you had been in an accident or had gone to the hospital. Your father has been glued to the phone. What happened? Adil wouldn't tell us anything. Did the presentations run long?"

"No. I stayed. I won first prize."

We're quiet for a few beats, engaged in a silent war.

"You stayed at the competition after we agreed you were to present and then come here immediately after?" Mother's voice is super low and dangerous.

"You said it, but I didn't agree with it."

Her eyes blaze. "This is not finished, Anayah," she hisses. "Get out of my sight."

She rushes to my father and has a brief conference with him and Priya.

Father gives me a look that could pierce organs while Priya's expression is completely blank.

I turn to run out of the room but collide with Balraj instead.

"Way to continue the drama," he says. "Wonder what'll happen at the wedding."

I mutter about needing the bathroom and rush out of the room. But I don't know where to go. I don't know this place. I don't know me.

"Nayah."

I've never been so relieved to hear that voice. I turn, and half fall into Will. "Mother hates me."

"Your mom does not hate you." He wraps his arms around me. "People don't hate each other for making mistakes."

"They do if the mistake is big enough." My hand is still throbbing in pain. "I hurt Priya to get what I wanted."

"No one is perfect, Nayah."

"Mother thinks Priya is."

"Your mom is probably stressed out. I'm sure she didn't mean to hurt you."

My chest is getting that hiccupy motion.

"Let it out," Will says gently. "No one else is back here."

The dam breaks. I'm a sobbing, hiccuping, snotting disaster all over Will's nice dress shirt. I can't remember the last time I cried this hard and never in front of someone.

"Talk to your mom. You'll make things right. You're supportive in your way and amazing when you are."

That was good of him to say. I sniff and drag my sleeve across my nose.

"That is really gross."

"Be a man and live with it."

"I'm grabbing food. Are you gonna be all right?"

"Eventually, but it'll be painful getting there."

Will and Kyra keep me company as I spend a good portion of the evening at a table in the corner of the room, trying to avoid my sister. It's not difficult; she's engaged in many duties as a bride-to-be.

182

Until Father walks over, unsmiling and eyes hard. "Anayah, do your duty and visit with the family and guests."

I rise from the table to circulate.

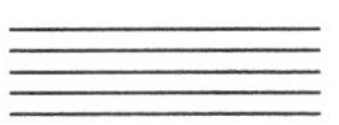

Dad sits at the desk in his office, his face unreadable. I'm sitting in the chair opposite the desk.

Mother paces Dad's office. "Anayah, I'm so livid, I don't have words. How could you do this to your sister?"

"The competition is important to me."

"Your sister's marriage is important to the whole family," Mother retorts. "We knew the presentation was important; that's why we agreed to let you meet later. Your standing would have been the same whether you left or not." She stops pacing. "Why did you stay?"

I glance at the family picture on the wall behind Father that we had taken when I was little. I'm in the center, and it's like my family had formed a tent over me.

"I will stand here until you give me an answer."

"I wanted my moment. Recognition for something I worked hard on."

Mother slowly shakes her head as she stands behind Father. "You'll place at nationals, which means much more recognition than you got today. What's the real reason?"

I'm silent as I break eye contact.

Mother starts pacing again.

"You're grounded," Father says quietly. "No car, no outings for the rest of the school year. Clearly, we can't trust you. You will give your sister and mother the reason for your absence."

"But, I just-"

"Enough!" He pounds his fist on his desk as his eyes grow cold. "That's not the complete story. You will give your sister, her fiancée, and his family apologies and gifts. I considered banning you from working at the lab for a time, but because of the importance of the research, I won't." He walks around the desk and stops before me, eyes boring into mine. "But I'm insisting your name be withheld from the lab paper."

"What?" I explode.

He jabs a finger at me. "Steal something precious from your sister, and I'll take something precious from you. You can join the ranks of bunches of other students who don't get the credit they deserve for their work."

My jaw drops.

He turns his back, returning to his desk. "Go to your room. Do some research on how to act with sense and compassion."

I run out of the office and to my room, slamming my door.

Everything has spiraled out of control.

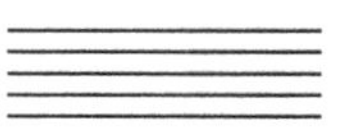

I'm sitting among the clothes strewn across my bed, staring absently at the shoes, papers, and books on the floor. Rub my throbbing hand.

There's a sharp knock on my door.

"Yeah."

Priya enters and slams the door. "Do you hate me that much? What have I done to you?"

"You wouldn't understand."

"I deserve an explanation, and I'm getting one from you."

I bite my lip. "I don't hate you, but I wanted you to look bad. Feel hurt."

The color drains from Priya's face, and her eyes grow glassy.

Yes, I am that awful. "All the time I hear, 'Priya this', and 'do this like Priya' and 'that was good, but Priya did it better' and 'can't you be more like Priya'. Perfect Priya. I'm always, always second. Less. Not good enough." I pick a shirt off my bed and throw it on the floor.

Priya's eyes narrow. "Do you know how much I have to hear about my amazing little sister?"

"What?"

"Let me tell you what I hear about Amazing Anayah." Priya puts her hands on her hips. "Your sister is so smart - she's going to be important one day, do something amazing. Your sister is so talented; she plays the flute better than anyone. Your little sister is quite the beauty. Someone said tonight it was a good thing I'm getting married because you'll steal all my prospects."

I blow hair out of my face.

"Yeah, that's a true story." She crosses her arms. "All I wanted was for tonight to be a fun, special night for my friends and family — especially my brothers and baby sister. One last celebration where we could remember how much fun it was to grow up together before my life changes forever and I leave everyone."

I stare at the bed.

"Or at least fun for me. I guess it wasn't for you. I only want my beautiful, intelligent, fearless baby sister to get as much out of life as she can. Because you have the circumstances to kill it, Anayah." Her voice wavers. "Is that so wrong?"

I feel like Copernicus. Like I just realized the universe doesn't revolve around the earth.

"No," I whisper. "Of course not."

Priya takes a step back. "I can't believe you hate me so much to plan this." Her voice is high and strained. "It's like I don't know you."

I get off the bed, but she thrusts her palm towards me, so I stop short. "Priya, I don't hate you. I'm sorry."

She looks like stone. Emotionless.

"Please." Ignoring her hand, I hug her.

She feels like stone.

"I didn't plan this." My voice wavers, the rhythm of my words increasing. "I only got the crazy idea this morning after an argument with Mother…"

Priya pushes me away. "I have to go."

She walks out of my room, shutting the door behind her.

Amazing Anayah has made a massive mess. When I finally feel closer to Priya, she's the furthest she's ever been.

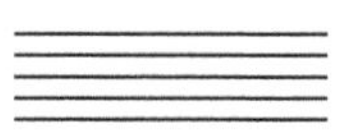

I'm in the tree house. It was difficult to drag my telescope up here with my hand throbbing, but I managed it. There's too much light pollution to see many stars, but I can comfort myself with a few sightings. My problems seem smaller compared to the universe.

A figure walks through the yard.

"Seth?"

He holds up an object. "I'll come up."

"Be careful. The rungs might be a little icy."

This winter hasn't been too snowy, so the tree house is unusually clear. I didn't have to clean up much to get in. A large expanse of white after a fresh snowfall is calming. If the sun is out and the sky is blue everything glitters and sparkles.

Seth hops on the platform and hands me a phone. "It was on a table at the party. It's freezing out here. Can't you do this inside? We could eavesdrop. My mom's talking to yours about you."

"Cold suits me. It's numbing."

We sit for a while, silent.

Priya's face flashes in my mind. The hurt. The coldness. "I stole a special moment from Priya. From everyone. How do I give that back?"

Can I? Is this so big Priya can't forgive me? Will my parents trust me again?

Priya will definitely be Mother's favorite, which I could swallow since I had Father. But I alienated him too.

"You can figure out a how," Seth says. "The question is will you put on the big girl pants and do it." Seth gives me a quick side hug. "Take care of yourself." He climbs down the ladder.

Find the big girl pants and do something amazing.

27

Brooke's Challenge

Gen and Matt leave history, barely speaking to me.

"Heading to the lab today?" asks Will, stopping by my desk.

I sigh. "Yeah."

"That's the first time you don't sound excited about being there."

I shrug. "I'm not feeling it today."

"Maybe you need a break, Nayah."

"I need to be there. This is bigger than SJRC, and there's a lot of work to do."

I need to maintain my presence if they're trying to edge me out. I stand and maneuver my bookbag over my shoulder. My hand is killing me. "You warned me. That I'd do this."

"Do what?"

"Choose research over my family and friends."

Will exhales. "You'll make it right. It's not like I told you in a way that was easy to take."

"You were kind at the competition and the engagement party."

"Friends look out for each other, Nayah. It's what you usually do."

I kind of wish he was doing more than looking out for a friend, no matter how nice that was. "I've lost me."

"You're just working out a few things. Getting ready to launch Nayah 5.0."

"Watch out world."

"Better believe it."

Our eyes lock.

"Thanks for looking out for me, Will."

"Always Nayah."

Will's words soothed me, but my research resolve wanes. I haven't felt well all day.

"No Gen or Will?" asks Adil as I slide into the car.

I shake my head.

"You want to get dropped at the lab?"

"No, please go home. I need a nap."

"You never take naps."

I shrug. "I want one today."

After sleeping for two hours, I didn't feel much better.

Father's office door is open. He's home early today. After asking him to take me to the lab, Dad gives me a quick visual once over, like he's conducting a body scan. He must not have liked what he saw, because he then asks to see my hand. "Anayah, I'm insisting on taking you to the hospital."

A few hours later, I come home with a cast on my hand. One more complication. This will make my chair challenge interesting.

"What happened to you?" Adil asks when we walk through the door.

"I chipped my thumb."

"How?"

"I punched my wall."

Adil's jaw drops, and then he laughs.

Dad stares at me like I'm somebody else. "Why did you punch your wall?"

I study the floor.

"Anayah, what is going on with you?" Dad asks. "Your behavior lately has been… I don't have a word to describe it."

"I got angry Saturday morning."

"At what?" Dad prods.

"Priya a little. Mother especially." I finally look at Dad. "Mother was driving me insane. She would not get off my back that morning, and I had it."

Dad regards me for a moment. "Why don't you lie down? You must be tired after the hospital."

"I am. Good night."

I feel their eyes on me as I exit the kitchen.

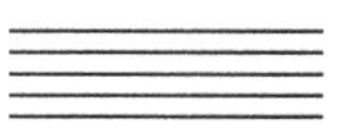

"What is that?" Brooke asks the next morning, pointing to my hand.

"A cast." I race after Brooke as she charges into the band office. "Why are you so upset? I'm the one who's injured."

"Look!" Brooke points at me.

Ms. Cortez looks startled. "I'm sorry about your hand, Anayah. I'll allow you to reschedule the challenge as long as it's okay with Brooke."

"I can still play. My hand just gets a little sore."

"No way," says Brooke. "We're rescheduling."

She's more worked up over this challenge than I am. I want first chair, but it's suddenly less important.

I'm tired of everything

"How long does the cast stay on?" Ms. Cortez asks.

"Four weeks."

"So let's say six weeks from today is the new date for the chair challenge. Is that good for you two?"

I nod.

Ms. Cortez pencils it in. "It's on the calendar. I gotta run and get something from the main office."

She walks out of the room.

Brooke whirls on me. "You better bring it in six weeks, because when I kick your tail, I'm not hearing any complaints."

Brooke marches out of the room, leaving me open-mouthed.

I've awakened the beast.

28

Butterflies

I massage my fingers after practicing my flute. They're free, even with the cast, but it's ten times harder to do the intricate runs for my music lessons. The walls of my room are closing in on me, and I need to get out of here.

Most of my friends have driver's permits except Will, who has his license. I feel awkward asking Will to drive me around, but no one is home, and I don't want to ask my family for favors anyway.

After he agrees to get me, I head to the kitchen for water, gazing at the sunlight pouring through the windows. Mother has a tiny prism hanging in the kitchen window. When it catches the light, it reflects a rainbow. I love how one object can completely change the way ordinary light appears.

"Sup Nayah?" Will says as I slide into the back seat of the car.

"Thanks for doing this."

"No problem." He backs out. "Kyra needed a ride to work anyway."

Kyra gives him a look. "When I asked, you said you were busy. Anayah calls and you're on her doorstep in twenty."

"Do you go to the science museum alone often?" Will asks me.

"I do it occasionally if no one is around."

He glances in his rear-view mirror when we come to a stoplight. "Do you want company? That's usually a group kind of place, and it feels wrong to just leave you there."

I chuckle. "Afraid something will happen to me?"

"That's not a joke, and if something is seriously wrong, you shouldn't go through that by yourself."

"I'll be fine, Will," I assure him more gently. "I need time to think, and the museum helps me do that."

He pulls into the parking lot ten minutes later.

Kyra hops out and gives me a long hug. "Call us anytime."

I hug her back hard and look past her to Will. "Actually, I changed my mind. Would you come?"

"Sure. I gotta drop Kyra off first."

"I'll wait for you in the lobby. I can get you in free on our family pass."

Kyra hops back in the car, grinning wide. "Have fun."

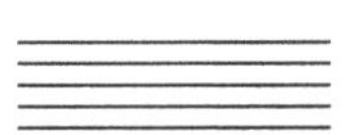

I enter the building and check out the planetarium show times. One will start shortly. Hopefully, Will gets back in time. I use the restroom and take a seat on a bench.

What was I thinking?

I've been a mess since the engagement party. My win was supposed to be my independence day, and so far, it's been a bizarre form of emotional torture. Destroying relationships. Being vulnerable and crying in front of people. Not wanting to be at the lab. Telling Will to join me at the science center.

What am I doing?

I sigh just as he appears in front of me.

"Regretting your decision?"

I toss my hair. "No. You?"

"Not yet. So what do you do here?"

"A planetarium show starts in five minutes. We can watch that."

We grab seats and get settled.

"Do you know the dialog to all these shows?" Will asks.

"How often do you think I come here?"

"You got a family pass, and you said you come here to help you think." He smirks. "I figure you need help with that regularly."

"Did you miss the fact I'm here for emotional solace, and you're supposed to be supportive?"

Will chuckles. "Sorry. It's hard to turn off. It's like automatic when I'm with you."

"Uh-huh."

As the lights dim, I slouch. Let the darkness engulf me as the night sky appears on the dome above. The universe that doesn't shout to be heard, but it's there for anyone who wants to see it.

So unlike me.

When did I start hurting others to get what I want? I don't like being this way. I feel so ugly.

The lights come back on. The show was short.

"You okay, Nayah?"

I shrug. "Let's go to the butterfly atrium."

"You like to watch butterflies?"

"Why do you find that so astounding?"

"Don't tell no one I sat and watched some butterflies with you."

"Not manly enough for you?"

"I'm man enough for anything."

I roll my eyes. "Let's go."

I can't explain it, but butterflies make me believe somehow everything will be okay. Compared to the rest of the center, this room is more open and sunny, kind of like a spherical greenhouse. I plop on a bench, and Will sits next to me.

If I was so out of line with Priya, maybe I'm way off base with Brooke too. I've never seen her like this. At first, I was pleased I was a threat in her eyes, but now I seem to be threatening more than a chair in band. Have I unwittingly taken something else from her?

She said her dad was finally there. I cringe. Okay, so if she wanted to show off for her dad, who never takes an interest and did for once that night, I totally destroyed that. And for no good reason.

Withdrawing the chair challenge is an option, but I never back down — that's part of who I am.

I start massaging my fingers. Brooke usually edges me out, and now I'm injured.

Why am I doing this?

"Is your car in the shop?" asks Will.

I shake my head, coming out of my thoughts. "The car is fine. I'm grounded and lost my driving privileges."

"You're allowed to be here?"

I didn't think about that. I groan and sag on the bench.

"Are you that new to grounding?" Will asks.

"Why don't you teach me the ways?"

"So no car. Grounded. Anything else?"

"I have to apologize to a bunch of people, and Father says I can't get named on the lab report."

Will winces. "They're really ticked."

"In my family, getting married is one of the most important events and decisions we'll make." I swallow. "I've treated it like it's nothing."

"I don't think you regard it as nothing. You were pretty mad when your sister's fiancée broke the engagement."

I shake my head. "I have to do something incredible. A sure-fire success. It'd have to be perfect to make up for this fiasco."

Will frowns. "Incredible. Perfection. Success. Why are you so hung up on winning all the time?"

"Winning is important."

"Not always. Effort counts too. So does the journey."

"You have an idealistic view of the world. People respect success. They pay attention to you if you win. Results matter."

"For a bunch of strangers, yeah. But the people who care about you don't need all that and think you're great. You don't have to spend every moment of the day proving it."

"Are you gonna yolo at me now? You think I'm uptight?"

"What will you do to me if I say yes?"

"If I told you, that would ruin the surprise."

He chuckles. "Just take a breath. And being awesome isn't the same as being first, best, or whatever other ideas of greatness you have. Let people see you."

A butterfly lands on Will's shoulder.

I smile. "It likes you."

"If you tell anyone about this, I will tell them you snotted all over my good shirt."

"Traitor. Fine. My lips are sealed." I pause. "Thanks for doing this. It helped a lot."

"Anytime, Nayah. This butterfly place will be our secret."

I stare at the butterfly still sitting on Will's shoulder. One day I hope I'll be as pretty as it is.

29

Tough Questions

"**I** want to throw Sangeet for Priya and David." I'm standing in front of Father's desk in his office Saturday afternoon.

He puts down the paper he's reading, takes off his glasses, and regards me for a moment. "That's a wonderful idea. What made you think of it?"

"I think Priya was headed in that direction with her dance routine. Given the drama I created for the engagement party, Sangeet might help bring the families together."

"Excellent thought. What help do you need?"

"Help?"

"It can get expensive. You'll probably need, at the very least, financial assistance."

"This might have to be an original Anayah Kapur brand Sangeet."

Dad laughs. "Wouldn't have it any other way. I'm sure Priya would feel the same."

I grimace. "I don't know about that."

"She'll come around, Anayah. But you hurt her immensely, and it'll take time for her to get over that."

I nod. "I have money in savings, but more to cover food would be helpful."

"DJ? Venue? Flowers and decorations?" A smile is playing on his face.

I fidget. "Yes, your financial assistance will be required and is greatly appreciated."

"Very good, and wait until you have everything planned before telling your mother. That'll cut down on the stress."

"Yes Dad, good idea." I pause. "Are you upset Priya's wedding isn't more traditional Indian?"

Dad regards me for a moment. "I don't have an answer for that, Anayah. Priya was born in the UK, lived for a short while in Canada, and then spent the rest of her childhood into adulthood in the United States, not India. And as for my upbringing, the village of my childhood differed greatly from the cities of my teens and the countries of my adult life. Besides some very blanket generalities, tradition was different in each place I lived, and it's not like your mother and I spent tons of time instilling even that in you. We were so busy with our careers." He shakes his head. "Priya's wedding needs to reflect who she is and who she will join her life with. I think we all lost sight of that for a while."

I bite my lip. "Are you upset she's not marrying someone who's Indian?"

Dad's eyes almost shot off his head. "No, but I'd be naïve not to acknowledge blending backgrounds and cultures will most likely present a few challenges." He pauses. "You're asking tough questions. What brought this on?"

"I don't know."

His face softens. "Remember what I said, daughter. You are the sun, the moon, and the stars. I don't care what nation he comes from, but he better get that right."

I grin. "Okay, Dad."

"On a much lighter note, I received a very interesting phone call from Mr. Cox, essentially requesting your babysitting services for his sixteen-year-old son at Nationals."

Dad chuckles as I burst out laughing.

"How much trouble will he get in at a national science competition?" he asks.

"Will is gifted. He could find plenty if he wanted, but I think his dad is going overboard on this one."

"I gathered that, but I told him it was fine. We'll pick Will up and take him to the bus depot, and you can keep an eye on him. If that's okay with you? I don't want to cause you any actual trouble."

"It's fine. Will and I are friends. We'd spend time together there anyway."

"Good." He smirks. "Is he why all the questions earlier?"

I grow inexplicably hot. "No. I was just curious."

"It's okay to be attracted to someone, Anayah."

I back up, stumbling into the chair behind me. "I have to talk to Priya and make sure they have the date I want free, or my idea will be dead in the water."

Dad gives me a wry smile. "Have fun with that."

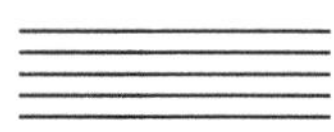

I knock on Priya's door.

"Come in," she yells.

I open the door, and her face turns frosty. "What do you need, Anayah?" She continues putting clothes away in her dresser drawers.

She only speaks to me when it's absolutely necessary, and then it's usually terse. No more hugs. No more trying to dress me or hang out with me. No more confiding. I took that all for granted until it was gone.

"Do you and David have the Saturday evening a month before your wedding free?"

"I'm not sure. I'll have to speak with him. Why?"

"I want to throw Sangeet for you that day."

"Really?"

I nod. "I know it's usually done much closer to the wedding, but my life is… we'll have to do a Kapur twist. It won't do any good if you can't be there."

Priya smiles a little. "I'll talk to David tonight. He'll need to consult his family too, right?"

"Yes, of course. I haven't told Mom yet. Dad said he'll make sure she doesn't plan anything for that day."

Priya snickers. "Smart idea. She'll try and take over."

"We could use your dance routine too, if you're willing to do it again."

The parade of emotions on Priya's face is priceless. "Of course. Thank you."

"It's the least I can do for acting so badly about the engagement party. I'll let you finish with your clothes."

I heave a sigh of relief after leaving her room. My big girl pants are on. Now I just have to make sure I don't trip on them.

30

Superwoman

My family is having dinner with the Baniks on Sunday. Priya was having dinner with David and his family, so she's not with us tonight.

"What news did you want to share?" Father asks about midway through dinner.

"There's an experimental therapy in California the doctor thought Nina may do well with," Mr. Banik replies. "Since this has been a rough year for her, we decided we should go for it."

"That's good," Father says. "When do you leave, and how long will you be gone?"

"We'll need to go in about two weeks, and we'll be gone for a month."

Seth stills. "Are we all going?"

"Of course, son," Mr. Banik says, clapping Seth's back. "All hands on deck."

Seth nods and shoves food around his plate.

"What about school?" Nina asks.

Is this the first time Nina and Seth are hearing about these plans?

"We're concentrating on getting you strong," answers her mom. "We'll worry about your schoolwork after we do that, and we can make special arrangements for Seth to study remotely."

Nina frowns as she resumes eating.

"The special jazz concert is in three weeks," I blurt out. I never blurt things out. Unless I'm angry. Or frustrated. Upset.

Seth gives me a warning look.

"He won't be able to see it," his dad says.

Did Seth never tell them he's in jazz band? Does this family tell each other anything?

"Why does Seth have to go?" asks Nina.

"So as a family, we can support you," Mrs. Banik replies.

Nina twists her face. "I'm tired of being a burden."

Seth's face falls as Mr. Banik throws him a dirty look.

"You're not. Nina, this might make you feel better," Seth says. "I want to help."

"Which is why I'm saying something because you never will. I love having Seth around, but I'll feel awful if he leaves school and band just to sit with me for a month."

"It's not a big deal," Seth says.

"Yes, it is." Nina's voice rises. "Don't act like I don't know everything you had to do for me this year to make things work. And I'm grateful for it, but this doesn't make sense. Seth should get to stay here."

I love this girl. It's like a thirty-year-old inhabits her little ten-year-old body.

Father appears uncomfortable. "It sounds like there's much to discuss."

"We go as a family," says Mr. Banik. "End of discussion."

Seth and Nina exchange pained glances, but Mrs. Banik looks at Nina thoughtfully.

"I'll clear the table." Mother grabs Adil's plate with his fork still in midair. "Anayah, why don't you help me?"

He hands me his fork as I walk by him.

I put the dishes in the sink.

"Anayah, why did you mention band?" Mother asks. "You know that's a sore point with them."

"It popped out."

"Since when does that happen? Words never pop out of you."

"I'm a bundle of surprises this year."

"Go back in there and fix it."

"Fix it?! I shouldn't have blurted that out, but this discussion was a long time coming. And what was Mr. Banik thinking, not telling his kids about this plan before announcing it to us?"

Mother sighs. "He's so burned out that he's not thinking clearly anymore."

Father walks into the kitchen and chuckles. "Are you two going to stay in here and keep gossiping?"

Mother crosses her arms. "What are you going to do about things out there, Kareem?"

"Absolutely nothing," he answers, amused. "It's none of our business, and they need to have this discussion. Nina is right; Seth will beat himself into the ground for her and never say anything about it. Let them work it out."

The adults remain in the dining room with coffee and dessert, so I join the boys in the living room after Nina heads to bed. The TV is on but Seth looks like he's staring into space.

"You never told them about being in jazz band, did you?" I ask quietly after sitting next to Seth on the sofa. Adil is on his other side.

"Nope."

"I hope that doesn't blow up in your face one day."

"It probably will."

"Did you guys reach any decisions?" I ask.

Seth pauses the show they're streaming. "No. The issue is tabled for tonight anyway."

"What do you want?"

"I want Nina to be well." Seth swallows and rubs his hands over his face. When he drops them, he's back to his usual collected self. "Dad is mad at me. He feels Nina said what she did because I have a bad attitude."

"You've been nothing but supportive, without complaining."

"I have complained."

"There's a difference between complaining and honestly telling people that you're worn out and need a break."

"I guess."

"What about your mom?"

"I think she gets it and is inclined to let me stay home, unless they need me for practical physical assistance. We're doing this for Nina; it does little good if she feels guilty."

"I'm sorry we had to overhear all of that," Adil says. "That must have made things even more awkward."

Seth shakes his head. "If anything, it made things less tense, and Nina probably felt better about speaking up. She thinks Anayah is a superwoman."

"If she only knew," Adil says.

I toss a pillow at him.

31

The Impossible

Dr. Reed has been unusually solemn during lab on Monday.

"What's wrong?" I finally ask him.

"Your employment is being blocked. This has never been a problem because Human Resources usually hires anyone I want, but technically, they need the director's approval."

"The director said no?" I ask incredulously.

"His argument is you're doing community outreach and don't need to be an employee of the University."

"If I never did SJRC, and you employed me as a lab tech, there would be no issue. This is unbelievable. The director has never even met me."

"I know."

"Some community outreach."

A small smile creeps onto Dr. Reed's face.

"Is it always like this?"

He sobers. "No, but you're taking the path less traveled, and that can cause people to show some different

206

sides." Dr. Reed rubs his face and then throws a pen on the counter, making a clanging noise. "I'm sorry, Anayah. We should be celebrating and nurturing your achievement, and instead, we're arrogantly showing you the door."

"Who's this we? You're fine. It's the director I want to kick in the pants. Are all directors like this?"

"No. The last one was very easy to work with, and to be fair, we don't know very much about the current one or what's going on. It's probably not just him, but we should collect more intel because he may be the one that we have to deal with."

I nod.

"You're going to have to come up with a way to show you're indispensable to this project," Dr. Reed continues. "Or, at least, demonstrate it's in their best interests to keep you rather than push you away."

I gawk at him. "How? What idea will do that?"

"I can't help you with that, Anayah. That will undermine your position in the end."

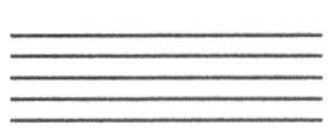

Prove I'm indispensable.

I bite my lip, staring at the papers strewn across the kitchen table.

Dr. Reed said they're finalizing the new budget, which will be released shortly. Once it's out, this battle will be harder than it already is. My time is disappearing, if it's not already too late.

The University switched into a new conference, and while most people think about that in terms of sports, it also has implications for research and academics. Fundraising needs to kick up to another level, and they've embarked on ambitious building plans to overhaul a few programs.

My research could bring funding.

I sit back. It's hard to fight them when I don't understand why they're fighting me. Why do I need to be out in order for this to happen? Do they believe I won't realize the project's full potential?

I have a mentor. It's not like I'm doing this on my own, and I made the discovery. I'm the one who combined the boost with the anti-inflammatory, not Dr. Reed. If I could do that, I could figure out what it takes to see this forward.

Does my being in charge impact the amount of funding that they can get?

Possibly.

Dr. Reed is a big name, but again, he's involved.

Is this really about not respecting me? That they can just take this?

Nothing is concrete. I feel like I did when Katie told me about not having solutions and answers to patients' problems. Working with emotions.

"Why are you calling me?" Balraj asks a few minutes later.

"Can't I want to talk to my older brother?" I smirk.

"Sure, if you actually talked to people."

"I talk to people."

"You're pretty much the worst person for chit-chat."

"Okay, Mr. Charming, The next time you're plowing through our fridge, take a breath, and demonstrate how one does this chit-chat you speak of."

He chuckles. "What's up?"

"What makes money?"

"That's a vague question."

"Come on, business major. Isn't that what you're studying?"

"Supposedly." He's quiet for a moment. "Sell products or your services, or invest, for an equally vague answer."

I have no skills to sell. At least nothing that would make the University money. I'm doing research. Trying to find cures. Pain relief.

Ding, ding, ding. The pinball machine goes off in my brain.

Sell something.

Time to do the impossible.

I need to make a drug.

32

Shifting Universe

I follow Ms. Cortez into the band office Friday after school. Brooke is there already, and Ms. Cortez tells me to take a seat as she shuts the door.

"I have the results of the chair challenge. Brooke, you will remain first chair."

"Congratulations, Brooke," I say in a tight voice.

"Thank you," she replies in an equally thin tone.

"Brooke will also be section leader for the flutes next year," Ms. Cortez announces. "It's unprecedented for a junior to take this position, but she has consistently displayed leadership qualities and is the most qualified on a technical level."

Of course.

Ms. Cortez hops up. "Now I have a jazz band that's waiting for me to begin rehearsal."

She leaves the office.

Brooke stretches out her hand towards me. "Truce?"

I stare at it. A part of me wants to.

I stand. "I gotta go."

"Seriously, Anayah?" Brooke exclaims.

"You got first chair. You got jazz band. You got section leader next year. You got Ms. Cortez's ear. What more do you need?"

Brooke gapes at me. "It's not like I can do things around here by myself."

"I get that. The whole links thing. I'll certainly do my part. It's not like I'll sabotage you or the band or anything."

Brooke exhales. "You don't get it."

"Yeah, I know. That seems to be the story of my life this year. Good but not enough." I leave the office.

I need to bury myself in my lab.

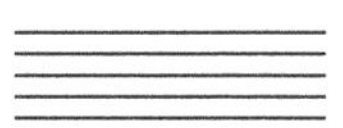

My stomach rumbles as I study the numbers on the screen.

Same results as before. That's the fourth trial I've personally done. At least I can feel like I'm in control right now. Numbers. Procedures. Data. That's what I'm good at.

I check the clock. It's almost seven, which is later than I expected. The lab is in the center of the building with no windows to the outside, only bright white fluorescent light. Easy to lose track of time.

"It's unusual for you to be here on a Friday, Anayah," Dr. Reed says as he enters the lab. "And nobody is usually around on a Friday evening."

"I know. It's good for thought. Clarity."

Dr. Reed seems to study me for a moment. "How's it going?"

"Good. I'm still able to duplicate the results. I'll spend the next couple of days writing up this trial."

"I've started contacting a couple of colleagues. We'll see if they can produce the same results in their lab. I'll get the ball rolling, but once they start, you'll do more of the correspondence."

My heart picks up. I suddenly feel inadequate. Again.

"Congratulations," Dr. Reed says. "You are an official employee of the University."

I squeal. "How?"

"Your colleagues may have something to do with that. You seem to have grown on them. They argued you have become an important part of the lab team, and your employment will encourage your continued presence and aid to their research. That's the good news…"

I close my eyes. What now?

"On a frustrating note, the department has rolled out an official agenda and, more importantly, a budget to include this project."

Time's out.

I barely understand the ramifications of this decision. "Am I not allowed to participate?"

"Participation, yes. They even threw you a bone and said you could use the experiments as the basis for your future SJRC projects, which would almost guarantee you a win."

"What would I give up?"

"The amount of control and credit you'll be given when all is said and done."

Those are high stakes and a huge sacrifice. A few months ago, I was set on winning SJRC. But now, I want to explore, learn, and help, and I feel the University's actions sully that. "If this continues along the path that's outlined, who has control and credit?"

"The University." He pauses. "And me."

I regard him carefully. "You have an intriguing conflict of interests here, don't you?"

"I do."

"You don't want credit? Or control?"

"I love credit and control, but I'm not taking more than I should. I don't need to — I have my own ideas and am good at what I do."

He sounds like me. Or at least the way I used to be before getting thrown.

"However, I'm an employee of the University with a lab team. Serious pushback from me will have consequences and repercussions that could affect not only me and my career, but other people's work."

"It's that big a deal?"

"Your research is that big a deal. You need to seriously consider that there may come a day when what's in your best interests may not be mine. That could color my opinions and guidance."

I don't want to think about that. "What grounds were given for taking the project? Or did they bother?"

"Their position is the primary reason for this project was SJRC. They argue that since your competition will soon be over, you'll no longer have a vested interest."

"That's not true. I started working here before the contest. Our initial agreement was to work in the lab. You agreed to be my mentor afterward."

"I know, but things can be twisted to appear you did the research for the competition, and that's it."

I cannot believe that SJRC, the thing I've worked so hard for, may derail what's real. But would I have this without SJRC pushing me?

I slam my hands on the counter. What is this game we're playing? "What happens if I fight them on this?"

"At best, status quo."

"I like the status quo."

"It's what I prefer as well. At worse, they could edge you out completely and make it so you can't even continue this line of research elsewhere."

My eyes widen. "They could do that? They would do that?"

Dr. Reed shrugs. "It's unusual, but things can get nasty, especially when prestige and money are involved."

This is way worse than I thought. I could make my situation worse by fighting them. For something I shouldn't have to fight over.

I set my jaw. "How much time do I have?"

Dr. Reed furrows his brow. "We usually run loose on time frames, but the tentative plan is for funds to be made available to me in June. Make your argument well before then, because once I have the money-"

"You'll be expected to use it as they direct."

It sounds like a lot of time, but it really isn't.

Dr. Reed taps his pen on the metal counter. "Remember what I told you. Make them need you and don't tell me anything. At heart, I'm on your side, but you'll do better if you view me as the enemy."

The guy who was almost in lieu of my father when I made the discovery has become my rival. A reluctant one, but a rival nonetheless.

How am I going to combat that?

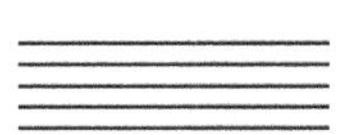

I sit on the swing at the lake, rocking gently. It's evening and not super warm since it's early March and dark outside. The smart thing would be to call for a ride, but I'm not ready to go home yet.

Make a drug. Much easier said than done; this will probably be impossible for me. I don't know the first thing about pharmacology. I'm going to be up to my ears in research, and I'll have to be careful about who I ask for help. For this to work, I need to do it without anyone affiliated with the University.

Can I really do this?

Dr. Reed, renowned researcher. Someone the University sees as worthy. Capable.

Who am I?

Why can't I answer that question without some medal hanging from my neck? I close my eyes. Swept to the side with no discussion. With no voice.

Everything I feared.

"What's up, Nayah?" Will asks.

I jump. I didn't even hear him. "Are you running again?"

He drops onto the swing next to me, and it rocks sharply under his weight.

"Yeah. I'm doing a cool down lap. Dad had another meeting," he explains. "I get it's the campus, but this is not the safest spot at night."

The patio lighting gives off a soft illumination, and the nearby path has lights, but this section isn't well lit. I was so distraught over Dr. Reed's news it hadn't occurred to me.

"I need a moment to think."

"Is something wrong?"

"I'll figure it out."

He frowns. "What's wrong?"

"Will…"

He sighs and stands. "Would you let me at least walk you to a place with more people and light?"

"No, thanks. I'll stay here."

Will looks exasperated. "Nayah…"

"Can you just stay here with me?"

"Yeah." He drops back on the swing, and we sit quietly for a bit.

"I hear I'm your babysitter for Nationals," I say just to break the silence.

"Dad wouldn't budge off me going to the competition. The whole competition."

"I can't believe it's the same week as the jazz workshop. You'll miss the whole thing, won't you?"

Will grimaces. "Yeah, pretty much. I'll get back in time for the concert, which will be an incredible experience. But I was really looking forward to working with the band during the week beforehand. I could have learned a lot."

"I'm so sorry, Will."

"Maybe we'll get another great artist next year."

We swing silently again.

"They're trying to take my work away from me," I say softly.

He stops the swing. "Who?"

"The University is trying to boot me off my research. Or, at least, they want to call the shots and get the credit."

"How?"

I shrug. "Some nonsense about how once I finish SJRC, my interest in my project will be done, and they can take it from there, since the research was done on their grounds."

"That's unbelievable."

"Right? You said someone could come and snatch it all away. Stupidly, I thought you were talking about yourself."

Will winces. "I didn't mean it so literally and so soon. You're fighting them on this, right?"

"Yeah."

"That sounds weak."

"I'm fighting them, but I'm not sure how. Or the how I came up with is next to impossible."

"I guess you're gonna have to do the impossible." Will leans forward. "What makes it so hard?"

"They're handing the project over to Dr. Reed."

"Who's Dr. Reed?"

"My mentor and an excellent scientist."

"What's your plan?"

"What makes you think I have one?"

"You're Nayah. You always have a plan. What's your plan?"

"Dr. Reed said to make them need me. Prove I'm indispensable." I bite my lip. "My goal is to make a drug."

"Nice. That should do it."

"I can't waltz into the kitchen and whip one up."

"It's your plan, so somewhere in there, you must think it can happen. What's involved in making a drug?"

"I barely know."

"Where can you find out? Who can you get that kind of info and help from?"

"I'm not sure. My usual go-tos are my competition and enemies."

"What about your dad? Can he help?"

"Possibly. But I can't be too dependent on him. I'm supposed to prove I'm indispensable. Running to Daddy to do the work will not help."

Will places his hands behind his head. "How long do you have?"

"Junish." The stars are unusually bright tonight. Like the cold, clear air immobilized the light. "Good but not good enough," I whisper.

"What?"

"They said I can still participate in the research and use it for future SJRC projects. I'll be named in papers and get great recommendations for schools. It's not a bad deal."

"Don't let them take what's yours, like you're nothing." His tractor-beam eyes bore into mine, backlit in the dark.

"Mine." I set my jaw. "And I fight for what's mine."

Will slaps his leg. "There she is. Anayah Kapur is back in the building."

I guess I don't need the actual drug, only the schematics. Just enough to sell myself to the University. Indispensable. They don't get my drug without me.

Nina pops into my mind. Hopefully, I can help make it a little more bearable for her.

"Finished planning the launch of Nayah 5.0?" Will asks.

"Not even close, but at least I'm sure there will be one." I pause. "You really think I can do this, don't you?"

"I do."

"It's ridiculous to believe a sixteen-year-old can develop a drug."

"It wouldn't be the first time we've been ridiculous together."

I chuckle.

"Nah, you'll be good." He gives me a warm smile. "You'll make it happen."

He just believes in Nayah.

I kiss his cheek.

What am I doing?

I feel his forehead on mine and exhale.

He's okay.

Everything fades. There's no University trying to take my research away, no SJRC, and no drug I have to find.

He kisses my forehead, and then his lips lightly brush mine. "Be you, and you'll be fine."

I open my eyes as he stands. "Are you ready?" His voice sounds rough. "I should find my dad, and I'm not leaving you here alone."

I nod, my voice gone. I take one more look at the stars.

The universe has shifted again.

33

Another Crisis

Felicia pokes her head into the room. "Anayah, you should go to the nurses' station."

The little girl in front of me has cystic fibrosis, and it's taking everything she has to breathe.

I put the puppet down and ask her if she still wants company.

"That puppet looks fun." Felicia takes my spot in the chair. "Tell me about her."

I walk to the station, and my stomach drops. Adil was supposed to sit with Nina this afternoon, but he's here.

"Is Nina okay?" I ask him.

"She was just moved from emergency, so I guess she's doing better." He heaves a ragged sigh. "I've never seen anything like that before."

"Are her parents on the way?"

"Yeah, and Seth too."

Mrs. Banik races down the hall. "Where is she?"

We follow Adil to her room. Nina is hooked up to a bunch of machines and she's sleeping. Her skin is pale and yellowish, her face pinched.

Mrs. Banik speaks with a nurse to get an update. After they leave, she asks where Seth is.

My brother and I exchange glances. Seth didn't tell them about the arrangements?

"Seth is at jazz band practice," Adil replies. "I was sitting with Nina this afternoon."

"I didn't know Seth was in jazz band," Mrs. Banik says.

Mr. Banik races into the room.

"She's stable," Mrs. Banik says quickly. "Adil saw trouble right when it started and could get here quickly."

I give him a proud pat.

"Thank you," Mr. Banik says to Adil. "But why isn't Seth here?"

"He'll be here any minute," Adil answers.

"From where?" Mr. Banik asks tightly.

"He was at jazz band," Mrs. Banik responds quietly.

Seth runs in. "How is she?"

Mr. Banik zeros in on him, eyes blazing. "We didn't have you quit soccer so you could join jazz band. We were very clear on this. You need to be at home with your sister."

"Nina was never left at home alone. There was always-"

"Don't you care at all about your sister?"

Seth recoils. "Of course, I do."

"Then how could you leave her like this? She could have died, Seth! All because you had to be at jazz band."

"Daddy, don't yell at Seth." A tear trickles down Nina's cheek.

We need to leave. Now. "We should talk about this outside, so we don't disturb Nina."

They freeze.

"You're absolutely right." Mrs. Banik leaves the room, dragging her husband briskly out.

"Be right back," I mouth to Nina and shut the door behind me.

Mr. Banik faces Seth like he's about to lay into him again.

"Mr. Banik, you and your wife can get information at the nurses' station about when the doctors are making their rounds."

They head over, and I direct my attention to Adil. "You need to take Seth home or back to our house."

"I can't leave," Seth whispers sharply. "My dad already feels like I don't care about Nina."

"Your Dad is frustrated, and he's taking it out on you," I say. "Nina does not need to hear you guys arguing. Adil can bring you back later, if necessary, and when things cool down."

After the boys decide to go to my house and leave, I scoot into Nina's room and shut the door. Her chest is rising and falling, and her cheeks are wet.

I sit at the edge of her bed and hold her hand. "They're just worried. They didn't mean anything."

"It's all my fault."

"No, Nina, none of this is your fault. Your family loves you very much and wants you to get better. Are you in tremendous pain?"

"It hurts a little, but nothing like it was before."

"I'll tell them. Can you try to fall back asleep?"

Nina nods and shuts her eyes for a moment before she opens them back up. "Can you stay with me until I do?"

I squeeze her hand. "Sure."

The Baniks decided to stay at the hospital, so Dad and I went to their house to get them a change of clothes and things for Nina. It's nearly ten at night when we get home. Faint sounds of a trumpet float through the air as we walk up to the house.

Priya and Mother are at the kitchen table, and Priya's eyes are red.

"What's wrong?" Father asks.

Mother sighs. "Seth has been playing for the last two hours."

"I'm sure he'll stop if you ask him to." I drop my bookbag by the counter and lean against it.

"It's not that," Mother replies. "The music he's playing is mournful. Anayah, you need to talk to him."

I close my eyes. I don't have anything to give. I open my eyes and realize everyone else looks just as tired.

Seth stops when I come down the rec room stairs.

"How's Nina?" he asks.

"She's resting comfortably."

"That's something at least. What brought this one on?"

"An infection that came on quick and hard, probably because she's been so sick this year."

Seth nods and swallows.

"Do you want to talk?" I ask.

Seth shakes his head.

"It sounds like you've been talking plenty through your trumpet."

Seth winces. "What time is it?"

"Ten."

"I'm sorry. I must be keeping everyone awake."

"Don't worry about that, but they are concerned about you."

Seth shrugs. "I'll be fine. It's Nina we need to worry about."

"You're important too, Seth."

He fingers the keys on his trumpet. "There are times when I look at Nina, terrified that we'll lose her and simultaneously angry with her for being sick and changing our lives. How messed up am I?"

I swallow. "Seth, I don't know what to do. I don't have any answers for you."

He pulls in a ragged breath and offers me a weak smile. "You stopped my dad from killing me in the hospital. You really are Superwoman."

I chuckle.

"You're here." He opens his trumpet case. "That's enough."

34

All the Voices

A week later, Nina is still in the hospital, so I stop by her room before checking in at the nurse's station.

Seth is there.

"Are you gonna keep me company?" Nina asks.

I hug her. "I have to work, but I'll definitely pop in."

"Okay. I had to leave Will in the playroom."

Will is here? I give Seth a questioning look.

"We went to the big playroom to hang out," Seth explains. "But while we were there, one of the nurses grabbed Nina for a couple of tests, and Will decided to wait there while I went with them."

Will is still here then. My heart rate picks up.

"I gotta go." Seth hugs Nina. "I should make sure the playroom is still standing."

"Can I come?" Nina asks.

"You need to rest." Seth smooths her hair down. "You're tired."

Nina pouts but doesn't argue, which means she's exhausted.

Seth and I start off. Since the swing happening, I feel conscious around Will, and we haven't had a real conversation beyond a short hello greeting. I hope all we need is a typical Will and Nayah exchange, and then I'll feel normal around him again.

As we approach the playroom, it sounds louder than usual. We round the corner and enter the room, where about seven kids are crowded into a corner, with Felicia standing near a window.

"Where's Will?" I ask.

Seth shrugs, and then a kid steps away.

I smile. Will is sitting on the floor with a group of children surrounding him. Whatever make-believe game they have going, they're enraptured in it.

Felicia walks over. "Can you get him to volunteer? He's great with those kids."

"He found some people he can relate to," I remark dryly.

A woman joins us. "I love the staff here. My little girl is usually very shy, and she took right to him." The woman points to Will and a little girl, who must have been her daughter, and then walks to the magazine table.

"We should extricate him before this fallacy gets perpetuated," I say.

"English, Anayah," says Seth.

Unfortunately, Amara is back in and stands as we approach the group. "Will can do all the voices superbly, Anayah. If he's willing, he can show you how."

I know she's a sick little girl, but it takes everything I have not to scowl at her.

"I'd be happy to show Nayah a few things," Will says to Amara. "There's a lot she can learn from me."

I scowl at him instead. "How about we find people your own age to play with, Will?"

"Speaking of, we need to get to rehearsal," says Seth.

The face falls on the little girl the woman had pointed to, and her lower lip trembles, as if sensing he's about to leave. Will stands, and the kids give a collective groan and start complaining.

"Sorry guys, carry on without me," Will says. "You got this."

He points to the little girl clutching his jeans and asks us where her mom is. After I point towards the magazines, Will guides the girl back and says a few words to her mother, who is all smiles.

How does he do that?

Will joins us again.

"Seriously, if you can volunteer here a couple of hours a week, the kids would love it," Felicia says to Will.

He glances at me. "I'll think about it."

"I'm sure Anayah wouldn't have any problems with it." Felicia gives me a pointed look.

I glance at Will.

His gaze is more intense than I expected. We were normal for a little, and then he looks at me like that.

I swallow. "No, none."

I really hope he'll do it.

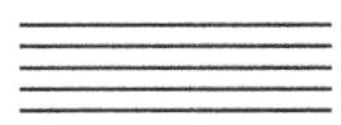

"Are you going to volunteer at the hospital?" I ask Will during lunch the next day.

"How would you feel if I did?"

"Does it matter?"

He shrugs. "The hospital is sort of your turf. I don't wanna trespass on anything you got going."

"It's a public facility. I don't own the place. Felicia is right — you'd be a good addition to the staff, and the kids love you. I'm surprised you're considering it."

"Why?" He sounds guarded.

"It's not like you get paid. Are you using this experience for college applications?"

"I guess I could; I hadn't thought about that. I figured I could find a couple of hours a week to play with sick children if it makes their day better, especially since I have my license and access to a car."

He's really just doing this to be nice? "Oh."

"Why do you volunteer?"

When Seth asked, I had no issues telling him my reasons. Will asks, and I'm ashamed that the welfare of those I'm helping didn't factor into my decision greatly. "I figured experience in a hospital would be good since my work might tie into it in the future."

"That's a very well thought out and developed reason."

Too bad it's only one of them and not the top one. I'm surprised by my relief that he thinks my reasons are good enough. Not that I don't care what Will thinks, but it shouldn't matter this much to me.

"You're okay with me volunteering there?" he asks.

"Why do you keep asking that?"

"Because you keep not answering it."

"Sure," I reply in a small voice. "I could even ask if you could be put on the same shift as me. If you wanted."

Will turns on the tractor beam. "Can the hospital take the two of us there together?"

I squirm. "Seth mentioned making sure the playroom was still standing yesterday, but I think they'll be up to the challenge."

"All right then. You have a new volunteer."

≡≡≡≡

A week later, Will rides with Adil and me for his first day of volunteering. Even though Will can drive, I offered a ride with us, and Dad and I could take him home. I'm surprised at how excited I am to have a buddy there.

"Do you only play with the kids?" Will asks me.

"No, I do other things. They didn't trust me with the children right away. You sound nervous."

"Yeah. This is new, and it's for a hospital. It's serious."

"It is, and it isn't," I say. "You were a camp counselor at a stay-away camp. Believe me — you'll be fine."

"You've had way more experience than Anayah," Adil adds.

"She knows about science and medicine."

"I had to learn about people, and that's more important."

Will turns. "You know people."

I shrug. "I had to go to the hospital and sell my volunteering services; they asked you. I'm a little jealous."

Since Felicia was the one who recommended he do this, Will put down our floors as his volunteer preferences. I'm glad they gave them to him. Katie has me give him the hospital tour to free her up. After the tour, he has orientation work, so I return to my volunteer duties.

Felicia and I leave the nurse's station to do a transport trip that requires two sets of hands.

"You're in an exceptionally good mood today," she remarks.

"Really?"

"You're smiling more and seem relaxed. Your cheeks are a little pink too. Is this going to happen every time Will volunteers?"

I stumble a little. "What does Will have to do with anything?"

"I wouldn't blame you. No wonder you requested he work on Wednesdays."

"I'm not looking at Will."

Felicia chuckles.

"I'm not," I insist. "We're just good friends, and it's nice to work with a good friend."

Felicia laughs hard.

Thankfully, by now, we're at the little girl's room and focus on her and the task at hand.

Focusing proved to be a problem for the rest of my shift. I kept wondering how Will's afternoon was going. I haven't seen him since we did the tour.

This kind of distraction is why I was so set about no boys. I firmly put him out of my head and get to work on the inventory sheets.

My shift ends a little early, and Dad is running late, so I try to work on my drug research. Katie got permission for me to use one of the tiny lab rooms in the hospital. I haven't made extensive use of the facilities yet, and it's taking time to get acclimated to my surroundings. This room is empty at present, but the hospital is much busier than BSRI, so I have to work harder to focus.

I also don't have a lab team to keep me company. I'm realizing how much I appreciate their energy because working on this alone is rather lonely. Not having Dr. Reed is downright nerve-wracking.

I read the emails I received. I still need colleagues, of sorts, and got a few bites from professors at other universities and colleges willing to lend a hand. But it's a hard go; I'm not their student or in their lab, and I'm only sixteen. The only reason they're talking to me is because I've worked with Dr. Reed, and the research I've done is substantial enough for them to sit up and take notice.

I exhale and close my eyes. "Just be me, and I'll be fine," I whisper.

I pull a pharm textbook out of my bag along with a chemistry one. I'm deep in thought when Will comes in.

"How did you know I was here?"

He pulls up a stool and takes a seat. "Katie told me when I finished."

"How was your first day?"

"Good. A lot of paperwork." He gestures toward my notebook. "What are you working on?"

"Chicken scrawl and notes for the drug. I have to work on it here, so I try to grab every opportunity I can."

"Why here?"

"I'm trying to create as many levels of protection as possible, though this might not be enough." Technically, I'm still using the fruits from my experiment but this is better than doing things on campus or at home.

Will points to another folder. "What's in there?"

"Those are papers Dr. Reed gave me about the University's plans, agenda, and budget."

"Can I see it?"

I give Will the folder and go back to work as he pages through the documents. I'm in the zone. Anchored.

He lets out a low whistle. "They're doing a serious program overhaul."

"Yes, and I guess my research can bring funding."

"It might also encourage people to give more."

"Isn't that the same thing?"

"Same end, different channels. There are different ways to spin your research and story to encourage alumni and others to give to the University."

"I never thought of that." I should have — it's not like both of my parents are not connected to academia. For some reason, I only thought of grants when I considered funding.

He holds up a sheet of paper. "What's this list of names?"

"People I want to meet with, decision makers."

"Money givers?"

I give him a look. "People who decide what projects to pursue."

"Yeah, the money givers. I don't mean to sound cynical, but you need a couple of people who hold some purse strings on that list to grab anyone's attention. And you should get at least one that's a woman."

Will makes some good points. "Where can I get that kind of list?"

He chuckles. "Maybe start with the names on the buildings. Do you want help?"

"With the research?" I ask hesitantly. I don't want to underestimate him, but at the same time, this is heady stuff.

"I gave you grief before about doubting my abilities, but let's not get ridiculous. I can't make a drug. You can."

I smile at him.

"I mean finding donors or people who might give you a hearing ear."

"That would be wonderful." That's more than being a cheerleader.

35

Prisms

It's strangely quiet in the house Saturday afternoon. I set a small box in front of Mother while she's reading a book on the porch. "I'm sorry I worried everyone and ruined Priya's engagement party."

She picks up the box. "Thank you. I still don't understand why you did it. It's completely unlike you. You were always the rational child."

"Even more than Adil?"

"Adil is levelheaded, but he'll sometimes cave to his emotions when making decisions, and that's not always wise."

"Yes, I'm so emotionless."

Mother raises an eyebrow. "I didn't say that, and clearly you had some pent-up emotion regarding Priya and this wedding. What's going on?"

I shrug. "I really did want to be at the competition."

"I know, and if that's all this was, I'd let it drop. You got grounded. It's finished." Mother studies me. "But what you did was very personal. Your aim was to hurt Priya, and you succeeded. Why?"

Their words that morning play through my mind. I rub my chest; my heart is back in that vise again. "I was tired of everything."

"Of what?"

"I feel like I'm living in Priya's shadow. Like I'm being compared to her and never measure up, or her activities are more important or exciting." I take a deep breath, but my throat is tight like my chest. "The day of the engagement party, you would not get off my back. Every time I turned around, you were yelling at me for something."

My own voice is raised.

Mother's eyes are wide, but she doesn't interrupt.

"It's like I exist to serve Priya, and I'm tired of it." My voice cracks. "I'm important too."

Mother sets her book on the end table next to her. "Anayah, I had no idea you felt that way." She takes her glasses off and regards me. "I apologize if anything I or anyone else has done contributed to it." She pauses. "I ask you to help Priya not to minimize your importance, but because you have a good effect on her."

My jaw drops. "What?"

"Have you ever noticed how all over the place Priya is?"

No… but at the same time, yes. I guess I've always focused on the confusion and annoyance that brought me instead of the state causing it. My eyes catch a rainbow on the porch wall, and I glance at the prism in the kitchen window.

"You're seeing it now, aren't you?"

I nod.

"You have a stabilizing effect on her, and she has come to depend on it. When her engagement was broken, she didn't come to me or her friends." Mom gives me a smile.

"She talked to you, because she knew you would somehow ground her, and you did."

I swallow and stare at the floor.

"All of you have a very important place in this family and different gifts. The four of you make up this beautiful kaleidoscope of hope, intelligence, talent, and ambition. I find it hard to believe that your father and I begot you all." She pauses. "As for Priya's things seeming more important… I love to write, and so does Priya, and I guess it creates a special bond." She grabs my hands. "But that in no way means I believe your accomplishments in music are less important. I've been a little jealous that you and your father share a similar interest in science, medicine, and research."

My eyes widen.

"When you two get going, I have no idea what's going on. The night you made that discovery in the lab, I understood it was important, and I was so proud. But I couldn't share the excitement the same way he could, and I really wanted to."

"I'm sorry, Mom."

She waves a hand. "It was beautiful to watch." She tightens the grip on my hands and gives them a shake. "I'm so happy you and your father can connect on that level. And Anayah-"

"Yes?"

"The next time you feel some kind of way, don't bottle it up. Talk to us." Mom opens her arms. "Come here."

I bend over, and she gathers me in a huge hug and kisses me on the head. "I love you very, very much."

I hug her back. "Love you too, Mom."

36
One Awkward to Another

I'm with Nina, and we're sitting on her bed working on my research. Nina is proudly typing the next phases as I dictate. Even though we're pretending the University hasn't done anything, I'm supposed to plan and document everything up to the hilt. On the positive side, I have real money to work with, so I can design a more elaborate experiment.

A door shuts, and Mr. Banik calls out.

He's home early.

I shoot Seth a text, and he tells me jazz band practice ran late, and Will is driving him home now. He comes up with the brilliant idea of us hiding in Nina's room, and he'll sneak in the back.

I roll my eyes.

There's a knock, and Mr. Banik pokes his head in.

Nina grins. "Hi, Daddy."

He kisses her cheek. "How do you feel?"

"Good. I'm helping Anayah with her research."

"That sounds important. I'll let you two ladies get back to work."

My phone goes off.

Seth: I'm here. Where is he?

Anayah: Just left Nina's room

The door pops back open.

"Where's Seth?" Mr. Banik asks.

I plaster on a smile. "He's here somewhere."

"I'll find him and ask what he wants for dinner." He shuts the door.

"Let's go downstairs," Nina suggests. "I don't want Daddy more mad at him than he already is. "

As I follow her downstairs, I see Will stepping onto the porch through a window. On a whim, I open the door as he's about to press the doorbell.

"What are you doing here?" I step outside and shut the front door quietly behind me. "Mr. Banik doesn't know Seth hasn't been here."

"Seth left his trumpet in my car."

I grab it from his outstretched arm and turn to go back inside, but the door is locked.

Will lets out a low chuckle. "Should I text Seth, or would you like to ring the doorbell?"

"This is not funny," I snap.

Will pulls out his phone as the door flies open.

"I thought I heard voices," Mr. Banik says. "Anayah, weren't you just inside the house? Hello, Will."

"Hi, Mr. Banik."

Seth appears behind him, and his eyes get large. "They're staying for dinner. Last minute thing."

Will and I exchange glances.

"Come in." Mr. Banik grins at me. "Or back in. We should order pizza instead, Seth. It'll be easier."

The three of us stand in the hall while Mr. Banik disappears into the kitchen.

"How did you forget your trumpet?" I shove it at Seth.

"I was panicking. Can you guys actually stay for dinner? I couldn't come up with anything better."

Will nods. "It was a good cover."

An hour and two slices of pizza later, I'm planning my exit.

Mrs. Banik asks Nina about her afternoon.

I still and glance at Seth, whose eyes have gotten wide again.

"Why wasn't Seth able to?" Mr. Banik asks curtly.

Nina bites her lip.

Mr. Banik glares at Seth. "Where were you this afternoon?"

"Jazz band practice."

Mr. Banik throws his napkin down on the table and looks toward me. "And you were covering for him?"

"Yes."

"What was your role in this whole charade, Will?" Mr. Banik asks.

"I dropped Seth off at home, sir. Came back to return his trumpet, which he accidentally left in my car."

"Sahar, it's okay-" Mrs. Banik starts.

"No, it's not. Seth has repeatedly shirked his responsibility during a time when we need him most. Stay with Nina. We aren't asking him to work. He's not taking her to doctor's appointments-"

"I like having different people sit with me," Nina says.

"How many people have been here?" Mr. Banik looks Will and me over. "I take it you two have been here often?"

We nod.

"And Adil, since he was at the hospital?" Mr. Banik further questions.

"Adil, Priya, Gen, Kyra," Seth answers. "Matt was here once or twice with Will-"

"That was fun." Nina lights up. "We played video games and ate ice cream for dinner."

"Nina!" Will exclaims.

I smack my hand on my forehead, but I notice Mrs. Banik looks amused.

"Were you ever here?" Mr. Banik asks Seth, his voice dripping with sarcasm.

"With all due respect, sir, he's been here a lot," Will says. "It's why we said we'd pitch in. It's taking a toll on him."

"Because he's doing too much." Mr. Banik points at Seth. "You have to quit jazz band."

Seth looks crushed.

"No, Daddy-" Nina cries.

"Tomorrow," Mr. Banik goes on. "With us leaving in a couple of weeks, it won't matter anyway."

"We need to talk about that," Mrs. Banik says quietly.

"Yes, we need to finalize the arrangements."

"We need to talk about Seth going."

"Why wouldn't he go?"

"Because it's not good for Seth or Nina."

"Will and I can leave." I slide out of my seat.

Will jumps up from the table. "Thanks for dinner."

"Please stay." Nina grabs my arm.

"You might as well." Mr. Banik glares at Seth. "Anayah and Will have apparently been here as much as the family."

We slide back into our chairs.

"How is this not good for them?" Mr. Banik asks incredulously.

"Seth's grades have dropped, he quit soccer, and now you want him to quit jazz band," Mrs. Banik answers. "He's had bags under his eyes for months. Seth is a sixteen-year-old boy, and Nina is his sister, not his daughter."

Mr. Banik sets his mouth in a thin line.

"He asked his friends to help him, and we should ask for help too," Mrs. Banik continues. "It sounds like Nina loves having different company."

Nina nods vigorously.

"Thank you so much for supporting us," Mrs. Banik says to Will and me.

"I still think he should go." Mr. Banik crosses his arms. "We need to be there for Nina."

"Daddy, I'm fine."

"Be there for Nina or be there for you?" Mrs. Banik asks gently.

Mr. Banik looks surprised. "What do you mean? For Nina of course."

"And you want to be surrounded by your family even more than Nina does when things are difficult," Mrs. Banik says.

Seth goes pale. "I'll come then. It's fine. I didn't realize—"

"Wait." Mr. Banik rubs his face. "What is Seth going to do by himself for a month?"

Will clears his throat. "He could stay with us."

"I'm sure we can arrange a place for Seth to stay," Mrs. Banik says. "If not with the Coxes, the Kapurs would certainly take care of him."

I nod. Mom would love it.

"I suppose you think he should stay too, Anayah?" Mr. Banik asks.

"I do, and I think you should let him remain in jazz band.

Mr. Banik raises an eyebrow.

"Jazz is how Seth releases tension," I continue, emboldened. "Take that away from him, and you may have expensive therapy bills in the future."

The corners of Will's mouth are twitching upwards again, and there's the barest hint of a smile on Mr. Banik's face. "That's a little dramatic, don't you think?"

"If you heard how he played his trumpet at my house the last time Nina was in the hospital, you wouldn't think so."

Mr. Banik sighs and seems to study Seth. "Since it's six to one, I better re-examine my position."

Nina wrinkles her brow. "It's five to one."

"Your mom counts as two people."

"Dad, if you want me there, I'll come," Seth says.

"I know you would," Mr. Banik replies. "But your mom is right. And I don't thank you for the contributions you've made, and that's wrong. We'll figure out something."

"Anayah and Will, if you two want to escape, Nina might be persuaded to release you," Mrs. Banik tells us.

Nina pouts. "Can't you stay a little longer? We can watch a movie."

It's cute how she's always trying to get us to keep her company.

"Another time, Nina." Will gets up. "I have homework to do."

"How did you get here, Anayah?" Mrs. Banik asks.

"Adil dropped me. Will can take me home. Actually, can you swing me by the lab, so I can give Dr. Reed the list of people I need to meet with?" I ask Will.

"I got you. Let's go."

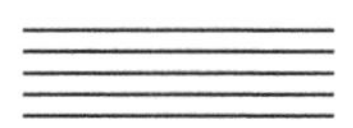

About ten minutes later, Will pulls out of the Banik's driveway.

"I don't have one of those fancy faculty staff parking tags, so we'll have to hike to your lab," he says.

I groan. I forgot about that. All of our vehicles are registered.

"You could do this on Friday when you go in," Will says.

"Then I'll lose the week, and time is important. Since you helped with some of the research, you could explain if he has questions."

"I go from one awkward to another."

"What's so strange about my lab?"

"I don't hang out at places like that."

"You'll be fine. You're doing SJRC, and it's not like we'll be talking science."

Will exhales. "How do you know he'll even be there still?"

"He's always there, but I won't rope you into another drama tonight. You can take me home."

"I want to help. It's fine." He merges onto a busy roadway.

"You really jumped into the fire back there," I say just to make conversation.

"I couldn't sit there and let Mr. Banik bag on Seth like that. It's not like you were real shy at the end either."

"Mr. Banik invited my opinion, and I freely gave it."

"I'm glad you said something, and I'm sure Seth loves you."

"Who does Seth like?"

"Super random, Nayah." Will's face goes blank. "Are you actually interested in him now?"

"Why would I like him and kiss you?"

He shrugs. "It's easy to get lost in the moment. And I kissed you."

"No. I did it first."

"Is everything a competition with you? You pecked my cheek, which could have been interpreted as only appreciation."

"Yours was more?"

Will shifts in his seat. "Like I said, it's easy to get lost in the moment."

"So it didn't matter to you?"

He scowls. "Of course, it mattered. I don't do that kind of stuff for entertainment, and based on your initial statement, I could conclude you only kiss guys you're interested in."

"That's a faulty line of reasoning. I was only pointing out the contradiction in liking one guy and then kissing another, but since I don't like the first guy, no conclusion could be drawn from my actions regarding the second."

Will shakes his head as he parks. "You have some serious problems."

After a five-minute walk to BSRI, I introduce Dr. Reed to Will, and Will shakes his hand.

"You interested in science?" Dr. Reed asks him.

"Not exactly," replies Will. "No offense, Dr. Reed. You guys do amazing work."

Dr. Reed seems amused. "Thanks. So what is your strong suit?"

"He's good at science." That popped out of my mouth.

They both look at me quizzically.

"Just because he doesn't like it doesn't mean he's not good at it," I clarify. "He placed second in regionals for SJRC and is going to Nationals."

Dr. Reed seems to consider Will with greater interest. "Congratulations. That sounds like a story for another time. I'm sure Anayah didn't bring you here for table talk."

I hand him my list. "I need to meet with these people."

He raises an eyebrow as he looks it over. "You're quite savvy. This is a good list. How did you come up with it?"

"A ton of detective work. Mom, Dad, and Will helped."

Dr. Reed glances at him again before directing his attention back towards the paper.

Mom gave me background on how giving can work. Dad was able to give me information on how companies and corporations can sometimes help with funding. It became clearer to me how important it is to follow the money trail. I listed a few decision makers, but more importantly, I included people who give money and have connections to others who give, as Will suggested. He came up with a couple of names on the list too. If they're unhappy, it'll make a lot of other people unhappy. I had to search high and low for women that might have a say. In the end, I only came up with two.

"These people have a tremendous amount of pull," Dr. Reed says. "If you can convince them, you'll have won your battle. Are you sure I should get this meeting together? Remember, you want me out of this as much as possible."

"They won't meet with me if I ask. You have a name and this research means something. If you ask, they'll probably grant your request. I don't want to fight before I actually start fighting."

"I'll see what I can do, Anayah. It was nice to meet you, Will. Something tells me it won't be the last time."

Dr. Reed's comment was innocuous enough, but my face heats as we leave the room.

"Is there anything else you need to do while we're here?" Will asks.

"Would you like to see my lab?" I ask, almost shyly.

"Sure. Dr. Reed is cool," Will remarks as we head down the hall. "You said he was a friend of your dad's?"

"Yeah, they studied together in London."

"I thought your parents were from India?"

"They invented this thing called the airplane—"

"Okay, stupid comment. It's just interesting how people end up where they are."

"True. My dad's family moved around. He lived in London for a short time as a teen and later did some studies at Oxford where he met Dr. Reed."

"How did your parents meet? College?"

I shake my head. "It was partially arranged through their parents."

Will's face has an odd expression. "People still do that?"

I snort. "It's not what you imagine. People know people and they talk and then introduce their kids to one another. Just another way of doing things."

"I wonder what Seth's parents was?"

"It wasn't arranged. Love match. Very much so, according to my mother. She wrote a poem based on their experience."

"You'd hardly know it from the looks of them. They're so…" he trails off.

I chuckle. "Cold? Mean?"

"No, but can you picture Seth losing his mind over a girl?"

"Not yet. But that doesn't mean he can't, and he'd probably display it differently if he did."

"So your parents' marriage isn't like love?"

"And you said I needed things spelled out. They love each other, it just wasn't boy-meets-girl stuff people talk about."

"How would you like to meet your future husband?"

"Seeing that my parents have no interest in husband hunting for me, I'll be on my own in that department."

"Is that what you actually want?"

I stop short, suddenly understanding what his question may be implying. "You mean because I can't possibly fall in love, would I prefer to be provided with a mate? Could you dehumanize me more?"

"I didn't mean that. It just seems like for something that important, you'd be determined to make the quote-unquote correct choice."

"Is there such a thing?"

"I don't know. What do you think?"

I shrug and pull on the door handle. "People aren't like numbers which is why I don't deal with that stuff yet. Here's my lab."

"Is there a particular spot where you usually work?"

"Yep." I walk to a counter and stop at the middle section.

"Very tidy and sanitized."

"It's a lab, Will. It has to be."

He grins. "In comparison, your station is overachieving."

"Whatever." I feel silly. In actuality, there isn't much to see. "You're probably itching to get home."

Will grows more serious. "I like that you wanted to show me something so important to you."

I flush with warmth. "It was just handing Dr. Reed a list, but it's critical. We can go." I pause. "Thank you. This was more fun than having Adil or my dad drop me."

"Sure, Nayah. I'm glad I could help."

There's something I'm dying to find out, but I don't know how to ask without sounding like it. Curiosity wins. "You still have a crush on Gen?" I ask during our walk back to his car.

"Why do you suddenly care about this? I thought you wanted to only deal with numbers?"

I shouldn't care, but I do. I shrug.

"I don't," he answers. "I never did."

"But you said—"

"You assumed, and I repeatedly told you I didn't."

"Who are you interested in?"

"It's not customary to ask people that."

"You're well aware how little I know about ordinary people customs, but you don't have to answer if you don't want. It's not my business."

He's quiet for a moment before starting the car. "I'm going to say no one."

"You sound unsure. You don't look and don't like to be looked at?"

"That wasn't your question. Of course, I do, and yes. But that doesn't mean I'm interested in being with anyone."

It's eerie how closely that mirrors my resolve. My own waning resolve.

"No one is shocked when you say you don't wanna be with no one," Will continues.

"That's because people see me as this cold-hearted, emotionless automaton—"

"That's not what I meant earlier."

"Others think so."

"It hurts when people imply that?" he asks quietly.

"Yes. I'm a very rational person, but I care about people."

"I know."

"Are you not interested in anyone because of Estelle? It's been almost a year."

Will exhales. "Yeah, but not in the way you mean." He pauses. "You're not actually interested in anyone, right? I assumed based on what you said before…"

"I just didn't like the idea of you thinking I'm incapable of falling in love. I choose not to right now because I can't be needlessly distracted with silly romances that won't last."

I swear the corners of Will's mouth twitch up for like a millisecond.

"Those are interesting caveats," he says.

"What?"

"Silly and won't last. So if it were a serious relation-ship that you felt could become permanent, you'd give it a shot?"

I fidget again. "What are the chances that's going to happen while I'm in high school? There are adults who can't make that happen."

"True, but there are people who are happily married to their high school sweetheart."

I shrug. "If they have the emotional maturity to handle all of that, then go for it. I sure don't."

"Less than a minute ago, you insisted that you could fall in love."

"I don't think that's necessarily the same thing as having a mature, adult-like relationship that could lead to marriage. But what do I know?"

"Probably more than you think."

"You're telling me you could handle that?"

"No, I can absolutely tell you I cannot."

I have a feeling there's a huge history there but I won't needle that out of him today. "Which is why I'm waiting until after I get my postdoc."

Will chuckles. "That degree will suddenly make you relationship and emotionally wise?"

I glare at him. "No. But then I should be in a good spot in my life where I can focus on a relationship."

"Got this all neatly planned out, don't you?" He glances at me, eyes twinkling, as he pulls into my driveway.

I tilt my chin up. "I do."

"I'd have fun watching someone mess up those plans."

"As the spectator or participant?" Why did I ask that? I dart a glance at Will.

He's staring straight out the windshield with an unread-able expression on his face.

I need to breathe, so I reach for the door handle.

"Nayah?" Will says urgently.

My heart thuds. "Yeah?"

"It should go without saying any information shared in this car stays in this car." He's still staring out the windshield.

I laugh but feel vaguely disappointed. "Obviously. See ya later."

"Good night, Nayah."

37

A Precious Gift

"Help, please?" Xiang is hanging precariously from a chair with the end of the last satin panel in her hand.

A trip to the emergency room is not how I want to start the evening.

I drop my tablet on a nearby table and rush over, pushing a small step ladder squarely beneath her. "It looks great. Why don't you call it a day?"

Xiang helped me plan and buy the decorations. We made it colorful and happy, borrowing heavily from Priya's rose and teal-themed bedroom. Father helped me rent space at a community center not too far away. It's not as nice as where Priya held her party, but it's large enough for everyone to be comfortable and small enough to feel hospitable. The room has a stage which will be perfect for the most important event of the night, at least to Priya.

Since Priya is always trying to get me 'gorgeous', I'm letting Gen and Xiang glam me up a little. I pull out the lehenga choli once we're in the bathroom to change.

"Oh Anayah, it's beautiful," breathes Gen.

"Priya has the same one in pink and gold." I bought a matching dupatta in pink and green for when we aren't dancing.

"Ready Xiang?" Gen asks. "Let's do this girl's hair and makeup."

Xiang pulls a straightener and blow dryer out of her bag with a flourish. "Ready!"

Forty-five minutes later, they're done, and I'm dressed.

Xiang stands behind me and puts her chin on my shoulder. "You look amazing."

Gen holds up a mirror. "Even you will like it."

To my relief, they were light on the makeup. My eyes pop, and my hair is full and shiny with soft waves cascading down my back — as Priya likes it.

"Thanks. This is perfect."

Xiang and Gen beam, and I leave them so they can get ready.

My father and I bought the food from an Indian restaurant and did buffet style to simplify things. Gen's mom offered to make a couple of desserts and salads and to ensure everything went smoothly in the food department. The food is set up in the back and smells delicious.

The jazz band had arrived and was setting up. With Ms. Cortez's permission, I begged them to perform tonight with the promise of good food and a small thank-you gift. Most were willing to come.

Seth and Joe are warming up on their trumpets, dressed in the traditional jazz band attire of white button-down shirt, black tie, and black slacks. Seth is staying with the Coxes while the rest of the Baniks are away.

"Who's in charge tonight?" I ask them.

"Me," Will replies.

I give him a look.

He laughs. "Joe will be calling the shots."

"I heard my name," a voice says behind me. Joe stops alongside me. "Anayah, you look gorgeous."

My face heats. I don't think a guy has ever been so forthright in saying that to me without sounding creepy. "Thank you. I wanted to talk to you about tonight's program."

"I'm all yours." He gives me a wide smile.

I shake my head. Seth seems amused but Will is scowling.

"You all right, Will?" I ask.

"Yeah." His face suddenly goes blank. "I'm gonna get a drink." He gets up from his chair with an unusual amount of energy and heads towards the refreshments.

"Why don't we go into the hallway, and you can tell me what you want done," Joe says.

I spend five minutes discussing the schedule for the evening and what songs I want played and when.

"I wasn't stepping on any toes earlier, was I?" Joe suddenly asks. "I asked Will before if he was into you."

I'm quiet for a moment. "What did he say?"

"He said you two were just good friends."

"That's true."

He chuckles. "You want me to talk some sense into him? He can't just wait around for a girl like you—"

I wave my arms. "Please, don't. I'm good, thank you, Joe."

"No problem. Let me know if you change your mind. About Will I meant." He winks and then walks off, chuckling.

I close my eyes for a moment, trying to collect myself again. Talk about complete derailment, and I need to be on my game tonight.

I re-enter the room and of course my eyes are immediately drawn to Will's and he's half-way across the room.

Thankfully, my family and David enter which helps me put my attention back where it belongs.

"Anayah, this is beautiful." Mom hugs me.

"Where's the food?" Balraj scans the room.

I point to the back of the room. "Talk to the Larsens. They'll set you up."

"Anayah, this is fabulous!" Priya holds me out at arm's length. "I knew you'd be stunning. Mom, doesn't she look great?"

"Yes. You've always had a good eye for those things, Priya."

It's funny how little that comment bothers me now.

"It's exactly what I wanted! The Kapur sisters - we'll be twins!" She turns and grabs David's hand and pulls him into the room, chatting excitedly.

Good, she seems happy so far.

I turn towards my parents. "I can take you to the family table."

There's a specially decorated table in the center of the room, in front of the stage, for our family and David's family to sit at. The other tables are in two semicircles surrounding it.

Before sitting down, Dad gives me a side hug. "I'm proud of you."

Balraj comes back with a plate of food. "Amazing Anayah does it again."

"I didn't personally cook the food, and is that a for real name you guys have for me?"

Adil grins. "Yep. Amazing Anayah pulled this off. You always do things well."

"Except for the engagement party fiasco." Balraj snickers. "But it's nice to know you aren't actually perfect all the time."

My mouth drops. "Perfect? Me? That's what I called Priya. Perfect Priya."

Balraj throws his head back, laughing. "Perfect Priya? Are you living in an alternate universe? Priya is so far from perfect it's not funny. I'm more perfect than Priya."

"Raj…" Dad smiles a little.

Balraj shoves a forkful of food into his mouth. "Priya can't find which end of the bag is up half the time." He points his fork at me. "If you'd been paying attention to this wedding, you'd know that."

"Balraj…" Dad rubs his face.

Am I that clueless?

"I have to go." I walk over to David's parents and show them around.

The guests arrive in full force, and I give the jazz band a cue to play. Operation Repair Priya Relationship underway. I step on the stage and welcome everyone. Then I introduce the families.

"As a special gift, Li Xiang has made jewelry for the special ladies."

Xiang offered to make jewelry for Priya and both moms. I bought the men cuff links. Matt presents David and Priya with a large caricature drawing of the two of them, which they loved.

"While everyone is finishing their appetizers, we'll provide you with entertainment," I announce. "I know everyone saw a dance performance at the engagement party, but that wasn't the full routine."

The dancers assemble themselves on the stage.

"The Kapur kids and their friends would like to perform the full dance for you." I gesture to Priya and David. "Priya and David, our guests of honor, could you join us here on stage?"

This is it, Priya. This is all I can give.

With David close behind, Priya bounds on the stage. The dance goes without a hitch. At the end, Priya grabs my brothers and me in a huge group hug and then makes

us take a bow with her. Then she grabs David and takes a
bow with him.

As the dancers clear off, I return to the mic. "Taylor
Vance and Brooke Campbell will do a cello and flute duet."

We called a truce and everything, but I was still
shocked when Taylor told me Brooke had agreed to do it.

After the applause dies down from Taylor and Brooke's
performance, the jazz band plays two selections. They'll be
the last performance of the evening.

The rest of the night will be for dinner, mingling, and
dancing.

Gen rushes up to me with a plate of food in her hand.
"You should eat with your family."

"Thanks!" I grab the plate from her. The chair between
Priya and Adil is open.

"Yaya!" Priya pats the chair. "I saved this seat for you."

I smile and slide into it. Food hasn't tasted this good in
weeks.

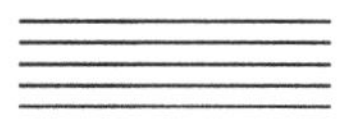

David's family leaves around ten. I walk them out the
door and then stay outside enjoying the cool air.

The night is going wonderfully. My family seems to like
me again. I never want to be on the outs like that.

Most importantly, maybe Priya has forgiven me. I'll
be the best little sister, the greatest maid of honor, and do
everything I can to make sure Priya's wedding is amazing,
and she's okay.

Will is sitting on a bench, some distance from the door.

I can't pass up an opportunity to harass him.

"Whatcha doing?" I ask as I plop on the bench beside
him. There's yelling and noise coming from his phone.

"Nothing."

254

I peer over his shoulder. "Don't look like nothing to me."

"It's hot in there."

"Yeah."

"And loud. Whhhaaaaaat?!" he exclaims at the phone.

I snicker. "Are you seriously watching a basketball game?"

"It's game five of the finals, Nayah."

I stare at him.

"I cheered you on, and I'm still here. I need a little sidebar. They're all in there, dancing. You don't need me for that."

"Guilty much?"

Will scowls.

I lean back, my tiredness hitting me like a ton of bricks.

He puts the game on silent. "Did things go the way you needed them tonight? Was everything a perfect success?"

"I think things went excellently, and Priya seems thrilled. But I get what you were saying — Priya would have been touched that I tried hard to make her happy, even if the evening went terribly wrong. She's good like that."

"You went out of your way to make her happy. That's good of you." He unmutes the game but turns down the volume.

I could fall asleep, but the bench is uncomfortable. I slide my head onto Will's shoulder. Improvement, but not by as much as I'd hoped.

"Warning?" he asks.

"What?" My eyes are shut.

"Your hair is all over my screen."

"You're such a whiner."

"What does all that hair feel like?"

"Like hair. What kind of question is that?"

"It probably doesn't feel like my hair."

"I can't say. I've never rubbed your head. Do you want to make a comparison?"

"Seriously?"

I finally open my eyes. "Yeah. I'll start."

I rub his head.

"Yo! Why are you so rough?" he exclaims.

"Why are you such a baby? Your hair is cool." I rub his head again. "You usually keep it close cut. If you grew it out, what would it look like?"

"Tight curls."

"Like Gen's hair?"

"No, smaller and tighter."

"Your turn."

He flicks the end of my hair.

"How are you gonna tell anything with that?" I ask. "My hand was all over your head."

"And it was weird."

"I'm giving you permission to make it as weird for me as I did for you."

A slow grin lights his features. "All right, Nayah. You'll have to sit up and turn around."

"Why?" Maybe I should have rephrased my invitation.

"You got to feel all my hair. I should get to feel all of yours."

I spin my body, so my back is facing him, and put my feet up on the bench in front of me.

"Your hair is super thick and long," Will comments. "Why do you cut it all the time?"

"Because I don't want to spend half my life maintaining it, and it gets in the way."

"Gen's hair is long."

"Has Gen told you her hair care schedule and procedure? It would rival a NASA launch."

"It's nice like this. It's a shame to ruin it."

"You sound like Priya."

Then his hands are in my hair, and I can't breathe, feeling every individual hair root as he slowly combs through to the end. Each nerve ending in my body is electrified, and I shudder.

I'm not sure weird is the word for this.

"You okay there, Nayah?" Will asks.

I gulp. "Yep. I'm fine. Nothing weird here. I don't know what you were talking about."

Will's fingers graze my neck as his hands go underneath my hair again. "Your hair is heavy, like a blanket. Isn't it tiring carrying all this around?"

"Uh-huh," I croak.

"You like this, don't you?" he asks, amusement in his voice.

"Girls put their hair up in the summer because it's literally hot under there. You have a sister. How do you not know more?"

"We don't talk about hair, and it's not like it's actually hers all the time." Will pulls his hands through my hair. "I'm good."

Nooooooo!! "Are you sure? You should do it one more time. I want to make sure you've done the full experimentation."

Will chuckles. "Is there something else I should do to broaden my hair-playing experience?"

I spin, fold my legs under me, and then flip my hair to cover my face. "You didn't do it from the front."

"How is that different from the back?"

"It'll be a completely different experience because of my face. You'll have to interact with my hair differently."

"You're a mess." His fingers comb back a huge swath of hair up and over the crown of my head.

I close my eyes. "You keep telling me that but it seems not to bother you."

"You're my mess."

Ordinarily, that kind of statement would rub me the wrong way, but Will said it with such affection that it brings a grin to my face. I open my eyes.

His tractor beam is going full force, holding me as his hand trails down the side of my face, over my cheek. My eyes drift shut as my lips touch his.

"Would you keep playing with my hair?" I ask shyly as he pulls away.

"Can I finish watching this game while I do it?"

I nod. "Can I lie on the bench? I'm tired."

He grabs his jazz band jacket and rests it against his leg. "This will be softer."

Two minutes later, Will is watching the game and playing with my hair, and I'm already drifting off.

I haven't felt this relaxed in ages. It's funny how Will can wind me up and then relax me better than anyone.

I'm glad I'm in the pretty lehenga.

A door bangs open.

Will and I jump.

I draw a ragged breath in, and Will wipes his hands on his thighs as some friends of David's family walk towards the parking lot.

I swallow. "I should get back inside."

"Good idea. I'll stay out here."

"Right." I leap from the bench and walk back inside without looking back.

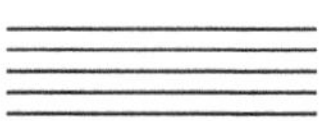

Later that night, I knock on Priya's door.

"Come in!" she sings.

I poke my head in.

"Come in, Yaya! Tonight was perfect. Sit with me."

After joining her on the bed, I put a small gift in her hand. "It's nothing, but I want you to have it. I'm so sorry."

"It's okay. We all had our moments with this wedding." She opens the box and pulls out a jade bracelet not unlike the necklace she gave me at the beginning of the year. "It's absolutely precious, Anayah."

I bite my lip. "I was so afraid…"

"You afraid?"

"Why does everyone say that? I do experience fear sometimes."

"Like when you were five, and there was a giant spider in your room?"

That's not funny — I don't even know where that thing came from. It's not like we live in the Amazon. "That was bad, but the night of the engagement party when you came into my room was much worse. I was afraid I had permanently damaged our relationship. I had never felt that kind of terror before."

Priya hugs me. "Let's not mention it again."

"Would you braid my hair?" I ask, after hugging her back hard. "For old times' sake."

"Of course, Yaya. Would you like pigtails?"

"How about we change it a little? Can you do one of those nice reverse fisherman type braids?"

Priya gives a hearty laugh.

38
Members of Great Merit

I follow Ms. Cortez into the band office Monday after school. She tells me to take a seat after shutting the door.

I am not happy to be here this time.

She studies me for a moment. "Anayah, I'd like to share a couple of things so you can direct your efforts and talent in a more fruitful manner. I have encouraged Brooke to work towards applying to Juilliard."

As good as I am, I'm not a contender for that school. Did I spend all this energy on getting first chair for nothing? I feel like my sailboat suddenly stopped in the middle of the sea because there is no wind.

A reminder of yet another battle I can't win.

"Don't conclude that you wasted your time," Ms. Cortez continues. "The two of you have entertained me with the battle for first chair, and I think it has benefited both of you."

"How so?" I ask.

"I believe you've become a much better flute player because you've tried to keep up with Brooke, and Brooke needed a nudge."

I snort. "A nudge? She's already the best."

"She's not, Anayah. But in this group, she has been and that can lead to a painful reckoning down the road. To pursue things as a jazz musician, she'll have to compete for it, and you've given her a taste of what it's like. Only her competitors will be mean, and they'll be just as good or even better than her." She winces. "No offense, Anayah."

"None taken." I know when I'm beaten, and I can take consolation in the fact that it rarely happens. "I thought I was pretty mean?"

Ms. Cortez chuckles. "You were competitive. I don't mind that; it's why the chair challenge arrangement exists. But you played within the rules and when you lost, you were done."

I tap my foot. "I wouldn't call a truce with Brooke when she asked."

"Yeah, she told me about that. I reminded her that it might be difficult for even gracious people to do so quickly after being defeated. She might have waited at least a few minutes, if not a day or so."

I chuckle.

"I need the rivalry to end," Ms. Cortez says quietly.

I exhale. "I want that too, but it's hard. I just want to be important."

"You are, and Brooke needs you."

"No, she doesn't."

"She does, and she knows it, especially after I asked her to be section leader next year. Being a section leader is difficult enough. But on top of that, next year's seniors might disagree with my decision, so Brooke may encounter pushback. And while Brooke can be firm, she doesn't have the same kind of backbone you possess. Together, you two can create an exceptional flute section, but not if you continue to fight each other."

Together?

"Anayah, this will be difficult for you, but I need you to support her," Ms. Cortez continues. "Support from someone who's cut from the same mold, shall we say, is the best kind. Can you do this?"

As much as it kills me to support Brooke, I'm not ignorant of the fact that Ms. Cortez has specifically asked me to essentially help her. It's not number one, but it's something. "It'll take time, but yes."

"Good. I knew you would. Even though I appointed Brooke as section leader, I'm not blind to your talents and abilities. You have an analytical mind and excellent ear, which is unmatched by anyone here, Brooke included. If you can use that skill to better the musical groups you're in, we'll have the opportunity to play selections that will set us apart. You can play in any of the ensembles you wish — pit, orchestra, wind ensemble, and I'll keep two flute players for jazz band. It's working well this year, and I'd be happy to have both of you for the next."

My jaw drops. I could be greedy and say all of them, but I have my research. "I'll let you know which groups I'm interested in."

"Great!" Ms. Cortez hops up. "I have a jazz band that's waiting for me to begin rehearsal."

She leaves the office.

For the first time in a long time, there's a twinge of excitement to work with Brooke. I like the sound of building an awesome flute section together.

My boat is sailing again.

Now I just need to encourage the captain.

I didn't know exactly what to expect at tonight's band banquet. Many of the awards are for the seniors. Everyone got a pin for their year in band, which can be worn on our uniforms. They also announced some of the officer positions for next year, which was exciting.

"Continuing with our merit awards," says Ms. Cortez from the podium on the stage. "This year, our sophomore class has sharply distinguished themselves. Sometimes, not in a good way…"

Quiet laughter fills the banquet hall.

She grins. "After a rocky start, the sophomores have shown a strong work ethic, resiliency, enthusiasm, and an amazing ability to work well together, bringing honor to our musical organization. I'm excited to see what they will continue to bring to the table. The next few merit awards will go to sophomores who highlight those accomplishments."

She pauses. "The next merit award goes to Will Cox."

He looks stunned.

I chuckle. I'm not surprised, but it's interesting to see the ordinarily self-assured Will is.

Gen turns in her chair, her face lit up with a smile. "Way to go!"

"Come on up here, Will." Ms. Cortez takes a step from the podium and claps her hands.

Will slowly makes his way to the stage while everyone applauds. He takes the award and shakes her hand with his mega-watt smile, even brighter than the one he wore on stage at regionals.

He starts to leave, but Ms. Cortez says, "Hold on, Will, let me talk about you for a minute."

Will stops short, eyes wide.

"Earlier, we mentioned people with boundless energy, and Will certainly fits the bill."

There's general laughter, cheers, and applause as the band acknowledges that fact wholeheartedly.

"Will infused his energy and positive attitude into the sophomore class during band camp when they certainly needed it. Along with a great work ethic, he is eager to learn and improve his trumpet technique by seeking help from others and practicing. He is a band member of great merit. Congratulations."

Will shakes her hand again, says thank you, and leaves the stage.

"The next award goes to a lady who was also instrumental in lifting the sophomores up during band camp this past summer, but in a different way. This young lady showed outstanding leadership both to her section and her class. Even when unsure of herself, she was always positive and ready to step up to the plate. She is also an outstanding musician, and I look forward to seeing great things from her in the future. Brooke Cauldwell, please come receive your merit award."

Brooke receives her award and sits down again. I check myself for feelings of jealousy and anger. I'm shocked to find there are none. Maybe a little disappointed, wishing I'd get one too. But not jealous.

"The last merit award goes to another outstanding musician. Anayah Kapur has consistently shown technical excellence in her flute playing."

My mouth drops. I should do that wishing thing more often.

"She has also distinguished herself in her abilities to troubleshoot. Despite her obvious talent, she has shown humility in supporting another flute player in taking the lead."

Will raises an eyebrow at me and mouths, "Humility?" and smirks.

I narrow my eyes at him, but I have to agree on this one. Humility has never been a word that people have used to describe me.

"Anayah Kapur, congratulations on your merit award."

I go to the stage while everyone applauds, shake the director's hand, and accept my award.

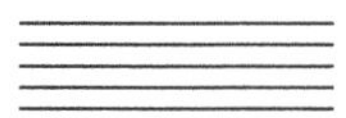

I run into Brooke when the evening draws to a close. "Congratulations, Brooke."

She looks surprised. "Thanks. You too."

I nod towards a woman that looks like her. "Is that your mom?"

Brooke nods. "Yeah, she's big on this kind of stuff."

"That's nice. Your Dad couldn't make it?"

Brooke's expression turns neutral. "He's playing at a series of festivals across the country for a few months. But even if he wasn't, he wouldn't have been that interested anyway."

"I'm sure he's proud of what you've accomplished, Brooke."

She shrugs. "He works and plays. That's what he does. That's what he'll always do. And that's cool in a way, but…" she trails off.

My family didn't come either but I pretty much told them it wasn't necessary. They would have been here if I had said otherwise, and they'll be happy to see my award.

"I'm sorry about what I did at the concert," I say. "I should have acted better and been less into me and my issues."

"Don't worry about it. Like Ms. Cortez said, it was really the oboe player's fault."

"Yeah, but I wanted to make you look bad and that's not right. When do you audition for Juilliard?"

"I'm not sure. I need to be sure that that's what I really want."

I'm shocked. "But it's a fantastic opportunity. You should go if you can."

"I know, but I want to make sure that I'm doing it for the right reasons. I can't do this half-hearted."

I'm quiet for a moment. "Was Ms. Cortez pushing this or something? Or your parents?"

Brooke shakes her head. "Ms. Cortez threw it out there and has been supportive, but has never pushed me into anything. My mom has been overly supportive, and my dad..." she trails off.

"Not so much."

Brooke nods. "I think the biggest reason I did this was to make him pay attention and follow in his footsteps." She gives me a little smile. "I'm very jealous of what you and your father have."

My jaw drops.

"Cya Monday, Anayah."

I stick my hand out. "Truce?"

She grins and hugs me. "Truce."

I watch Brooke and her mom walk out of the building.

39

Something Great

I put the finishing touches on my poster exhibit at Nationals. It took longer because I'm distracted with a giddy, jumpy excitement that's more than just my research.

The organizers encouraged us to explore the other exhibits if we finish setting up early. Satisfied with my display, I amble. As usual, everyone brought their A-game. I give a contented sigh.

I arrive at Will's station, where he's adjusting his poster board. His display is in a similar style to his report - clean, clear, and accessible. Don't realize the brilliance of the project until you think about it.

He's never looked better to me.

How do you act around a guy you kissed, who is your friend, and not your boyfriend, and have no intention of making one? We've done a spectacular job of pretending nothing happened on that bench the night of Sangeet. But there's this constant low-level hum with me, and my nerve endings are on fire every time I see him. I get why people go for this stuff, but I don't like this out-of-control sensation. So much has fallen into place, and I don't want to knock anything out of balance.

"You done already?" Will asks me.

"I'm letting the project speak for itself and didn't bring too many materials this year."

"Nice. You seem calm."

"My research is good."

Will chuckles. "Yes, we know. But you'll be the best and still tense."

I eye him. "You seem nervous."

He adjusts his tie. "I am."

"Your project is excellent." I smirk. "It came in second only to mine."

"Yeah, but I don't do this." He waves a hand around. "This is Kyra's scene, and my Dad will be on me if I screw up."

"Screw up like not place high?"

"No, like be me with a lot of extra thrown in to make people forget actual me."

I contemplate him for a moment and then chuckle. "Your dad isn't even here."

"He'll find out somehow. It's like he's all knowing or something. He even looks like a superhero. Completely wasted on him; he doesn't even appreciate it."

I laugh. Will really is nervous; he seldom rambles.

A voice comes through the PA announcing that poster presentations are about to begin, so I return to my station.

Time flies when I'm in my element. I think of little Nina when explaining why I did the project. Appreciate Dr. Reed's priceless guidance and Chen's assistance as I explain the experiment. My hiccup with the drug drew some laughs. Relive how I felt when my research turned up something unexpected and describe how overwhelming the implications were and still are. Thrilled to be able to add to the body of scientific knowledge, and express how eager I am to continue.

I want to win because that's how I'm wired. But this is much more than that, and for once, that's burning brighter than any prize. I'm so into it, I don't realize it's past the allotted time for presentations. There's still a steady stream of people stopping by.

When the last three people leave my booth, Will walks up to me, applauding and beaming. "That was outstanding."

I flush. "You're congratulating a fellow competitor?"

Will leans against my table. "It takes a truly secure guy to do that — one with poise and good upbringing."

I roll my eyes.

"You really love this, don't you?" he asks.

I grow warm and squirm, tucking a piece of hair behind my ear. "Yes, why do you think I keep doing these things?"

"You're smart, like to win, and this is another area to assert dominance."

"Wow, Will, that was completely unflattering."

"It's not your motivation for being here, so it's not true. You like love the whole thing."

He says it like it's incredible.

"You know this. Remember throwing it in my face on the trip?"

Will winces. "It's different seeing you live and love it." He plays with a piece of my display. "Lights you up in a different way."

I swallow. "You don't like research at all?"

Will gives a short laugh. "No. The results are interesting, and I like the idea that it could help others. But doing the science?" He shakes his head. "I didn't hate it, but I'll be perfectly fine if I never have to do it again."

"So I guess I don't have to worry about trying to beat you next year?"

"Not if I can help it."

"Trying to beat you is the most fun I've had at this competition." I'm surprised at how disappointed I am. It's like suddenly the next two competitions aren't as exciting anymore.

"Let's go out with a bang," he says. "Make sure you're fresh for tomorrow's presentations. Can't have my competition slacking off."

I salute him. "Early bedtime for me."

"Catch ya later, Nayah."

"See ya, Will."

I sit on the bed, studying my outfits for today. What would I wear if I dressed for me? Without worrying about everyone else?

I can't buy a new wardrobe for this trip, but sneaky Priya threw a couple of things in my bag. I pull out a black and white pinstripe jacket and skirt, but it's not exactly a business suit.

If I left my hair out and curled it, I'd look good — like girl good. I'd like to present my mind-bending research at this great competition and, to borrow Priya's thinking, be gorgeous while doing it.

That's the real me.

Nayah 5.0.

Something else catches my eye in the bag. A pair of black Mary Janes with a note attached.

'I would have worn strappy, stilettos with this, but I figured that would be too much. These will be more comfortable. Knock 'em dead — with your smarts and looks!'

"Someone owns the world," Will says when I meet him.

I walk to the elevators, head high. "The sun is out, I present my awesome research project today which will win me a fat scholarship prize, and I'm pretty. Need I say more?"

Will laughs. "No, Nayah. Go ahead."

We gather in a large lecture hall on campus for announcements and instructions. Then we're given our room assignments. Will is in a separate building in the quad, so we part ways.

The room is almost full when I arrive. I find an open seat and sit down. Kids are skimming their materials.

There's a snicker behind me. "What does she think she's dressed for?"

Are they laughing at me?

My heart picks up as I try to hear what they're saying.

"We'll be bored to tears with her project."

"Always easier when you got looks to get by."

They wouldn't be saying anything if I had worn the boring blue suit dress. But my looks are not why I'm here. The University is trying to take over my project it's so off the charts.

I relax in my chair. Let them hate. Soon it'll be for a completely different reason.

Two hours later, I stand when they announce me. Give my hair a toss and stare down the girls who snickered.

One of them smirks.

I square my shoulders and walk to the front of the room.

Make eye contact with the presenters. "Let me tell you about my friend Nina…"

"In the future, I plan on continuing this investigation with the university as part of their lab team," I conclude. "Eventually, we plan on publishing papers based on our findings. We also hope to develop a new drug based on this research, but that's much further down the road. Meanwhile, I hope to be back next year to share what else we discover."

The snicker girls can't look me in the eye but I barely care now. I absolutely love talking about my work. I return to my seat, crossing my legs and leaning back to listen to the rest of the presentations.

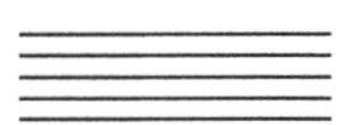

I look for Will in the multi-purpose room where dinner is served. There's raucous laughter in a corner, and guess who's at the center?

How does Will do it? He's never been to Nationals before, and three days in, he's got a crowd around him already. I sigh and search for another place to sit.

"Nayah!" Will calls and waves me over.

As I approach the table, a girl taps a chair. "Will said to save you a seat."

She resumes her conversation with the guy by her as I plop in the chair next to Will.

"How did it go?" he asks me.

"How do you think it went?"

Will grins. "Don't get full of yourself."

"How did yours go?"

"Like I said, don't get too full of yourself."

One of the guys asks me what my project was. After telling him, he exchanges a glance with the boy next to him. "Told you it was her."

"What do you mean?" I ask.

He turns red. "My roommate couldn't stop talking about the beautiful girl with the unbelievable experiment. He said he wants to marry you." The guy looks towards Will. "Figures you two are friends. I heard your project was good too."

Will seems surprised.

See Will? Be a beast about your smarts.

He recovers and leans back in his chair, putting his hands behind his head. "She knows a good thing when she sees it."

I give him a light smack on his stomach, causing him to drop his hands as the other guy laughs.

A couple of hours later, Will walks me back to where we're staying.

"So how does it feel?" I ask.

"Feel what?"

"To be Will?"

"It's hard work being smart and stuff. So much easier being a goofball."

"You fit right in. I couldn't believe it when I walked in, and you were the center of the loudest area of the room. How do you do that everywhere you go?"

"It's not hard, Nayah. They're like everyone else, just more into science. You heard the one kid wants to marry you. Normal, teenage, hormone stuff like any other guy."

"It's all about looks."

"No you don't, Nayah. He liked your brains first. Your looks were a bonus."

"I suppose. You meet any cute science girls here? There may be a special one who can really talk photosynthesis to you."

"Okay Nayah, you need to go to bed."

"Photosynthesis not your thing? How about ATP? Meiosis? Quantum mechanics? AI?" I grin. "Genetics?"

"I might know a special genetics girl." He winks.

I giggle, and then sober because I sound like one of those silly girls at school that are always trying to get his attention. "Why do you act like such a goofball all the time?"

"All the time? That's exaggerating."

"Stop avoiding the question."

"Why does it bother you so much?"

"It's a waste of talent and intelligence, and people underestimate you. I'm surprised you're not upset by that given your reaction when I did it."

"There's a difference between you and some random person on the street. I want people to feel comfortable around me."

"You're acting like someone you're not so people like you? You told me to be myself."

"I'm not acting. I'm just accentuating one part of my personality to avoid drawing attention to another."

I give him side-eye. "You don't expect me to believe that, do you?"

"I get good grades. I'm in honors classes and an AP course. I'm not exactly underperforming."

"But we could be fighting for number one in our class!" My heart thumps harder. Fighting with Will over valedictorian would be such an amazing rush.

Will chuckles. "And as exciting as that sounds-"

"It's one thing if you're going after something else, but what are you really doing?"

Will groans. "Nayah, I don't need all that. I want to be part of things that are great. Being with my friends and family is great. I might sound like a nerd, but I think learning things in school is great. Being part of an awesome band — one of the best experiences in my life. What good is achievement if I'm the only one benefiting?"

This guy is so nice it's almost sickening. "Why did you work so hard to win this competition?"

Will smirks. "To teach you a lesson."

"Will!"

His smile turns more genuine. "Wasn't this something great?"

My breath catches. "Yes, Will, it was." I pause. "We could be something great together."

He doesn't break eye contact, almost like I'm the one with the tractor beam. "We need to talk."

"We are."

He gives me a look and then exhales. "I keep kissing you."

I'm not sure how to interpret that. "Yes. So you regret it and wished you hadn't?"

"No, not exactly. More like I don't want to date right now, so I shouldn't be kissing you."

"I told you before I didn't want to be in a relationship until further down the road. I have a lot of important things on the line."

"I was afraid I was sending mixed signals, in case you changed your mind. So we're still on the same page?"

He makes a good point; it is kind of mixing me up. "As long as it's more of a 'shouldn't' as opposed to a 'don't want'."

"I pretty much want, which is why it's an issue. You?"

That set my body on fire, but I play it off and shrug. "It was all right."

The corners of Will's mouth quirk up.

I can't fight the ridiculously enormous grin spreading across my face. I'm in serious danger of violating this non-whatever it is.

"I mean it's probably completely selfish not to want to be with you, but still want you to care for me."

"I'll always care for you, but I'm not ready for all that may encompass."

"It's just like, Will."

"Like can lead to a lot of things, especially with a girl like you."

I flip that around my brain, feeling like he's talking on another level with this and blowing it out of proportion. But if he says he can't, then I'll absolutely respect that. Especially since I decided not anyway. What am I doing trying to convince him… I don't even know what I'm trying to talk Will into.

"Are we okay?" he asks.

Shake it off. "Yeah, of course. I don't know what came over me."

"Good night, Nayah," he says quietly. He turns and takes off down the hallway.

I whirl around, having difficulty unlocking the door to my room. Ridiculous teenage romances that won't last distracting me.

Stay in the game.

I'm most nervous for the Sunday Q&A session, though in reality, it's usually easier than presenting. It's the hardest to prepare for, and not knowing who your panel will be and what kinds of questions they may ask is nerve-wracking. While everyone involved is in a science and technology field, there's a big difference between being asked generic questions from someone outside of biochemistry and a research scientist in the same field as your project digging into you.

Will had texted me to say he was running late and that I should go without him. I'm not sure if that was entirely true, but I'm not devastated by his text either. We could both use a breather from each other after last night. I'm totally conflicted, and despite his firm insistence, Will seemed frustrated too.

The awards presentation is a banquet in the multi-purpose room about three hours after the Q&A is finished. My session ran very long, so I didn't get a chance to see Will before the ceremony began. Our spots at the banquet are assigned, and I'm not seated with him.

There are overall prizes, which get very large, and there are prizes within the divisions. Will placed second in our division and 36th overall. Both placements come with scholarship prizes.

I got top place in our division and second place overall. I'll have to corner first place and ask what his project was about. Probably cured some disease.

I finally catch up with Will when the banquet ends, and we congratulate one another.

"You did fabulously for your first time doing this," I tell him.

"I did better here than I thought I would."

"There's nothing wrong with actual you, Will. I think I prefer it."

He grins.

"Can't you just drop all the extra you throw in? At least some of the time?"

He stares at me. "All right. As long as you don't let anyone stop you from being Nayah, because she's something else."

I beam for a second and then my smile fades. The next battle. My work is great, but I doubt myself because others doubt me.

Will tilts my chin up, his brown eyes searching mine. "Don't let anyone take your self-respect."

"Yes, I know, but I need the reminder. You're my own personal cheerleader. They're gonna hear me."

40

I Am Hear

"Are you ready for this?" Dr. Reed asks as we gather the last of our papers in his office.

I nod. Today is the day I make my argument. Dr. Reed had to pull some strings to get this meeting. The director said he wanted to be there, which is a huge deal.

My phone goes off. Will. "I should take this. It's unusual for him to actually call."

"Go ahead."

"What's up?" I ask into the phone.

"Ms. Cortez wanted me to talk to you about being an usher for the percussion workshop concert."

He's been a little distant since we returned from Nationals, and I hate it. Will is becoming the second voice inside my head, and when it's gone, I feel the absence.

"You okay?" I ask.

"Yeah. Why?"

"You sound uncomfortable."

"Sorry, I'm tired."

Will is never tired.

Dr. Reed looks exasperated.

The thing with Will is important, but not now. "I want to, but can I call you back later? I'm leaving to argue for my research."

"That's today? You got this, Nayah. Nobody messes with you."

I smile. There he is. "Thanks. I'll let you know how it goes."

Dr. Reed and I walk down the hall.

"I'm surprised your father didn't mention anything about you dating," he says.

"Because I'm not."

Dr. Reed snorts as we get on the elevator.

"I don't have a boyfriend," I insist. "There's too much work to do"

Dr. Reed gives me a curious glance. "I'll drop it. It'll look informal because that's how we do things around here."

We exit the elevators on the first floor and head to one of the conference rooms. I stop short and put my hand on Dr. Reed's arm. "Give me a moment."

He stops, and I close my eyes, taking a deep breath.

Your research. Your love. Nina.

Will said to take them down.

That iron reserve locks into place. "Let's go."

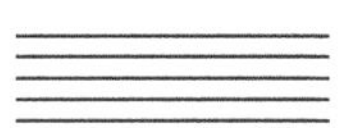

I follow Dr. Reed into the room and he introduces me to everyone. We take our seats and they discuss a few other minor matters of business.

"Now for the real reason we're gathered today." The director looks towards me seemingly amused. "Ms. Kapur,

I hear you have a few things to say about the direction of
our research.”

“The direction of your research is your business,” I
reply evenly, all my carefully prepared comments flying out
the window at the tone of his voice.

“Then why do you have us here?”

“I will be heard about taking my work.”

Dr. Reed raises his eyebrows at me.

Diplomacy has never been one of my strong suits. Add
it to the list.

The director’s smirk is gone. “The project was done
here, which makes it the University’s research.”

“I signed no papers to the understanding that my
project would become the property of the University.”

“Nobody drafts papers for community outreach
programs.”

“Then perhaps you should stop underestimating your
community and start.”

Dr. Reed gives me an exasperated look.

“We’re not inclined to have you participate in this
research,” the director declares. “The implications are far
outside of your experience and expertise.”

“You wouldn’t have this research without my so-called
inadequate experience and expertise-”

“Anayah…” Dr. Reed says under his breath.

“Winning a high school science fair does not prepare
you for this level of research,” the director snaps. “What
have you actually accomplished in your life? You do not
have what it takes to see this through.”

“Some people are perceptive enough to see the
potential without the accolades. Fortunately, you have Dr.
Reed to do that for you, so you and this University can
have a part in something great.”

The guy’s face turns red.

Dr. Reed winces. “Anayah…” he breathes.

Attacking the director personally is not the way to win. Pull back.

I take a deep breath. "I may lack experience, and I'll always work to increase my knowledge," I say in a calmer tone. "But do not say I'm not good enough. Even if my work didn't produce these results, no one should be subjected to that kind of disrespect."

I'm hear.

The woman at the table nods.

Another guy clears his throat. "Dr. Reed, you've been unusually silent. What is your position?"

Dr. Reed leans back in his chair. "I see no need to change the current arrangement. And I'm alarmed at the heavy-handedness with which the University has handled these extraordinary circumstances. This is first and foremost an academic institution. What exactly are we teaching Miss Kapur?"

The woman at the table nods again.

"The University has increased funding to your lab, and yet you resent their so-called heavy-handedness," the director retorts.

"I don't need to be bought."

And Dr. Reed thinks I lack diplomacy.

"Young lady, you haven't presented a strong enough case other than your displeasure over the direction of the research," the director says. "Your goal was to do a project for a science competition. That competition has been completed, and you got your prize. It's not as though you won't be involved, and it's time to allow someone else to take the reins so that the full value of this work can be realized. This is more than you, and its benefits can be enjoyed by countless others."

That's the first sensible thing he's said yet, but it's not enough.

"I'm fully aware of that which is why I'll have to take my drug elsewhere." I look at Dr. Reed. "Shall we go? Our business here has been completed."

Dr. Reed stares at me like I've lost my mind.

Perhaps I have. This is a serious gamble. If they don't bite, I've essentially walked out the door and let them have my work.

"Drug?" The woman asks. "Nobody said anything about a drug."

"Nobody mentioned it." The director looks towards me. "How do you have a drug?"

"I'm very resourceful."

"Can we see the paperwork and research on this so-called drug that you supposedly have?" the director asks.

I shake my head. "Not until my research is named as mine."

"How can we be sure that what you have is real? And if it was done here-"

"It was not. All my research was done at the hospital, and those consulted have no affiliation with this university. I have correspondence from them that will vouch for the validity of what I have. It's technically not the full formula, but it's the main chemical compound that should provide the foundation for one based on the experiment."

Silence.

Dr. Reed gives me a broad grin.

"As an employee of the University-"

"I'm technically an employee of the hospital, which predates my employment here. If the matter were pressed, they could call dibs, and I can easily terminate my employment here."

"I'm done watching you men posture." The woman stands. "If you're smart, you'll let Miss Kapur continue her work."

She hands me a card. "If that doesn't happen, make sure you contact me. I have connections with a couple of pharmaceutical companies that would love to hear what you have to say. I wish you well."

"Thank you." If I lose my research project, at least I have a plan B of sorts.

The woman narrows her eyes at the director. "I'll be in touch. A gift has practically fallen into your lap. If you can't handle that right, it doesn't give me confidence in how you will handle my money."

She leaves the room.

The director pushes his chair back from the table. "We've discussed all the pertinent matters. Dr. Reed, we'll inform you of our decision."

We say our goodbyes and disperse.

"What do you think?" I ask Dr. Reed as we head back to the lab.

"I think you won."

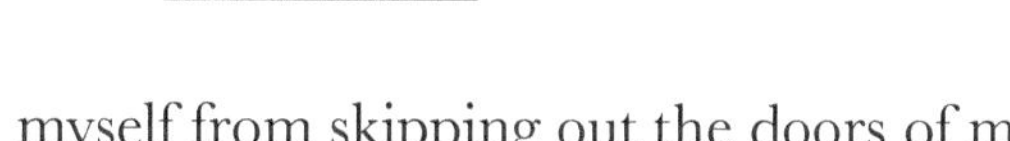

I have to stop myself from skipping out the doors of my building. Because that would look silly.

"You must be losing your touch, Nayah." Will is sitting on the bench outside. "I expected you out here faster."

"Will!" I stop short and beam. "What are you doing here?"

"I wanted to hear about the conquest and didn't trust you to call me back anytime soon. You get sucked into the lab."

"Dr. Reed kicked me out. Told me to have fun or play or something."

"You're already getting a rep." He pats the bench next to him. "Tell me about it."

"Not this bench. The one by the pond. I need the proper setting."

Will laughs. "The proper setting?"

I toss my hair. "I was glorious, and I need to tell my story in the right place."

Will stands, still chuckling. "Where's your Dr. Reed? I may need a more impartial account."

To my surprise, Dr. Reed comes out of the building.

"You get your wish. Dr. Reed, Will asked for an objective account of our amazing meeting."

"That's not how you put it," Will says.

"It was exciting," Dr. Reed replies. "Though I'd be interested to hear how Anayah tells the tale."

"I'd be factual." I can't help the smile playing on my lips.

Dr. Reed nods towards Will. "Is he your not boyfriend you were talking to earlier?"

My face heats. Way for Dr. Reed to get a dig in, and it does look suspicious that Will is here.

Will raises an eyebrow.

I glare at Dr. Reed. "He is the one I was speaking to earlier."

"It's nice to see you, Will. Anayah, I'll let you know as soon as I have news."

He walks away, and I grab Will's hand, my boldness returning. "Let's go so I can tell you about my glorious battle."

We go to the pond, still hand in hand.

Twenty minutes later, we're sitting next to each other on the bench by the reservoir. Will is shaking his head. "Can I believe anything you're telling me?"

"You can ask Dr. Reed."

"I'm just playing, Nayah. I'm very happy for you. Where do you go from here?"

I explain the next steps depending on the University's decision. "But I need to know more, especially if I try to move forward on that drug. It's like I'm operating in a knowledge vacuum."

Will seems to consider that. "How do people get into that line of work? They have to start somewhere. I'm sure they took the classes you're taking in high school."

"It's not enough. The information is too general and the problems aren't hard enough. I need better math skills. The topics aren't completely relevant. There's a huge gap, and I don't know how to fill it other than pursuing this beyond high school."

"Can't you?"

"Eventually but that won't help me now."

"I mean, can't you take college courses? To help fill the gap?"

"You mean like AP?"

"No, Nayah, actual college courses. You work at a University. Don't they have special programs where you could take a course free or at a reduced cost or something?"

I gasp. "You're right. It's genius."

"I keep trying to tell ya."

The wheels in my brain are going triple time. "I'll have to talk to Dr. Reed about that. I wonder if the high school would let me do it during school hours in lieu of a class or two."

"I'd give it a shot, because if you're trying to do it after school, that may be a lot. Contrary to popular belief, you are only human." He pulls something from his pocket. "I got you a little 'we won' gift."

I squeal and snatch it from him. It's a scrunchy covered with equations and a cloth hairband with stars and the moon on it.

It's an odd gift, but I can't help smiling because he obviously gave thought to it. "Are you afraid I don't have the proper hair accouterments?"

"This way you can pull your hair back when you do your research, and then you don't have to cut it off."

"Should we schedule another hair playing session?"

"Maybe."

I lay my head on his shoulder, and Will takes my hand in his.

I watch the ducks in the reservoir for a while, enjoying having Will here with me like this. Enjoying the quiet.

"I should go, Nayah," he says, voice deep.

"Me too. I have homework to do."

I glance at our hands still clasped.

"Congratulations," Will says. The tractor beam is back.

"Thank you," I whisper and place my forehead on his. "Thank you for believing in me."

His hands go in my hair and cradles my head, and he gives me a long kiss.

Will pulls back.

I take a deep breath and gulp. "We'll chalk that up to celebration and euphoria, and things can return to normal."

Will jumps up. "Right, so I'll see ya."

"Yep."

He nods and then walks away.

What is normal anymore?

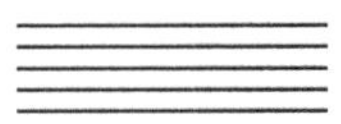

"Anayah," Dr. Reed calls after me a few weeks later when I'm on my way to the lab. "Come into my office, please. The department has released a new agenda and budget."

"And?" I'm almost breathless.

"Your research is on it, as your research."

My grin almost splits my face.

"Congratulations. But they've practically eliminated the money they were giving us to pursue it. They're not helping you at all."

"So this issue may be revisited?"

"You learn quickly. Yes, if it's perceived that you cannot fulfill this research's potential, it may be revisited."

"Got it."

"Let's not worry about that. It was a low-cost investigation to begin with. Let's see how long we can keep it that way. Another challenge for you, and as a lab, we may be able to find ways to help fund."

"Maybe I should contact the woman with the pharmaceutical connections."

"That's not a bad idea." He points a pen at me. "You may survive in this world."

"And here I thought my scientific intelligence would carry me."

Dr. Reed snorts. "The idealism of youth."

I resist the urge to stick my tongue out at him.

"Speaking of youth, I convinced your father to allow your name to be included on the lab paper. What on earth did you do to make him so angry?"

"It's a long story and one I'd rather not share."

"It must have been spectacular. That's apparently your M.O. Your name will be on the paper, but you have to do some form of laboratory drudgery this summer in addition to your research, per your father's orders."

"Thank you, Dr. Reed. I appreciate you negotiating on my behalf."

"You're welcome. This was your investigation. You deserve at least a little credit. I'm excited to see where we go from here."

Chen pops in. "Speaking of the lab paper, I think I deserve a lot of credit too."

Dr. Reed closes his eyes. "Chen."

"Without my excellent tutelage, our young scientist wouldn't be where she is today."

I work hard to suppress my laughter.

"Chen."

"Leaving."

I start to follow him out of the room.

"Anayah," Dr. Reed says. "Don't grow up too fast. Or get too absorbed in this world."

I stop short. "What?"

"A word from someone who's been there. You have more to offer than just your brains. Enjoy your youth."

"I enjoy this."

"Make sure it stays that way. At least for now."

I look towards the floor. "The other stuff is scary, even if I want it a little."

"Relationships are definitely new territory, aren't they?"

I nod.

"Easier to hide in here."

"Is that what you did?" I ask.

"Like I said, take it from someone who knows."

"So you regret your choice?"

"No, but I wish things had turned out a little differently. I envy your father occasionally. He seems to have gotten it all."

"I don't know about that. I have a feeling there were times, especially this year, when he wished he were you."

Dr. Reed gives a hearty laugh. "Have a good night, Anayah."

"Good night, Dr. Reed."

41

Wedding

“I’m getting married today.”

“You are.” I try to fix the hairpiece Priya asked me to put in. I need Xiang and Gen for this; I’m no good at these things.

“I’m getting married today,” Priya repeats in a high-pitched voice.

“Yes, Priya. Marriage. Today.” What is her problem?

“I’m scared.”

“Your wedding will be fine. You guys planned everything to perfection.” I eye the hairpiece. That should do.

“I’m scared of being married.”

I still. “You don’t think David is the one?”

“No, he’s the one.”

“Then what’s wrong?”

Priya smiles. “I forgot who I’m talking to. Amazing Anayah. What pearls of wisdom do you have for me on my wedding morning?”

“Don’t do it.”

“Seriously, Anayah?”

"Ask a ridiculous question, and you'll get that answer back. I have no marriage advice. I don't plan on looking until after I have my doctorate."

Priya laughs hard.

"How come every time I say that, the other person laughs?" I ask.

"People change their minds."

"I can't afford that kind of distraction. Stand up. Something is going on with your skirt."

The families compromised on a white and pink lehenga with a western veil. Priya is radiant in it.

"You could find someone who'll support you in your endeavors," Priya says.

"Not likely." Though Will supported me in my most recent science endeavor in a huge way.

I smooth down her dress and adjust things.

"Seth has turned into a nice young man. Handsome too."

A pair of backlit light brown eyes fill my vision. Will is better looking.

Focus on Priya.

"He already admitted to looking at you," she says.

So did Will. I'm his Nayah. "Seth is like my third brother."

I rearrange the veil. Now it's right.

Perfect Priya.

This time the phrase fills me with satisfaction.

"Are you sure about that?" Priya asks.

Yes, Will said it, but both of us agreed not to — I shake my head again. Priya is still talking about Seth. I have to stop thinking about Will. "Can we, please, finally, get you married today?"

Priya laughs so hard she has tears. "You win, Anayah. I feel so much better." She crushes me in a hug and then grabs my hand as we walk to her door. "Let's tell them we're ready and get this show on the road."

Epilogue

Ten months later

I run out of my lab building and race towards the lake. It actually happened.

Will is already there. Excellent. I wouldn't be able to sit still through a wait. He's changed from his school clothes to dark gray sweatpants and a matching gray long-sleeve shirt. For lounge clothes, they fit him well. I swallow as my heart rate picks up.

Will's brown eyes light up. "What's going on, Nayah? Why do you have me out here?"

I throw myself on the swing next to him making it rock sharply.

"You're going to break this thing. "

"I have exciting news!" I jump out of the swing and whip out a science journal publication. "I'm a published scientist!" I give a whoop.

"Congratulations! Can I see it?"

Absolutely. I open to the page and hand the journal to Will.

He directs his full attention towards it as I sit back down, still giddy.

"You did this?" Will asks after a bit.

That gaze… it's like wonder mixed with admiration mixed with something else that makes my body flush with warmth. "The lab helped, but yeah, that's my experiment right there."

He's still giving me that look. "This is absolutely amazing." He hugs me. "Not that I have anything to do with anything, but I'm proud of you."

I grin. He had something to do with almost everything. I give another whoop. "We need to celebrate."

Will chuckles. "I'm not on college student schedule here. I got to be up for school."

The high school allowed me to change my schedule so I could take a couple of classes at the university this year. My school day is a little different from my friends.

"But it's not that late, and it doesn't have to be big. I just want to be with my friends."

Will kisses my forehead. "I got you, Nayah. But why don't we plan something for the weekend? Everyone is busy tonight."

Forget everyone else. That was perfect.

I pull another journal out of my messenger bag. I'm suddenly self-conscious as I thrust the journal towards him. "I wanted you to have this one. I wrote a note in there. You can read it later."

Tractor beam. What is with his eyes? This reaction is going to become one of the laws of the universe soon.

"Thank you." He stands, shutting off the beam. "I should get back home. Congratulations again, Nayah." He taps the journal. "This is phenomenal."

"Thank you."

I wrap my arms around him, and he tightens his hold, pulling me closer to him.

Every thought I had in that message I wrote him is coming out in this embrace. My appreciation for him standing behind me and giving me courage. How happy I am we could do this wonderful thing together. And how much I hope he'll continue to stay behind me and support me.

I want to break the shouldn't.

My brain is foggy with all these thoughts and emotions that are more than what I can process. Handle.

"I have to go," I mumble as I whirl and run across the green.

"Nayah!" Will yells.

He'll text me later, and I'll smooth things over then. But right now - get a hold of yourself, Anayah. It was only a hug.

I swallow. That's a lie.

I really care for Will, and he was right; the way I feel this second, like can lead to a lot of things.

He's always right. I hate that.

I can't do this to myself. I just published my first experiment. There's plenty of work on the horizon. I can't let myself be distracted like this. I spend less than an hour with Will, and I'm a basket case.

What did we start?

Self-Portrait

Instrumental Book 3

Self-Portrait is a work in progress and working title for the third book in the Instrumental series. It's a dual POV story featuring Xiang and Matt. The following is an excerpt.

Chapter 6

Matt

"Good. You're home," Mom says to me when I walk through the door Thursday after school.

"You're home early." I jump as I notice Grandpa on the couch. "Hi, Grandpa. Is something wrong?"

He chuckles. "Does there need to be a problem for me to visit?"

I give him a hug. "Of course not."

"We do have something we want to talk about after dinner," Mom says. "Alex is spending the next few days with your father so this is a good time."

That explains why he told me to get another ride home. It's a holiday weekend so we have Friday and the following Monday off. Then we start exams a week from today.

I grimace. "I shouldn't have yelled at him."

"I wouldn't go that far," Mom says. "While your display at the mall was uncalled for, your brother has been asking for it. I was wondering how long you would put up with his garbage."

I'm without words.

"Just try to keep things in the privacy in our own home and out of public," Mom continues. "Don't put one another in the hospital, and don't get the cops called on us."

We're eating dessert when Grandpa says, "I hear you're interested in an art camp."

I stare at him. "How did you know?"

"Your mother told me."

"How did you know?" I ask Mom.

"I could tell when you mentioned it the other day after you told me you'd be working the music camp."

"The arts camps are expensive. I had already decided not to go."

"I want to pay for it," Grandpa says.

I glance at Mom, and she nods.

This is a big deal. Mom is funny about asking her dad for financial assistance, and she rarely does. She has to be between a mountain and a hard place. I never quite understood it. He's not mean about giving money and seems happy to help when given the chance.

"What's going on?" I ask quietly.

"We're a little concerned about you, Matt," Mom begins tentatively. "You're very to yourself."

"I have friends."

"I know, and good ones, but they're the only people you talk to."

I shrug. "It's better than the no one I was spending time with a few years ago."

Mom winces. "Yes, but we think it'd be good for you to spread your wings a little. And aren't a lot of your friends going away this summer - to camps of their own?"

I nod.

"So your already tiny circle will be dwindling," Mom points out. "We feel this arts camp will be a good opportunity for you to meet new people and broaden your horizons."

"I'll pay for room and board so you can get the full experience," Grandpa says.

I want to do art, but meeting new people is far less appealing.

"That's unnecessary," I say. "It's not that far to drive."

"And who will drive?" Mom asks.

"You?" I ask hesitantly.

Mom shakes her head. "I won't be able to swing that. So unless you make nice with your brother or coordinate something with your friends who will still be around, transportation will be a real issue."

"Should have let me buy the car," Grandpa says lightly.

I had told them it wasn't worth it if Alex was going to rail against it. Grandpa had let it drop, though I could tell he was disappointed.

I make a face. "I'm trying to be responsible."

"I know, and I love you for it," Mom says. "But I'm trying to be a parent so would you please just listen to me for one moment?"

I can't help but grin and nod.

"Let us set you up to do this," Mom says.

"Can I think about it first?"

"Yes," Mom replies. "But then do it."

I chuckle.

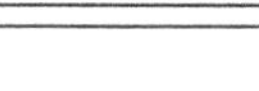

Xiang

I've been plotting excuses to call Matt for the longest time. He doesn't do chit-chat, and there's never been a real need otherwise. It's a bit of a long shot but my jewelry does require metal work, and Matt is familiar with that because of some of the models he does.

The school year is drawing to a close, and I feel this need to sorta create a closer connection to Matt before the time comes when I don't see him every day. We have the same circle of friends, and we are friends, but I can envision us only seeing and talking to each other maybe every other week.

That's just not enough.

So on Tuesday, our first half day of school, I'm going to work the jewelry angle. Just how to phrase it so I come off as wanting help but not sounding overly needy. Or desperate for his attention. And totally creating a situation just to spend time with him which I am.

I'm rendered momentarily speechless when he answers.

"Xiang? This is you, right?"

I inhale. Knock it off, Xiang, it's not like you never talk to him. "Yep! Sorry, you sound different on the phone. Like older."

There's silence on the other end.

What am I saying?

"Do I usually sound young?" Matt asks slowly.

"No, not at all. You just sounded like a man."

"So I usually sound like a girl?"

"No, like man, not a boy."

"Oh. Thank you?"

I shake my head. Now that I've made him feel weird… "I have a favor to ask you."

"Sure. Shoot." He sounds relieved.

"I could use a second opinion about some of the chains or metals I use for my necklace and bracelet pieces."

Silence again.

"Would you be up for that?" I ask.

"But I know nothing about jewelry."

"You don't have to. Remember I'm just asking for help with the metal stuff." For now. "You use metal for your models, right?"

"Yeah, but I'm sure it's not the-"

"You'll do fine."

"Okay. What do you want me to do?"

"Are you busy this afternoon?"

"No."

"Great! I'm kidnapping you on a trip to the craft store."

A few hours later, I pick up a string of beads at the store. It's a franchise so some of the stock is a little generic, but these will work. Hopefully, I can hit up a nice bead store or better yet, a bead show. I want beads or pendants and some pretty stones.

"Xiang? I thought we were looking at metal."

I turn to Matt, who looks really uncomfortable. He's going to regret coming here with me if I don't make this work better. "I'm sorry. I'll try and make sure it doesn't happen again."

Matt laughs. "You just looked like you left me there for a minute, which you can do it as much as you like. Just leave me in a more interesting aisle."

By now, we're standing in front of some of the chains and ropes of metal. I have an idea of what I want, but Matt has a better idea of what kinds of metal will hold what kind of weight.

But overall, he's quiet today. Quieter than usual, which means he's nearly silent, and it's awkward.

"Everything okay, Matt?" I ask.

"I'm sorry. I'm not very good company." He pauses. "My grandpa and mom want me to do the arts camp along with working at the music camp. And they want me to stay on campus."

No way. My decision is made.

I grab his hands and jump up and down. "That's what I'm doing! We'll be camp buddies!"

"What?"

"My parents conned me into doing this arts camp instead of the one in New York if they paid for everything including my supplies and room and board and if I took the college credit class. This is so perfect! I was kinda dreading this but now it's totally worth it. Our summer is going to be so awesome!"

And here I was afraid I'd hardly see Matt. I'll get to see him every day if things work out. I love my parents now.

A slow smile spreads across Matt's face, but he still looks thunderstruck. "I guess I'll tell them I'm doing it. I was hesitant because I was uneasy about meeting new people, but if you're there, that'll be great."

I'm trying not to jump up and down again, so I'm doing this odd little shuffle in the craft store aisle. "Best summer ever! So why are they so set on you doing this? My parents want me to be this serious person that I'm totally not, but I can show them I am a focused, goal-oriented fashion student."

"They think I need more friends."

"Really?"

"They didn't say that, but I think that's what it boils down to. Mom mentioned something about spreading my wings and broadening my horizons."

"Oh, well, that sounds a little more involved, but no worries, since you're going. And I think you're perfect as you are."

"Thanks." Matt's smile seems suddenly strained.

"Don't worry about camp. We're going to have a blast. Did you want to look at anything while we are here?"

Matt looks thoughtful. "Actually yeah."

We move into another aisle and he stops in front of some boxes. He kneels and picks one up. "I've been thinking of getting these."

They're the most adorable collection of building house kits. "They're so cute, Matt. You should totally get it."

He frowns. "They're pricey, but I have a little money. I might splurge." His frown deepens as he puts the box back. "Even though I shouldn't."

I study his face. I don't want to get into his business. "Are things okay at home?"

He sighs. "Yeah. They're not bad. Just a little tight from time to time." He shakes his head and gets up. Gives me a small smile. "That's all you're getting?"

"Yep. I'm good."

I am so good.

═══════

I was excited to tell my parents I decided to go to the camp of their choice. Not so much because I wanted to go there, though Matt was a game changer, but it's nice to do things that please my parents. It feels like it gets harder and harder the older I get.

But before I could launch into my news, Mama was excited about my older brother calling her. We don't talk to or see him much so it was exciting to hear what he's up to. He's about twelve years older than me and lives in Hong Kong with his wife, who's a half Nigerian and and half British expat. Long story how they met and ended up where they are.

They're good company, and I enjoy visiting them once every couple of years, but we've never been close. He reads more like an uncle than a brother to me. A nice one, but nothing like the relationships Kyra and Will have as twins, or Taylor and John as siblings a little closer in age, or even Anayah with her brothers and sister. And definitely nothing like the hero worship little Nina has for Seth.

My brother is a chef, which wasn't the career my parents had envisioned for him. But since he seems to be making a decent living doing it, they don't complain too loudly. I'm thankful they don't hold him up as some paragon of excellence I need to live up to.

They seem able to create an imaginary one perfectly fine.

I was about to tell Mama again, but then she taste tests the soup and proceeds to spend the first half of dinner commenting on how much better the soup would be if it had bok choi. The bok choi I forgot to pick up on my way home from school today. That was part of the deal for me having the van to take to school since Taylor had scheduled extra cello lessons right after. I may have gotten sidetracked by the colorful and artful fruit salads. The one was a serious work of art sculpture. How could I leave that in the store?

While Mama appreciated my fruit contribution, it was not enough of a distraction from the bok choi omission. She had pointed out kiwi and watermelon were not suitable substitutes.

"But I put the anise and fennel in," I explain again. "I think I did pretty good there."

Mama gives me a look.

"I'll do the Southerland arts camp, since you offered to pay for it," I tell them, hoping to shift the topic to something they might be happy about.

"Excellent," says Bàba. "I knew if you thought about it, you'd see the wisdom in our proposal."

"Thank you for making it." Being the dutiful daughter. Actually, I should stop being a rat. They are letting me have a good opportunity. And it's good he didn't ask what the real clincher was. Chasing after a boy would not go over well. My parents are wary of me dating, given my track record with other interests the past sixteen years, even though I don't fly through people like that. Though they liked what they've seen of Matt, I don't think he's the kind of guy they envisioned me with.

"If you don't do well enough to earn the college credits, then you have to pay back the money," Bàba says.

My jaw drops. "There's some fine print," I mutter.

"I just want to ensure you remain focused."

"I am focused. I'm serious about the fashion and jewelry."

"We'll see," Dad says.

I have to be serious now. If I botch this, not only will I have wasted the summer on a camp I didn't really want, but I'll lose all of my hard earned money on it too. And it'll be just that much harder for me to study in the future because without my parents financial support, I'll be footing the bill for that too.

Chapter 7

Matt

"Matt, thanks for coming by early. I know today is a pretty big day for your family with Alex graduating and everything."

I nod. It's gonna be real interesting. I'm appreciating this distraction.

"No problem. What did you want to talk to me about?"

She points to a chair, and I take a seat.

We're in the band room. There's a few other kids milling around, but most won't probably be here for another twenty minutes or so and it's still fairly quiet..

"As you know Miguel is graduating," she begins. "For the past two and a half years, he's been doing the artwork for our programs, t-shirts, and other things. He said you were surprised to be nominated to take over."

I nod.

"I asked your art teacher to point out your work. You're quite good."

I grin. "Thanks."

"Are you interested? It's yours if you want it."

"You don't need a sample or auditions or something?"

Ms. Cortez chuckles. "This is one of those things that's important but it's not. It's visual; your work will be on t-shirts and paperwork and things, so it does need some attention. But in the grand scheme of things — I don't make this a huge deal. I pick a student I trust to take care of it and then forget about it. I think you'll do this well, but I don't know what else you have going on."

I shake my head. "No, I don't have anything else going. I told Miguel I don't think I'm good enough for this."

"He said you might need some encouragement." She grinned. "You'll be fine. Otherwise, I wouldn't have asked."

I mull it over, surprised at my mounting excitement over the job. It would be awesome to use my skills for something I care as much about as I do the band. It's like a great combination of my favorite things. "I'd be honored."

Ms. Cortez pats my shoulder, and I follow her into the office. "Great. This is the info for a logo for the band shirts. I'll need it by the first day of band camp so we can get them printed and distributed by the first football game."

She hands me a sheet of paper with dimensions and instructions.

"If you could have a few mock-ups done by the middle of July that would be great. That way you can incorporate any suggestions I might have."

I nod. "Sounds good."

The middle of July will put me right smack in the middle of camp. I'll have to get started on this ASAP.

"Questions?"

I shake my head. "Not right now. I'll read this over and start brainstorming."

"Excellent. E-mail me with any questions and the mock-ups. Unless you want to bring the actual mock-ups here. I know you artists are particular about your mediums and presentation."

I grin. "I'll probably keep it simple so e-mail should be fine. Thank you."

"No, thank you."

<hr>

Yeah, graduation is real interesting.

Mostly because my dad is here. I haven't seen him in two years. It annoys me that he looks good. His dark hair is just starting to gray around the temples, and it looks like he stayed in shape. I was also annoys me that my looks are favoring his. I might have Mom's dark blue eyes and smaller stature but everything else about me is him.

Hopefully, our personalities will remain completely different.

My brother has dark red hair like my mom and brown eyes like my dad. He has my dad's build too.

Alex is happy he's here, and for Alex's sake, I'm glad Dad showed.

Fortunately, the band plays all through graduation, so my contact is greatly reduced.

When the ceremony concludes, I hang out with my friends for a little and then find my family.

Mom and Grandpa are in the stands. Mom is smiling but it looks a little strained.

"Are you okay?" I ask her.

Her smile widens but still looks forced. "Of course. This is a big day."

I nod as we all dance around the elephant in the stands.

"Your father was looking for you," Grandpa finally says.

"I'll go find him."

He's with Alex in the concourse near the main gates.

"Matt!" Dad waves his arms around and has a huge grin on his face. "I'd like to take you boys out for dinner tonight. I have some exciting news."

Doing graduation was one thing, spending real time with only him and Alex is another.

Alex's grin fades as his eyes narrow at me.

I shouldn't mess this up for him, and I'm curious about Dad's news. "Sure."

An hour later, a hostess seats us at an Italian restaurant, and we order drinks.

"What have you been doing with yourself, Matt?" Dad asks. "I never hear from you or see you."

Like it's my responsibility to arrange visitation. I shrug. "Not much. I did band like Alex this year so thats cool. I'm attending an arts camp and working at a music camp for the summer."

"Still doing your models and drawing?" Dad asks.

"Yep."

He chuckles.

"Why are you laughing?" I ask.

"No reason," Dad replies. "Any sports?"

"Climbing."

"No real sports?"

"Climbing the side of a mountain? It doesn't get much realer than that."

Alex snorts. "When you actually get out of the climbing building and onto a real mountainside, let me know."

"Shut up, Alex. I've climbed outside."

"Okay, boys," Dad says.

The waitress brings bread and asks for our orders. It's family style — many groups get a few dishes and share.

"Spaghetti and meatballs." Dad gives me a mock punch on the shoulder. "I remember you love that."

Yeah, when I was eight.

Alex and Dad order appetizers and two more dishes and then the waitress leaves to put in the order.

"What's your news, Dad?" I'm not in the mood for idle chit-chat.

"You get straight to the point, Matt. I like that," Dad says. "I'm getting remarried."

Alex and I sit silently for a moment. That wasn't what I was expecting and definitely newsworthy. Somebody wants to marry him?

"So you and Cindy are finally making it official?" Alex asks.

"Cindy Rossnagle?" I exclaim. "As in Miss Rossnagle, my old teacher?"

"Yes, Matt, that Cindy."

I take a sharp inhale and turn to Alex. "And how did you know?"

"I actually call my father every once in a while," he sneers.

Heat roars through my body. "It would be nice if our father bothered to call us every once in a while."

Dad winces. "About that…"

"Never mind." I glance at a family that just erupted into laughter next to us. They are so not what we are.

"When is this wedding supposed to take place?" I ask Dad.

"September. And I would love it if you and Alex would be my best men." Dad looks proud of himself.

My jaw drops. It's like being betrayed all over again. "No, absolutely not."

Alex glares at me, jaw clenched.

The waitress quickly drops the appetizers on the table and scurries away.

"Matt, just please think about it and give me an answer later," Dad says. "I know it's sudden and maybe a little hard to take. Just please understand."

"What is there to understand?" Alex asks angrily. "I don't know why you have to be such a jerk about everything, Matt."

I've had enough, but can't do a repeat of the mall, so I throw my napkin on the table. "Obviously, you two don't understand anything. I'm going to the restroom."

"Matt," Dad calls after me.

I rush through the restaurant and restroom door, my heart hammering. I cannot believe my father. Is he that selfish? Clueless? Heartless?

The year Dad left and Grandma died was the worse at

school. That was when I really started drawing pictures of superheros. Tons of them. I guess I was looking for someone to save me.

Miss Rossnagle was one of the few adults I told about the harassment. While sympathetic, she didn't really do anything at first. When a shoving match sent me down some stairs, finally people started taking action. But it was a little late by then.

That was when Mom decided we were moving — to be closer to Grandpa and to get out of town and start over.

Of all the women for Dad to pick, why her? Did he really not take what happened to me seriously?

Food was on the table by the time I return. It looks good, but I have no appetite. I try to make my way through a meatball.

"It's funny you mention that you're getting married," Alex says. "I plan on asking Alicia myself this summer."

I shouldn't have, but I snort out a laugh. "And what are you two going to live on? Love?"

"Why are you even here, Matt?" Alex snaps. "It's not like you want to be."

"He's here because I asked him to be," Dad says. "And though he could have been nicer about it—" Dad cuts me a look. "He raises a valid point."

"I thought you'd be happy for me," Alex says, poking at his food.

"I am, very happy you found someone. Just make sure you're right for each other and take your time doing it."

Alex smirks. "I get you. Don't want to make the same mistake you made with Mom."

"More like the other way around," I mumble.

Dad is quiet for a moment. "I wouldn't have you two without your mom, so not another word about it. Let me enjoy this meal with my two sons on this great day."

I can't say I loved the rest of dinner, but at least there was no more arguing.

C.E.J., writing as Elizabeth Borae, resides in Pennsylvania, U.S.A. Besides writing, she also works as a literacy and mathematics tutor, working with children who have learning challenges. A former marching band flute player with a B.A. from Rutgers University majoring in Economics and Art History, her stories about relationships and family keeps it sweet and clean, but still real.